The Metallic Muse

The Metallic Muse

A Collection of Science Fiction Stories by

Lloyd Biggle, Jr.

WILDSIDE PRESS

THE TUNESMITH: first published in *IF—Worlds of Science Fiction*, August 1957. Included in *The Best Science Fiction Stories and Novels*, Ninth Series, Edited by T. E. Dikty (Advent Publishers, 1958). Copyright 1957 by Quinn Publishing Company, Inc.
LEADING MAN: first published in *Galaxy Science Fiction*, June 1957. Copyright 1957 by Galaxy Publishing Corporation.
SPARE THE ROD: first published in *Galaxy Science Fiction*, March 1958. Copyright 1958 by Galaxy Publishing Corporation.
ORPHAN OF THE VOID: first published in *Fantastic Science Fiction Stories*, September 1960, as "The Man Who Wasn't Home." Copyright © 1960 by Ziff-Davis Publishing Company.
WELL OF THE DEEP WISH: first published in *IF—Worlds of Science Fiction*, March 1961. Copyright 1961 by Digest Productions Corporation.
IN HIS OWN IMAGE: first published in *The Magazine of Fantasy and Science Fiction*, January 1968. Included in *The Best from Fantasy and Science Fiction*, Eighteenth Series, Edited by Edward L. Ferman (Doubleday, 1969). Copyright © 1967 by Mercury Press, Inc.
THE BOTTICELLI HORROR: first published in *Fantastic Science Fiction Stories*, March 1960. Copyright © 1960 by Ziff-Davis Publishing Company. Illustration appearing in the Introduction to "The Botticelli Horror," Copyright © 1960 by Ziff-Davis Pub. Co. By permission of Ultimate Publishing Company, Inc.

Published by
Wildside Press, LLC
P.O. Box 301
Holicong, PA 18928-0301 USA
www.wildsidepress.com

Wildside Press Edition: MMIII

Contents

THE TUNESMITH   4

LEADING MAN   49

SPARE THE ROD   64

ORPHAN OF THE VOID   87

WELL OF THE DEEP WISH   138

IN HIS OWN IMAGE   160

THE BOTTICELLI HORROR   177

(Introduction)

The question is so inevitable that Science Fiction writers learn to wait expectantly for it. It comes variously phrased, sometimes administered with the practiced skill of the physician who distracts one's attention while aiming a needle at the buttocks, sometimes thrown out with the subtlety of a professional football lineman blitzing a quarterback, but it forms an important if not irreplaceable prop for almost every TV, radio or newspaper interview. Not infrequently it encompasses the entire Science Fiction knowledge of the interviewer.

So where *do* we get those crazy ideas?

From the same place that you get them, gentle reader. The Science Fiction writer's ideas, or at least the experiences that give rise to them, are no different from anyone else's. The difference lies in his ability to recognize a crazy idea when he sees one and to make use of it.

Anyone who has watched—or attempted to watch—the Late Late Show on television has been irked by the number as well as the placement of TV commercials. Many who have consciously noted this unabashed greed with which a TV station will push commercials at its viewers must have entertained the fleeting thought that the station would show nothing but commercials if it thought it could get away with that.

Few of these viewers take the next logical mental step and ask themselves, "What would happen if it did show nothing but commercials?" This is fortunate; otherwise, the Science Fiction profession would be far more crowded than it is at present.

Among their other sterling virtues, Science Fiction writers are inveterate viewers-with-alarm, in which role they perform an important public service. Their speculations frequently fix upon genuine dangers to our civilization that are ignored or unseen by others. Long before atomic tests in the atmosphere were a subject of public concern, a card was circulating in Science Fiction circles that read, "The Atomic Energy Commission wants to give every school child a hot lunch." Such dangers as DDT in the environment, or strontium 90 in our milk supply, or voter apathy, or atmospheric pollution, or crime in the streets have long been viewed with alarm by Science Fiction writers, and these writers have asked themselves, "What will happen if this goes on?"

They have supplied speculative answers.

Please note that they do not predict. They are not saying, "This *will* happen." They are saying, "*If* something or other continues, this is what *could* happen."

I viewed with alarm that trend toward more numerous TV commercials. Obviously if this is projected without faltering it has an inevitable end: programs that consist entirely of commercials. I also detected a companion trend, well worth noting, in that the dramatic content of some commericals was vastly superior to that of the programs that carried them.

I wrote "The Tunesmith." It describes a future where there is no entertainment except the TV commercial—which thus must constitute the only surviving form of artistic expression in music, art, literature and the drama. At no time did I anticipate that the human animal would ever tolerate such foolishness. I was not predicting. I was satirizing a contemporary trend by projecting it, exaggerated, into the future. This is a venerable literary device. An eighteenth-century writer of Science Fiction, Jonathan Swift, satirized his contemporary Englishmen by transposing them to Lilliput or Brobdingnag; in the succeeding 250 years the Earth has become almost too crowded for even fictional societies, and the modern Science Fiction writer is more likely to place his satires in the distant future or in outer space.

"The Tunesmith" was published in the magazine *IF*, it was included in T. E. Dikty's *The Best Science Fiction Stories and Novels, Ninth Series,* and translations appeared in several foreign countries, including (without my consent!) the Soviet Union. In the meantime I took my non-predicting to other areas.

And within the next few years I saw an impressive picture story in a nationally-circulated magazine concerning European television stations that were offering highly artistic programs consisting of nothing but commercials, and I happened onto a small but equally terrifying newspaper item about a new Los Angeles FM station scheduled to broadcast nothing but commercials twenty-four hours a day.*

Predictions, in our society, have become so authoritative and so widely publicized as to constitute a peculiar kind of menace. Consider

---

* The Los Angeles radio station, KADS (FM), gave up the all-advertising format after losing $86,393.02 in a six-month period. The failure was not blamed on the incessant advertising, just on the fact that the station failed to discover a mode of presentation that would make the ads palatable.

the sinister implications of the joke, "Tomorrow has been cancelled due to lack of interest." Lately there have been expressions of concern that predicting a thing may actually make it happen. If all of the leading economists were unanimous in their prediction of a business slump, for example, corporation presidents would tend to hold back —just a little—on expansion plans and inventory build-up. Wholesalers and retailers might delay their orders—just a little—until they could find out what was going to happen. Workers might postpone installment purchases until they could find out for certain that they would be able to go on working. The economy would turn downward—just a little—and this would be viewed by everyone as the beginning of the predicted slump. More cutbacks would follow, and in very short order the slump would be a reality with the economists attempting to explain why it arrived ahead of schedule.

Predicting it made it happen.

I didn't mean to do it.

1

THE TUNESMITH

Everyone calls it the Center. It has another name, a long one, that gets listed in government appropriations and has its derivation analyzed in encyclopedias, but no one uses it. From Bombay to Lima, from Spitsbergen to the mines of Antarctica, from the solitary outpost on Pluto to that on Mercury, it is—the Center. You can emerge from the rolling mists of the Amazon, or the cutting dry winds of the Sahara, or the lunar vacuum, elbow your way up to a bar, and begin, "When I was at the Center—" and every stranger within hearing will listen attentively.

It isn't possible to explain the Center, and it isn't necessary. From the babe in arms to the centenarian looking forward to retirement, everyone has been there, and plans to go again next year, and the year after that. It is the vacation land of the Solar System. It is square miles of undulating American Middle West farm land, transfigured by ingenious planning and relentless labor and incredible expense. It is a monumental summary of man's cultural heritage, and like a phoenix, it has emerged suddenly, inexplicably, at the end of the twenty-fourth century, from the corroded ashes of an appalling cultural decay.

The Center is colossal, spectacular and magnificent. It is inspiring, edifying and amazing. It is awesome, it is overpowering, it is—everything.

And though few of its visitors know about this, or care, it is also haunted.

You are standing in the observation gallery of the towering Bach Monument. Off to the left, on the slope of a hill, you see the tense spectators who crowd the Grecian Theater for Euripides. Sunlight plays on their brightly-colored clothing. They watch eagerly, delighted to see in person what millions are watching on visiscope.

Beyond the theater, the tree-lined Frank Lloyd Wright Boulevard curves into the distance, past the Dante Monument and the Michelangelo Institute. The twin towers of a facsimile of the Rheims Cathedral rise above the horizon. Directly below, you see the curious landscaping of an eighteenth-century French *jardin* and, nearby, the Molière Theater.

A hand clutches your sleeve, and you turn suddenly, irritably, and find yourself face to face with an old man.

The leathery face is scarred and wrinkled, the thin strands of hair glistening white. The hand on your arm is a gnarled claw. You stare, take in the slumping contortion of one crippled shoulder and the hideous scar of a missing ear, and back away in alarm.

The sunken eyes follow you. The hand extends in a sweeping gesture that embraces the far horizon, and you notice that the fingers are maimed or missing. The voice is a harsh cackle. "Like it?" he says, and eyes you expectantly.

Startled, you mutter, "Why, yes. Of course."

He takes a step forward, and his eyes are eager, pleading. "I say, do you like it?"

In your perplexity you can do no more than nod as you turn away—but your nod brings a strange response. A strident laugh, an innocent, childish smile of pleasure, a triumphant shout. "I did it! I did it all!"

Or you stand in resplendent Plato Avenue, between the Wagnerian Theater, where the complete *Der Ring des Nibelungen* is performed daily, and the reconstruction of the sixteenth-century Globe Theatre, where Shakespearean drama is presented morning, afternoon and evening.

A hand paws at you. "Like it?"

If you respond with a torrent of ecstatic praise, the old man eyes you impatiently and only waits until you have finished to ask again, "I say, do you like it?"

But a smile and a nod is met with beaming pride, a gesture, a shout.

In the lobby of one of the thousand spacious hotels, in the waiting room of the remarkable library where a copy of any book you request is reproduced for you free of charge, in the eleventh balcony of Beethoven Hall, a ghost shuffles haltingly, clutches an arm, asks a question.

And shouts proudly, "I did it!"

* * *

Erlin Baque sensed her presence behind him, but he did not turn. Instead he leaned forward, his left hand tearing a rumbling bass figure from the multichord while his right hand fingered a solemn melody. With a lightning flip of his hand he touched a button, and the thin treble tones were suddenly fuller, more resonant, almost clarinet-like. ("But God, how preposterously unlike a clarinet!" he thought.)

"Must we go through all that again, Val?" he asked.

"The landlord was here this morning."

He hesitated, touched a button, touched several buttons, and wove weird harmonies out of the booming tones of a brass choir. (But what a feeble, distorted brass choir!)

"How long does he give us this time?"

"Two days. And the food synthesizer's broken down again."

"Good. Run down and buy some fresh meat."

"With what?"

Baque slammed his fists down and shouted above the shattering dissonance. "I will not rent a harmonizer. I will not turn my arranging over to hacks. If a Com goes out with my name on it, it's going to be *composed*. It may be idiotic, and it may be sickening, but it's going to be done right. It isn't much, God knows, but it's all I have left."

He turned slowly and glared at her, this pale, drooping, worn-out woman who'd been his wife for twenty-five years. Then he looked away, telling himself stubbornly that he was no more to be blamed than she. When sponsors paid the same rates for good Coms that they paid for hackwork . . .

"Is Hulsey coming today?" she asked.

"He told me he was coming."

"If we could get some money for the landlord—"

"And the food synthesizer. And a new visiscope. And new clothes. There's a limit to what can be done with one Com."

He heard her move away, heard the door open, and waited. It did not close. "Walter-Walter called," she said. "You're the featured tunesmith on today's *Show Case*."

"So? There's no money in that."

"I thought you wouldn't want to watch, so I told Mrs. Rennik I'd watch with her."

"Sure. Go ahead. Have fun."

The door closed.

Baque got to his feet and stood looking down at his chaos-strewn worktable. Music paper, Com-lyric releases, pencils, sketches, half-finished manuscripts were cluttered together in untidy heaps. Baque cleared a corner for himself and sat down wearily, stretching his long legs out under the table.

"Damn Hulsey," he muttered. "Damn sponsors. Damn visiscope. Damn Coms."

Compose something, he told himself. You're not a hack, like the other tunesmiths. You don't punch out silly tunes on a harmonizer's keyboard and let a machine complete them for you. You're a musician, not a melody monger. Write some music. Write a—a sonata, for multichord. Take the time now, and compose something.

His eyes fell on the first lines of a Com-lyric release. "If your flyer jerks and clowns, if it has its ups and downs—"

"Damn landlord," he muttered, reaching for a pencil.

The tiny wall clock tinkled the hour, and Baque leaned over to turn on the visiscope. A cherub-faced master of ceremonies smiled out at him ingratiatingly. "Walter-Walter again, ladies and gentlemen. It's Com time on today's *Show Case*. Thirty minutes of Commercials by one of today's most talented tunesmiths. Our Com spotlight is on—"

A noisy brass fanfare rang out, the tainted brass tones of a multichord.

"Erlin Baque!"

The multichord swung into an odd, dipsey melody Baque had done five years before, for Tamper Cheese, and a scattering of applause sounded in the background. A nasal soprano voice mouthed the words, and Baque groaned unhappily. "We age our cheese, and age it, age it, age it, age it, age it the old-fashioned way . . ."

Walter-Walter cavorted about the stage, moving in time with the melody, darting down into the audience to kiss some sedate housewife-on-a-holiday, and beaming at the howls of laughter.

The multichord sounded another fanfare, and Walter-Walter leaped back onto the stage, both arms extended over his head. "Now listen to this, all you beautiful people. Here's your Walter-Walter exclusive on Erlin Baque." He glanced secretively over his shoulder, tiptoed a few steps closer to the audience, placed his finger on his lips, and then called out loudly, "Once upon a time there was another composer named Baque, spelled B-A-C-H, but pronounced Baque. He was a real atomic propelled tunesmith, the boy with the go, according to them that know. He lived some five or six or seven hundred years ago, so we can't exactly say that that Baque and our Baque were Baque to Baque. But we don't have to go Baque to hear Baque. We like the Baque we've got. Are you with me?"

Cheers. Applause. Baque turned away, hands trembling, a choking disgust nauseating him.

"We start off our Coms by Baque with that little masterpiece Baque did for Foam Soap. Art work by Bruce Combs. Stop, look—and listen!"

Baque managed to turn off the visiscope just as the first bar of soap jet-propelled itself across the screen. He picked up the Com lyric again, and his mind began to shape the thread of a melody.

"If your flyer jerks and clowns, if it has its ups and downs, ups and downs, ups and downs, you need a WARING!"

He hummed softly to himself, sketching a musical line that swooped and jerked like an erratic flyer. Word painting, it was called, back when words and tones meant something. Back when the B-A-C-H Baque was underscoring such grandiose concepts as Heaven and Hell.

Baque worked slowly, now and then trying a harmonic progression at the multichord and rejecting it, straining his mind for some fluttering accompaniment pattern that would simulate the sound of a flyer. But then—no. The Waring people wouldn't like that. They advertised that their flyers were noiseless.

Urgent-sounding door chimes shattered his concentration. He walked over to flip on the scanner, and Hulsey's pudgy face grinned out at him.

"Come on up," Baque told him. Hulsey nodded and disappeared.

Five minutes later he waddled through the door, sank into a chair that sagged dangerously under his bulky figure, plunked his briefcase onto the floor, and mopped his face. "Whew! Wish you'd get yourself a place lower down. Or into a building with modern conveniences. Elevators scare me to death!"

"I'm thinking of moving," Baque said.

"Good. It's about time."

"But it'll probably be somewhere higher up. The landlord has given me two days' notice."

Hulsey winced and shook his head sadly. "I see. Well, I won't keep you in suspense. Here's the check for the Sana-Soap Com."

Baque took the card, glanced at it, and scowled.

"You were behind in your guild dues," Hulsey said. "Have to deduct them, you know."

"Yes. I'd forgotten."

"I like to do business with Sana-Soap. Cash right on the line. Too many companies wait until the end of the month. Sana-Soap wants a couple of changes, but they paid anyway." He unsealed the briefcase and pulled out a folder. "You've got some sly bits in this one, Erlin my boy. They like it. Particularly this 'sudsy, sudsy, sudsy' thing in the bass. They kicked on the number of singers at first, but not after they heard it. Now right here they want a break for a straight announcement."

Baque nodded thoughtfully. "How about keeping the 'sudsy, sudsy' ostinato going as a background to the announcement?"

"Sounds good. That's a sly bit, that—what'd you call it?"

"Ostinato."

"Ah—yes. Wonder why the other tunesmiths don't work in bits like that."

"A harmonizer doesn't produce effects," Baque said dryly. "It just—harmonizes."

"You give them about thirty seconds of that 'sudsy' for background. They can cut it if they don't like it."

Baque nodded, scribbling a note on the manuscript.

"And the arrangement," Hulsey went on. "Sorry, Erlin, but we can't get a French horn player. You'll have to do something else with that part."

"No horn player? What's wrong with Rankin?"

"Blacklisted. The Performers' Guild nixed him permanently. He went out to the West Coast and played for nothing. Even paid his own expenses. The guild can't tolerate that sort of thing."

"I remember," Baque said softly. "The Monuments of Art Society. He played a Mozart horn concerto for them. Their final concert, too. Wish I could have heard it, even if it was with multichord."

"He can play it all he wants to now, but he'll never get paid for playing again. You can work that horn part into the multichord line, or I might be able to get you a trumpet player. He could use a converter."

"It'll ruin the effect."

Hulsey chuckled. "Sounds the same to everyone but you, my boy. I can't tell the difference. We got your violins and a cello player. What more do you want?"

"Doesn't the London Guild have a horn player?"

"You want me to bring him over for one three-minute Com? Be reasonable, Erlin! Can I pick this up tomorrow?"

"Yes. I'll have it ready in the morning."

Hulsey reached for his briefcase, dropped it again, leaned forward scowling. "Erlin, I'm worried about you. I have twenty-seven tunesmiths in my agency. You're the best by far. Hell, you're the best in the world, and you make the least money of any of them. Your net last year was twenty-two hundred. None of the others netted less than eleven thousand."

"That isn't news to me," Baque said.

"This may be. You have as many accounts as any of them. Did you know that?"

Baque shook his head. "No, I didn't know that."

"You have as many accounts, but you don't make any money. Want to know why? Two reasons. You spend too much time on a Com, and you write it too well. Sponsors can use one of your Coms for months—or sometimes even years, like that Tamper Cheese thing. People like to hear them. Now if you just didn't write so damned well, you could work faster, and the sponsors would have to use more of your Coms, and you could turn out more."

"I've thought about that. Even if I didn't, Val would keep reminding me. But it's no use. That's the way I have to work. If there was some way to get the sponsors to pay more for a *good* Com—"

"There isn't. The guild wouldn't stand for it, because good Coms mean less work, and most tunesmiths couldn't write a really good Com. Now don't think I'm concerned about my agency. Of course I make more money when you make more, but I'm doing well enough with my other tunesmiths. I just hate to see my best man making so little money. You're a throwback, Erlin. You waste time and money collecting those antique—what do you call them?"

"Phonograph records."

"Yes. And those moldy old books about music. I don't doubt that you know more about music than anyone alive, and what does it get you? Not money, certainly. You're the best there is, and you keep trying to be better, and the better you get the less money you make. Your income drops lower every year. Couldn't you manage just an average Com now and then?"

"No," Baque said brusquely. "I couldn't manage it."

"Think it over."

"These accounts I have. Some of the sponsors really like my work. They'd pay more if the guild would let them. Supposing I left the guild?"

"You can't, my boy. I couldn't handle your stuff—not and stay in business long. The Tunesmiths' Guild would turn on the pressure, and the Performers' and Lyric Writers' Guilds would blacklist you. Jimmy Denton plays along with the guilds and he'd bar your stuff from visiscope. You'd lose all your accounts, and fast. No sponsor is big enough to fight all that trouble, and none of them would want to bother. So just try to be average now and then. Think about it."

Baque sat staring at the floor. "I'll think about it."

Hulsey struggled to his feet, clasped Baque's hand briefly, and waddled out. Baque closed the door behind him and went to the drawer where he kept his meager collection of old phonograph records. Strange and wonderful music.

Three times in his career Baque had written Coms that were a full half-hour in length. On rare occasions he got an order for fifteen minutes. Usually he was limited to five or less. But composers like the B-A-C-H Baque wrote things that lasted an hour or more—even wrote them without lyrics.

And they wrote for real instruments, among them amazing-sounding things that no one played any more, like bassoons, piccolos and pianos.

"Damn Denton. Damn visiscope. Damn guilds."

Baque rummaged tenderly among the discs until he found one bearing Bach's name. *Magnificat.* Then, because he felt too despondent to listen, he pushed it away.

Earlier that year the Performers' Guild had blacklisted its last oboe player. Now its last horn player, and there just weren't any young people learning to play instruments. Why should they, when there were so many marvelous contraptions that ground out the Coms without any effort on the part of the performer? Even multichord players were becoming scarce, and if one wasn't particular about how well it was done, a multichord could practically play itself.

The door jerked open, and Val hurried in. "Did Hulsey—"

Baque handed her the check. She took it eagerly, glanced at it, and looked up in dismay.

"My guild dues," he said. "I was behind."

"Oh. Well, it's a help, anyway." Her voice was flat, emotionless, as though one more disappointment really didn't matter. They stood facing each other awkwardly.

"I watched part of *Morning with Marigold*," Val said. "She talked about your Coms."

"I should hear soon on that Slo-Smoke Com," Baque said. "Maybe we can hold the landlord off for another week. Right now I'm going to walk around a little."

"You should get out more—"

He closed the door behind him, slicing her sentence off neatly. He knew what followed. Get a job somewhere. It'd be good for your health to get out of the apartment a few hours a day. Write Coms in your spare time—they don't bring in more than a part-time income anyway. At least do it until we get caught up. All right, if you won't, I will.

But she never did. A prospective employer never wanted more than one look at her slight body and her worn, sullen face. And Baque doubted that he would receive any better treatment.

He could get work as a multichord player and make a good income—but if he did he'd have to join the Performers' Guild, which meant that he'd have to resign from the Tunesmiths' Guild. So the choice was between performing and composing, the guilds wouldn't let him do both.

"Damn the guilds! Damn Coms!"

When he reached the street, he stood for a moment watching the crowds shooting past on the swiftly moving conveyer. A few people glanced at him and saw a tall, gawky, balding man in a frayed, badly fitting suit. They would consider him just another derelict from a shabby neighborhood, he knew, and they would quickly look the other way while they hummed a snatch from one of his Coms.

He hunched up his shoulders and walked awkwardly along the stationary sidewalk. At a crowded restaurant he turned in, found a table at one side, and ordered beer. On the rear wall was an enormous visiscope screen where the Coms followed each other without interruption. Around him the other customers watched and listened while they ate. Some nodded their heads jerkily in time with the music. A few young couples were dancing on the small dance floor, skillfully changing steps as the music shifted from one Com to another.

Baque watched them sadly and thought about the way things had changed. At one time, he knew, there had been special music for dancing and special groups of instruments to play it. And people had gone to concerts by the thousands, sitting in seats with nothing to look at but the performers.

All of it had vanished. Not only the music, but art and literature and poetry. The plays he once read in his grand-father's school books were forgotten.

James Denton's *Visiscope International* decreed that people must look and listen at the same time, and that the public at-tention span wouldn't tolerate long programs. So there were Coms.

Damn Coms!

When Val returned to the apartment an hour later, Baque was sitting in the corner staring at the battered plastic cabinet that held the crumbling volumes he had collected from the days when books were still printed on paper—a scattering of biographies, books on music history, and technical books about music theory and composition. Val looked twice about the room before she noticed him, and then she confronted him anxiously, stark tragedy etching her wan face.

"The man's coming to fix the food synthesizer."

"Good," Baque said.

"But the landlord won't wait. If we don't pay him day after tomorrow—pay him everything—we're out."

"So we're out."

"Where will we go? We can't get in anywhere without paying something in advance."

"So we won't get in anywhere."

She fled sobbing into the bedroom.

The next morning Baque resigned from the Tunesmiths' Guild and joined the Performers' Guild. Hulsey's round face drooped mournfully when he heard the news. He loaned Baque enough money to pay his guild registration fee and quiet the landlord, and he expressed his sorrow in eloquent terms as he hurried Baque out of his office. He would, Baque knew, waste

no time in assigning Baque's clients to his other tunesmiths—
to men who worked faster and not so well.

Baque went to the Guild Hall, where he sat for five hours
waiting for a multichord assignment. He was finally summoned
to the secretary's office and brusquely motioned into a chair.
The secretary eyed him suspiciously.

"You belonged to the Performers' Guild twenty years ago,
and you left it to become a tunesmith. Right?"

"Right," Baque said.

"You lost your seniority after three years. You knew that,
didn't you?"

"I did, but I didn't think it mattered. There aren't many
good multichord players around."

"There aren't many good jobs around, either. You'll have to
start at the bottom." He scribbled on a slip of paper and thrust
it at Baque. "This one pays well, but we have a hard time keeping a man there. Lankey isn't easy to work for. If you don't
irritate him too much—well, then we'll see."

Baque rode the conveyer out to the New Jersey Space Port,
wandered through a rattletrap slum area getting his directions
hopelessly confused, and finally found the place almost within
radiation distance of the port. The sprawling building had
burned at some time in the remote past. Stubby remnants of
walls rose out of the weed-choked rubble. A walk curved toward a dimly lit cavity at one corner, where steps led uncertainly downward. Overhead, an enormous sign pointed its
flowing colors in the direction of the port. The LANKEY-
PANK OUT.

Baque stepped through the door and faltered at the on-
slaught of extraterrestrial odors. Lavender-tinted tobacco smoke,
the product of the enormous leaves grown in bot-domes in
the Lunar Mare Crisium, hung like a limp blanket midway
between floor and ceiling. The revolting, cutting fumes of
blast, a whisky blended with a product of Martian lichens, staggered him. He had a glimpse of a scattered gathering of tough
spacers and tougher prostitutes before the doorman planted
his bulky figure and scarred caricature of a face in front of him.

"You looking for someone?"

"Mr. Lankey."

The doorman jerked a thumb in the direction of the bar and noisily stumbled back into the shadows. Baque walked toward the bar.

He had no trouble in picking out Lankey. The proprietor sat on a tall stool behind the bar. In the dim, smoke-streaked light his taut pale face had a spectral grimness. He leaned an elbow on the bar, fingered his flattened stump of a nose with the two remaining fingers on his hairy hand, and as Baque approached he thrust his bald head forward and eyed him coldly.

"I'm Erlin Baque," Baque said.

"Yeah. The multichord player. Can you play that multichord, fellow?"

"Why, yes, I can play—"

"That's what they all say, and I've had maybe two in the last ten years that could really play. Most of them come out here figuring they'll set the thing on automatic and fuss around with one finger. I want that multichord *played*, fellow, and I'll tell you right now—if you can't play you might as well jet for home. There isn't any automatic on my multichord. I had it disconnected."

"I can play," Baque told him.

"All right. It doesn't take more than one Com to find out. The guild rates this place as Class Four, but I pay Class One rates if you can play. If you can really play, I'll slip you some bonuses the guild won't know about. Hours are six P.M. to six A.M., but you get plenty of breaks, and if you get hungry or thirsty just ask for what you want. Only go easy on the hot stuff. I won't go along with a drunk multichord player no matter how good he is. Rose!"

He bellowed the name a second time, and a woman stepped from a door at the side of the room. She wore a faded dressing gown, and her tangled hair hung untidily about her shoulders. She turned a small, pretty face toward Baque and studied him boldly.

"Multichord," Lankey said. "Show him."

Rose beckoned, and Baque followed her toward the rear of the room. Suddenly he halted in amazement.

"What's the matter?" Rose asked.

"No visiscope!"

"No. Lankey says the spacers want better things to look at than soapsuds and flyers." She giggled. "Something like me, for example."

"I never heard of a restaurant without visiscope."

"Neither did I, until I came here. But Lankey's got three of us to sing the Coms, and you're to do the multichord with us. I hope you make the grade. We haven't had a multichord player for a week, and it's hard singing without one."

"I'll make out all right," Baque said.

A narrow platform stretched across the end of the room where any other restaurant would have had its visiscope screen. Baque could see the unpatched scars in the wall where the screen had been torn out.

"Lankey ran a joint at Port Mars back when the colony didn't have visiscope," Rose said. "He has his own ideas about how to entertain customers. Want to see your room?"

Baque was examining the multichord. It was a battered old instrument, and it bore the marks of more than one brawl. He fingered the filter buttons and swore softly to himself. Only the flute and violin filters clicked into place properly. So he would have to spend twelve hours a day with the twanging tones of an unfiltered multichord.

"Want to see your room?" Rose asked again. "It's only five. You might as well relax until we have to go to work."

Rose showed him a cramped enclosure behind the bar. He stretched out on a hard cot and tried to relax, and suddenly it was six o'clock and Lankey stood in the door beckoning to him.

He took his place at the multichord and fingered the keys impatiently. He felt no nervousness. There wasn't anything he didn't know about Coms, and he knew he wouldn't have trouble with the music, but the atmosphere disturbed him. The haze of smoke was thicker, and he blinked his smarting eyes and felt the whisky fumes tear at his nostrils when he took a deep breath.

There was still only a scattering of customers. The men were mechanics in grimy work suits, swaggering pilots, and a few

civilians who liked their liquor strong and didn't mind the surroundings. The women were—women; two of them, he guessed,
for every man in the room.

Suddenly the men began an unrestrained stomping of feet
accented with yelps of approval. Lankey was crossing the platform with Rose and the other singers. Baque's first horrified
impression was that the girls were nude, but as they came closer
he made out their brief plastic costumes. Lankey was right, he
thought. The spacers would much prefer that kind of scenery
to animated Coms on a visiscope screen.

"You met Rose," Lankey said. "This is Zanna and Mae. Let's
get going."

He walked away, and the girls gathered about the multichord. "What Coms do you know?" Rose asked.

"I know them all."

She looked at him doubtfully. "We sing together, and then
we take turns. Are you sure you know them all?"

Baque flipped on the power and sounded a chord. "Sing any
Com you want—I can handle it."

"Well—we'll start out with a Tasty-Malt Com. It goes like
this." She hummed softly. "Know that one?"

"I wrote it," Baque said.

They sang better than he had expected. He followed them
easily, and while he played he kept his eyes on the customers.
Heads were jerking in time with the music, and he quickly
caught the mood and began to experiment. His fingers shaped
a rolling rhythm in the bass, fumbled with it tentatively, and
then expanded it. He abandoned the melodic line, leaving the
girls to carry on by themselves while he searched the entire
keyboard to ornament the driving rhythm.

Feet began to stomp. The girls' bodies were swaying wildly,
and Baque felt himself rocking back and forth as the music
swept on recklessly. The girls finished their lyrics, and when
he did not stop playing they began again. Spacers were on their
feet, now, clapping and swaying. Some seized their women and
began dancing in the narrow spaces between the tables.
Finally Baque forced a cadence and slumped forward, panting
and mopping his forehead. One of the girls collapsed onto the

stage. The others hauled her to her feet, and the three of them fled to a frenzy of applause.

Baque felt a hand on his shoulder. Lankey. His ugly, expressionless face eyed Baque, turned to study the wildly enthusiastic customers, turned back to Baque. He nodded and walked away.

Rose returned alone, still breathing heavily. "How about a Sally Ann Perfume Com?"

Baque searched his memory and was chagrined to find no recollection of Sally Ann's Coms. "Tell me the words," he said. She recited them tonelessly—a tragic little story about the shattered romance of a girl who did not use Sally Ann. "Now I remember," Baque told her. "Shall we make them cry? Just concentrate on that. It's a sad story, and we're going to make them cry."

She stood by the multichord and sang plaintively. Baque fashioned a muted, tremulous accompaniment, and when the second verse started he improvised a drooping countermelody. The spacers sat in hushed suspense. The men did not cry, but some of the women sniffed audibly, and when Rose finished there was a taut silence.

"Quick!" Baque hissed. "Let's brighten things up. Sing another Com—anything!"

She launched into a Puffed Bread Com, and Baque brought the spacers to their feet with the driving rhythm of his accompaniment.

The other girls took their turns, and Baque watched the customers detachedly, bewildered at the power that surged in his fingers. He carried them from one emotional extreme to the other and back again, improvising, experimenting. And his mind fumbled haltingly with an idea.

"Time for a break," Rose said finally. "Better get something to eat."

An hour and a half of continuous playing had left Baque drained of strength and emotion, and he accepted his dinner tray indifferently and took it to the enclosure they called his room. He did not feel hungry. He sniffed doubtfully at the food, tasted it—and ate ravenously. Real food, after months of synthetics!

When he'd finished he sat for a time on his cot, wondering how long the girls took between appearances, and then he went looking for Lankey.

"I don't like sitting around," he said. "Any objection to my playing?"

"Without the girls?"

"Yes."

Lankey planted both elbows on the bar, cupped his chin in one fist, and sat looking absently at the far wall. "You going to sing yourself?" he asked finally.

"No. Just play."

"Without any singing? Without words?"

"Yes."

"What'll you play?"

"Coms. Or I might improvise something."

A long silence. Then—"Think you could keep things moving while the girls are out?"

"Of course I could."

Lankey continued to concentrate on the far wall. His eyebrows contracted, relaxed, contracted again. "All right," he said. "I was just wondering why I never thought of it."

Unnoticed, Baque took his place at the multichord. He began softly, making the music an unobtrusive background to the rollicking conversation that filled the room. As he increased the volume, faces turned in his direction.

He wondered what these people were thinking as they heard for the first time music that was not a Com, music without words. He watched intently and satisfied himself that he was holding their attention. Now—could he bring them out of their seats with nothing more than the sterile tones of a multichord? He gave the melody a rhythmic snap, and the stomping began.

As he increased the volume again, Rose came stumbling out of a doorway and hurried across the stage, perplexity written on her pert face.

"It's all right," Baque told her. "I'm just playing to amuse myself. Don't come back until you're ready."

She nodded and walked away. A red-faced spacer near the platform looked up at the revealed outline of her young body and leered. Fascinated, Baque studied the coarse, demanding lust in his face and searched the keyboard to express it. This? Or—this? Or—

He had it. He felt himself caught up in the relentless rhythm. His foot tightened on the volume control, and he turned to watch the customers.

Every pair of eyes stared hypnotically at his corner of the room. A bartender stood at a half crouch, mouth agape. There was uneasiness, a strained shuffling of feet, a restless scraping of chairs. Baque's foot dug harder at the volume control.

His hands played on hypnotically, and he stared in horror at the scene that erupted below him. Lasciviousness twisted every face. Men were on their feet, reaching for the women, clutching, pawing. A chair crashed to the floor, and a table, and no one noticed. A woman's dress fluttered crazily downward, and the pursued were pursuers while Baque helplessly allowed his fingers to race onward, out of control.

With a violent effort he wrenched his hands from the keys, and the ensuing silence crashed the room like a clap of thunder. Fingers trembling, Baque began to play softly, indifferently. Order was restored when he looked again, the chair and table were upright, and the customers were seated in apparent relaxation except for one woman who struggled back into her dress in obvious embarrassment.

Baque continued to play quietly until the girls returned.

At 6 A.M., his body wracked with weariness, his hands aching, his legs cramped, Baque climbed down from the multichord. Lankey stood waiting for him. "Class One rates," he said. "You've got a job with me as long as you want it. But take it a little easy with that stuff, will you?"

Baque remembered Val, alone in their dreary apartment and eating synthetic food. "Would I be out of order to ask for an advance?"

"No," Lankey said. "Not out of order. I told the cashier to give you a hundred on your way out. Call it a bonus."

Weary from his long conveyer ride, Baque walked quietly into his dim apartment and looked about. There was no sign of Val—she would still be sleeping. He sat down at his own multichord and touched the keys.

He felt awed and humble and disbelieving. Music without Coms, without words, could make people laugh and cry, and dance and cavort madly.

And it could turn them into lewd animals.

Wonderingly he played the music that had incited such unconcealed lust, played it louder, and louder—

And felt a hand on his shoulder, and turned to look into Val's passion-twisted face.

He asked Hulsey to come and hear him that night, and later Hulsey sat slumped on the cot in his room and shuddered. "It isn't right. No man should have that power over people. How do you do it?"

"I don't know," Baque said. "I saw that young couple sitting there, and they were happy, and I felt their happiness. And as I played everyone in the room was happy. And then another couple came in quarreling, and the next thing I knew I had everyone mad."

"Almost started a fight at the next table," Hulsey said. "And what you did after that—"

"Yes. But not as much as I did last night. You should have seen it last night."

Hulsey shuddered again.

"I have a book about ancient Greek music," Baque said. "They had something they called *ethos*. They thought that the different musical scales affected people in different ways—could make them sad, or happy, or even drive them crazy. They claimed that a musician named Orpheus could move trees and soften rocks with his music. Now listen. I've had a chance to experiment, and I've noticed that my playing is most effective when I don't use the filters. There are only two filters that work on that multichord anyway—flute and violin—but when I use either of them the people don't react so strongly. I'm wondering if maybe the effects the Greeks talk about were produced by their instruments, rather than their scales. I'm wondering if the tone of an unfiltered multichord might have something in common with the tones of the ancient Greek *kithara* or *aulos*."

Hulsey grunted. "I don't think it's the instrument, or the scales either. I think it's Baque, and I don't like it. You should have stayed a tunesmith."

"I want you to help me," Baque said. "I want to find a place where we can put a lot of people—a thousand, at least—not to eat, or watch Coms, but just to listen to one man play on a multichord."

Hulsey got up abruptly. "Baque, you're a dangerous man. I'm damned if I'll trust any man who can make me feel the way you made me feel tonight. I don't know what you're trying to do, but I won't have any part of it."

He stomped away in the manner of a man about to slam a door, but the room of a male multichordist at the Lankey-Pank Out did not rate that luxury. Hulsey paused uncertainly in the doorway, gave Baque a parting glare, and disappeared. Baque followed him as far as the main room and stood watching him weave his way impatiently past the tables to the exit.

From his place behind the bar, Lankey looked at Baque and then glanced after the disappearing Hulsey. "Troubles?" he asked.

Baque turned away wearily. "I've known that man for twenty years. I never thought he was my friend. But then—I never thought he was my enemy, either."

"Sometimes it works out that way," Lankey said.

Baque shook his head. "I'd like to try some Martian whisky. I've never tasted the stuff."

Two weeks made Baque an institution, and the Lankey-Pank Out was jammed to capacity from the time he went to work until he left the next morning. When he performed alone, he forgot about Coms and played whatever he wanted. He even performed short pieces by Bach for the customers, and received generous applause, but the reaction was nothing like the tumultuous enthusiasm that followed his improvisations.

Sitting behind the bar, eating his evening meal and watching the impacted mass of customers, Baque felt vaguely happy. He was enjoying the work he was doing. For the first time in his life he had more money than he needed.

For the first time in his life he had a definite goal and a vague notion of a plan that would accomplish it—would eliminate the Coms altogether.

As Baque pushed his tray aside, he saw Biff the doorman step forward to greet a pair of newcomers, halt suddenly, and back away in stupefied amazement. And no wonder—evening clothes at the Lankey-Pank Out!

The couple halted near the door, blinking uncertainly in the dim, smoke-tinted light. The man was bronzed and handsome, but no one noticed him. The woman's beauty flashed like a meteor against the drab surroundings. She moved in an aura of shining loveliness, with her hair gleaming golden, her shimmering, flowing gown clinging seductively to her voluptuous figure, and her fragrance routing the foul tobacco and whisky odors.

In an instant all eyes were fixed on her, and a collective gasp encircled the room. Baque stared with the others and finally recognized her: Marigold, of *Morning with Marigold*. Worshiped around the Solar System by the millions of devotees to her visiscope program. Mistress, it was said, to James Denton, the czar of visiscope. Marigold Manning.

She raised a hand to her mouth in mock horror, and the bright tones of her laughter dropped tantalizingly among the spellbound spacers. "What an odd place! Where'd you ever hear about a place like this?"

"I need some Martian whisky, damn it," the man said.

"So stupid of the port bar to run out. With all those ships from Mars coming in, too. Are you sure we can get back in time? Jimmy'll raise hell if we aren't there when he lands."

Lankey touched Baque's arm. "After six," he said, without taking his eyes from Marigold Manning. "They'll be getting impatient."

Baque nodded and started for the multichord. The tumult began the moment the customers saw him. They abandoned Marigold Manning, leaped to their feet, and began a stomping, howling ovation. When Baque paused to acknowledge it, Marigold and her escort were staring openmouthed at the nondescript man who could inspire such undignified enthusiasm. Her exclamation rang out sharply as Baque seated himself at the multichord and the ovation faded to an expectant silence. "What the hell!"

Baque shrugged and started to play. When Marigold finally left, after a brief conference with Lankey, her escort still hadn't got his Martian whisky.

The next evening Lankey greeted Baque with both fists full of telenotes. "What a hell of a mess this is! You see this Marigold dame's program this morning?"

Baque shook his head. "I haven't watched visiscope since I came to work here."

"In case it interests you, you were—what does she call it?—a 'Marigold Exclusive' on visiscope this morning. Erlin Baque, the famous tunesmith, is now playing the multichord in a queer little restaurant called the Lankey-Pank Out. If you want to hear some amazing music, wander out to the New Jersey Space Port and listen to Baque. Don't miss it. The experience of a lifetime." Lankey swore and waved the telenotes. "Queer, she calls us. Now I've got ten thousand requests for reservations, some from as far away as Budapest and Shanghai. And our capacity is five hundred, counting standing room. Damn that woman! We already had all the business we could handle."

"You need a bigger place," Baque said.

"Yes. Well, confidentially, I've got my eye on a big warehouse. It'll seat a thousand, at least. We'll clean up. I'll give you a contract to take charge of the music."

Baque shook his head. "How about opening a big place uptown? Attract people that have more money to spend. You run it, and I'll bring in the customers."

Lankey caressed his flattened nose thoughtfully. "How do we split?"

"Fifty-fifty," Baque said.

"No," Lankey said, shaking his head slowly. "I play fair, Baque, but fifty-fifty wouldn't be right on a deal like that. I'd have to put up all the money myself. I'll give you one-third to handle the music."

They had a lawyer draw up a contract. Baque's lawyer. Lankey insisted on that.

In the bleak gray of early morning Baque sleepily rode the crowded conveyer toward his apartment. It was the peak rush load, when commuters jammed against each other and snarled grumpily when a neighbor shifted his feet. The crowd seemed even heavier than usual, but Baque shrugged off the jostling and elbowing and lost himself in thought.

It was time that he found a better place to live. He hadn't minded the dumpy apartment as long as he could afford nothing better, but Val had been complaining for years. And now when they could move, when they could have a luxury apartment or even a small home over in Pennsylvania, Val refused to go. Didn't want to leave her friends, she said.

Mulling over this problem in feminine contrariness, Baque realized suddenly that he was approaching his own stop. He attempted to move toward a deceleration strip—he shoved firmly, he tried to step between his fellow riders, he applied his elbows, first gently and then viciously. The crowd about him did not yield.

"I beg your pardon," Baque said, making another attempt. "I get off here."

This time a pair of brawny arms barred his way. "Not this morning, Baque. You got an appointment uptown."

Baque flung a glance at the circle of hard, grinning faces that surrounded him. With a sudden effort he hurled himself sideways, fighting with all of his strength. The arms hauled him back roughly.

"Uptown, Baque. If you want to go dead, that's your affair."

"Uptown," Baque agreed.

At a public parking strip they left the conveyer. A flyer was waiting for them, a plush, private job that displayed a high-priority X registration number. They flew swiftly toward Manhattan, cutting across air lanes with a monumental contempt for regulations, and they veered in for a landing on the towering

Visiscope International building. Baque was bundled down an anti-grav shaft, led through a labyrinth of corridors, and finally prodded none too gently into an office.

It was a huge room, and its sparse furnishings made it look more enormous than it was. It contained only a desk, a few chairs, a bar in the far corner, an enormous visiscope screen—and a multichord. The desk was occupied, but it was the group of men about the bar that caught Baque's attention. His gaze swept the blur of faces and found one that he recognized: Hulsey.

The plump agent took two steps forward and stood glaring at Baque. "Day of reckoning, Erlin," he said coldly.

A hand rapped sharply on the desk. "I take care of any reckoning that's done around here, Hulsey. Please sit down, Mr. Baque."

A chair was thrust forward, and Baque seated himself and waited nervously, his eyes on the man behind the desk.

"My name is James Denton. Does my fame extend to such a remote place as the Lankey-Pank Out?"

"No," Baque said. "But I've heard of you."

James Denton. Czar of Visiscope International. Ruthless arbiter of public taste. He was no more than forty, with a swarthy, handsome face, flashing eyes, and a ready smile.

He tapped a cigar on the edge of his desk and carefully placed it in his mouth. Men sprang forward with lighters extended, and he chose one without looking up, puffed deeply, and nodded.

"I won't bore you with introductions to this gathering, Baque. Some of these men are here for professional reasons. Some are here because they're curious. I heard about you for the first time yesterday, and what I heard made me want to find out whether you're a potential asset that might be made use of, or a potential nuisance that should be eliminated, or a nonentity that can be ignored. When I want to know something, Baque, I waste no time about it." He chuckled. "As you can see from the fact that I had you brought in at the earliest moment you were —shall we say—available."

"The man's dangerous, Denton!" Hulsey blurted.

Denton flashed his smile. "I like dangerous men, Hulsey.

They're useful to have around. If I can use whatever it is Mr. Baque has, I'll make him an attractive offer. I'm sure he'll accept it gratefully. If I can't use it, I aim to make damned certain that he won't be inconveniencing me. Do I make myself clear, Baque?"

Baque, looking past Denton to avoid his eyes, said nothing.

Denton leaned forward. His smile did not waver, but his eyes narrowed and his voice was suddenly icy. "Do I make myself clear, Baque?"

"Yes," Baque muttered weakly.

Denton jerked a thumb toward the door, and half of those present, including Hulsey, solemnly filed out. The others waited, talking in whispers, while Denton puffed steadily on his cigar. Finally an intercom rasped a single word. "Ready!"

Denton pointed at the multichord. "We crave a demonstration of your skill, Mr. Baque. And take care that it's a good demonstration. Hulsey is listening, and he can tell us if you try to stall."

Baque nodded and took his place at the multichord. He sat with fingers poised, timidly looking up at a circle of staring faces. Overlords of business, they were, and of science and industry, and never in their lives had they heard real music. As for Hulsey —yes, Hulsey would be listening, but over Denton's intercom, over a communication system designed to carry voices.

And Hulsey had a terrible ear for music.

Baque grinned contemptuously, touched the violin filter, touched it again, and faltered.

Denton chuckled dryly. "I neglected to inform you, Mr. Baque. On Hulsey's advice, we've had the filters disconnected."

Anger surged within Baque. He jammed his foot down hard on the volume control, insolently tapped out a visiscope fanfare, and started to play his Tamper Cheese Com. Denton, his own anger evident in his flushed face, leaned forward and snarled something. The men around him stirred uneasily. Baque shifted to another Com, improvised some variations, and began to watch the circle of faces. Overlords of industry, science and business. It would be amusing, he thought, to make them stomp their feet. His fingers shaped a compelling rhythm, and they began to sway restlessly.

He forgot his resolution to play cautiously. Laughing silently to himself, he released an overpowering torrent of sound that set the men dancing and brought Denton to his feet. He froze them in ridiculous postures with an outburst of surging emotion. He made them stomp recklessly, he brought tears to their eyes, and he finished off with the pounding force that Lankey called, "Sex Music."

Then he slumped over the keyboard, terrified at what he had done.

Denton stood behind his desk, face pale, hands clenching and unclenching. "Good God!" he muttered.

He snarled a word at his intercom. "Reaction?"

"Negative," came the prompt answer.

"Let's wind it up."

Denton sat down, passed his hand across his face, and turned to Baque with a bland smile. "An impressive performance, Mr. Baque. We'll know in a few minutes—ah, here they are."

Those who had left earlier filed back into the room, and several men huddled together in a whispered conference. Denton left his desk and paced the floor meditatively. The other men in the room, including Hulsey, gravitated toward the bar.

Baque kept his place at the multichord and watched the conference uneasily. Once he accidentally touched a key, and the single tone shattered the poise of the conferees, halted Denton in midstride, and startled Hulsey into spilling his drink.

"Mr. Baque is getting impatient," Denton called. "Can't we finish this?"

"One moment, sir."

Finally they filed toward Denton's desk. The spokesman, a white-haired, scholarly-looking man with a delicate pink complexion, cleared his throat self-consciously and waited until Denton had returned to his chair.

"It is established," he said, "that those in this room were powerfully affected by the music. Those listening on the intercom experienced no reaction except a mild boredom."

"I didn't call you in here to state the obvious," Denton snapped. "How does he do it?"

"We can only offer a working hypothesis."

"So you're guessing. Let's have it."

"Erlin Baque has the ability to telepathetically project his emotional experience. When the projection is subtly reinforced by his multichord playing, those in his immediate presence share that experience intensely. The projection has no effect upon those listening to his music at a distance."

"And—visiscope?"

"He could not project his emotions by way of visiscope."

"I see," Denton said. A meditative scowl twisted his face. "What about his long-term effectiveness?"

"It's difficult to predict—"

"Predict, damn it!"

"The novelty of his playing would attract attention, at first. While the novelty lasted he might become a kind of fad. By the time his public lost interest he would probably have a small group of followers who would use the emotional experience of his playing as a narcotic."

"Thank you, gentlemen. That will be all."

The room emptied quickly. Hulsey paused in the doorway, glared hatefully at Baque, and then walked out meekly.

"Obviously you're no nonentity," Denton said, "but whatever it is you have is of no use to me. Unfortunately. If you could project on visiscope, you'd be worth a billion an hour in advertising revenue. Fortunately for you, your nuisance rating is fairly low. I know what you and Lankey are up to. If I say the word, you'll never in this lifetime find a place for your new restaurant. I could have the Lankey-Pank Out closed down within an hour, but it would hardly be worth the trouble. If you can develop a cult for yourself, why—perhaps it will keep the members out of worse mischief. I'm feeling so generous this morning that I won't even insist on a visiscope screen in your new restaurant. Now you'd better leave, Baque, before I change my mind."

Baque got to his feet. At that moment Marigold Manning swept into the room, radiantly lovely, exotically perfumed, her glistening blonde hair swept up into a new and tantalizing hair style.

"Jimmy, darling—oh!" She stared at Baque, stared at the multichord, and stammered, "Why, you're—you're—Erlin Baque! Jimmy, why didn't you tell me?"

"Mr. Baque has been favoring me with a private performance," Denton said brusquely. "I think we understand each other, Baque. Good morning."

"You're going to put him on visiscope!" Marigold exclaimed. "Jimmy, that's wonderful. May I have him first? I can work him in this morning."

Denton shook his head. "Sorry, darling. We've decided that Mr. Baque's talent is not quite suitable for visiscope."

"At least I can have him for a guest. You'll be my guest, won't you, Mr. Baque? There's nothing wrong with giving him a guest spot, is there, Jimmy?"

Denton chuckled. "No. After all the fuss you stirred up, it might be a good idea for you to guest him. It'll serve you right when he bombs."

"He won't bomb. He'll be wonderful on visiscope. Will you come in this morning, Mr. Baque?"

"Well—" Baque began. Denton was nodding at him emphatically. "We'll be opening a new restaurant soon. I wouldn't mind being your guest on opening day."

"A new restaurant? That's wonderful! Does anyone know? I'll give it out this morning as an exclusive!"

"It isn't exactly settled, yet," Baque said apologetically. "We haven't found a place yet."

"Lankey found a place yesterday," Denton said. "He's having a contractor check it over this morning, and if no snags develop he'll sign a lease. Just let Miss Manning know your opening date, Baque, and she'll arrange a spot for you. Now if you don't mind—"

It took Baque half an hour to find his way out of the building, but he plodded aimlessly along the corridors and disdained asking directions. He hummed happily to himself, and now and then he broke into a laugh.

The overlords of business and industry—and their scientists —knew nothing about overtones.

"So that's the way it is," Lankey said. "You seem to have no notion of how lucky you were—how lucky we were. Denton should have made his move when he had a chance. Now we know what to expect, and when he finally wises up it'll be too late."

"What could we do if he decided to put us out of business?"

"I have a few connections myself, Baque. They don't run in high society, like Denton, but they're every bit as dishonest, and Denton has a lot of enemies who'll be happy to back us. Said he could close me down in an hour, eh? Unfortunately there's not much we could do that would hurt Denton, but there's plenty we can do to keep him from hurting us."

"I think we're going to hurt Denton," Baque said.

Lankey moved over to the bar and came back with a tall glass of pink, foaming liquid. "Drink it," he said. "You've had a long day, and you're getting delirious. How could we hurt Denton?"

"Visiscope depends on Coms. We'll show the people they can have entertainment without Coms. We'll make our motto NO COMS AT LANKEY'S!"

"Great," Lankey drawled. "I invest a thousand in fancy new costumes for the girls—they can't wear those plastic things in our new place, you know—and you decide not to let them sing."

"Certainly they're going to sing."

Lankey leaned forward, caressing his nose. "And no Coms. Then *what* are they going to sing?"

"I took some lyrics out of an old school book my grandfather had. Back in those days they were called poems. I'm setting them to music. I was going to try them out here, but Denton might hear about it, and there's no use starting trouble before it's necessary."

"No. Save all the trouble for the new place—after opening day we'll be important enough to be able to handle it. And you'll be on *Morning with Marigold*. Are you certain about this overtones business, Baque? You really could be projecting emotions, you know. Not that it makes any difference in the restaurant, but on visiscope—"

"I'm certain. How soon can we open?"

"I got three shifts remodeling the place. We'll seat twelve hundred and still have room for a nice dance floor. Should be ready in two weeks. Baque, I'm not sure this visiscope thing is wise."

"I want to do it."

Lankey went back to the bar and got a drink for himself. "All right. You do it. If your stuff comes over, all hell is going to break loose, and I might as well start getting ready for it." He grinned. "Damned if it won't be good for business!"

Marigold Manning had changed her hair styling to a spiraled creation by Zann of Hong Kong, and she dallied for ten minutes in deciding which profile she would present to the cameras. Baque waited patiently, his awkward feeling wholly derived from the fact that his dress suit was the most expensive clothing he had ever owned. He kept telling himself to stop wondering if perhaps he really did project emotions.

"I'll have it this way," Marigold said finally, waving a hand screen in front of her face for a last, searching look. "And you, Mr. Baque? What shall we do with you?"

"Just put me at the multichord," Baque said.

"But you can't just play. You'll have to say *something*. I've been announcing this every day for a week, and we'll have the biggest audience in years, and you'll just *have* to say *something*."

"Gladly," Baque said, "if I can talk about Lankey's."

"But of course, you silly man. That's why you're here. You talk about Lankey's, and I'll talk about Erlin Baque."

"Five minutes," a voice announced crisply.

"Oh, dear," she said. "I'm always so nervous just before."

"Be happy you're not nervous during," Baque said.

"That's so right. Jimmy makes fun of me, but it takes an artist to understand another artist. Do you get nervous?"

"When I'm playing, I'm much too busy."

"That's just the way it is with me. Once my program starts, I'm much too busy."

"Four minutes."

"Oh, bother!" She seized the hand screen again. "Maybe I would be better the other way."

Baque seated himself at the multichord. "You're perfect the way you are."

"Do you really think so? It's a nice thing to say, anyway. I wonder if Jimmy will take the time to watch."

"I'm sure he will."

"Three minutes."

Baque switched on the power and sounded a chord. Now he *was* nervous. He had no idea what he would play. He'd intentionally refrained from preparing anything because it was his improvisations that affected people so strangely. The one thing he had to avoid was the Sex Music. Lankey had been emphatic about that.

He lost himself in thought, failed to hear the final warning, and looked up startled at Marigold's cheerful, "Good morning, everyone. It's *Morning with Marigold!*"

Her bright voice wandered on and on. Erlin Baque. His career as a tunesmith. Her amazing discovery of him playing in the Lankey-Pank Out. She asked the engineers to run the Tamper Cheese Com. Finally she finished her remarks and risked the distortion of her lovely profile to glance in his direction. "Ladies and gentlemen, with admiration, with pride, with pleasure, I give you a Marigold Exclusive, Erlin Baque!"

Baque grinned nervously and tapped out a scale with one finger. "This is my first speech. Probably it'll be my last. The new restaurant opens tonight. Lankey's, on Broadway. Unfortunately I can't invite you to join us, because thanks to Miss Manning's generous comments this past week all space is reserved for the next two months. After that we'll be setting aside a limited number of reservations for visitors from distant places. Jet over and see us!

"You'll find something different at Lankey's. There is no visiscope screen. Maybe you've heard about that. We have attractive young ladies to sing for you. I play the multichord. We know you'll enjoy our music. We know you'll enjoy it because you'll hear no Coms at Lankey's. Remember that—*no Coms at Lankey's*. No soap with your soup. No air cars with your steaks. No shirts with your deserts. *No Coms!* Just good food, with good music played exclusively for your enjoyment—like this."

He brought his hands down onto the keyboard.

Immediately he knew that something was wrong. He'd always had a throng of faces to watch, he'd paced his playing according to their reactions. Now he had only Miss Manning and the visiscope engineers, and he was suddenly apprehensive that his success had been wholly due to his audiences. People were listening throughout the Western Hemisphere. Would they clap and stomp, would they think awesomely, "So that's how music sounds without words, without Coms?" Or would they turn away in boredom?

Baque caught a glimpse of Marigold's pale face, of the engineers watching with mouths agape, and thought perhaps everything was all right. He lost himself in the music and played fervently.

He continued to play even after the pilot screen went blank. Miss Manning leaped to her feet and hurried toward him, and the engineers were moving about confusedly. Finally Baque brought his playing to a halt.

"We were cut off," Miss Manning said tearfully. "Who would do such a thing to me? Never, never, in all the time I've been on visiscope— George, who cut us off?"

"Orders."

"Whose orders?"

"My orders!" James Denton strode toward them, lips tight, face pale, eyes gleaming violence and sudden death. He spat words at Baque. "I don't know how you worked that trick, but no man fools James Denton more than once. Now you've made yourself a nuisance that has to be eliminated."

"Jimmy!" Miss Manning wailed. "My program—cut off. How could you?"

"Shut up, damn it! I just passed the word, Baque. Lankey's doesn't open tonight. Not that it'll make any difference to you."

Baque smiled gently. "I think you've lost, Denton. I think enough music got through to beat you. By tomorrow you'll have a million complaints. So will the government, and then you'll find out who really runs Visiscope International."

"I run Visiscope International."

"No, Denton. It belongs to the people. They've let things

slide for a long time, and they've taken anything you'd give them. But if they know what they want, they'll get it. I gave them at least three minutes of what they want. That was more than I'd hoped for."

"How'd you work that trick in my office?"

"That wasn't my trick, Denton—it was yours. You transmitted the music on a voice intercom. It didn't carry the overtones, the upper frequencies, so the multichord sounded dead to the men in the other room. Visiscope has the full frequency range of live sound."

Denton nodded. "I'll have the heads of some scientists for that. I'll also have your head, though I regret the waste. If you'd played square with me I'd have made you a live billionaire. The only alternative is a dead musician."

He stalked away, and as the automatic door closed behind him, Marigold Manning clutched Baque's arm. "Quick! Follow me!" Baque hesitated, and she hissed, "Don't stand there like an idiot! He's going to have you killed!"

She led him through a control room and out into a small corridor. They raced the length of it, darted through a reception room and passed a startled secretary without a word, and burst through a rear door into another corridor. She jerked Baque after her into an anti-grav lift, and they shot upward. At the top of the building she hurried him to an air car strip and left him standing in a doorway. "When I give you a signal, you walk out," she said. "Don't run, just walk."

She calmly approached an attendant, and Baque heard his surprised greeting. "Through early this morning, Miss Manning?"

"We're running a lot of Coms," she said. "I want the big Waring."

"Coming right up."

Peering around the corner, Baque saw her step into the flyer. As soon as the attendant's back was turned, she waved frantically. Baque walked carefully toward her, keeping the flyer between the attendant and himself. A moment later they were airborne, and far below them a siren was sounding faintly.

"We did it!" she gasped. "If you hadn't got away before that alarm sounded, you wouldn't have left the building alive."

"Well, thanks," Baque said, looking back at the Visiscope International building. "But surely this wasn't necessary. Earth is a civilized planet."

"Visiscope International is not civilized!" she snapped.

He looked at her wonderingly. Her face was flushed, her eyes wide with fear, and for the first time Baque saw her as a human being, a woman, a lovely woman. As he looked, she turned away and burst into tears.

"Now Jimmy'll have me killed, too. And where can we go?"

"Lankey's," Baque said. "Look—you can see it from here."

She pointed the flyer at the freshly painted letters on the strip above the new restaurant, and Baque, looking backward, saw a crowd forming in the street by Visiscope International.

Lankey floated his desk over to the wall and leaned back comfortably. He wore a trim dress suit, and he'd carefully groomed himself for the role of a jovial host, but in his office he was the same ungainly Lankey that Baque had first seen leaning over a bar.

"I told you all hell would break loose," he said, grinning. "There are five thousand people over by Visiscope International, and they're screaming for Erlin Baque. And the crowd is growing."

"I didn't play for more than three minutes," Baque said. "I thought a lot of people might write in to complain about Denton cutting me off, but I didn't expect anything like this."

"You didn't, eh? Five thousand people—maybe ten thousand by now—and Miss Manning risks her neck to get you out of the place. Ask her why, Baque."

"Yes," Baque said. "Why go to all that trouble for me?"

She shuddered. "Your music does things to me."

"It sure does," Lankey said. "Baque, you fool, you gave a quarter of Earth's population three minutes of Sex Music!"

Lankey's opened on schedule that evening, with crowds filling the street outside and struggling through the doors as long as there was standing room. The shrewd Lankey had instituted an admission charge. The standees bought no food, and Lankey saw no point in furnishing free music, even if people were willing to stand to hear it.

He made one last-minute change in plans. Astutely reasoning that the customers would prefer a glamorous hostess to a flat-nosed elderly host, he hired Marigold Manning. She moved about gracefully, the deep blue of her flowing gown offsetting her golden hair.

When Baque took his place at the multichord, the frenzied ovation lasted for twenty minutes.

Midway through the evening Baque sought out Lankey. "Has Denton tried anything?"

"Nothing that I've noticed. Everything is running smoothly."

"That seems odd. He swore we wouldn't open tonight."

Lankey chuckled. "He's had troubles of his own to worry about. The authorities are on his neck about the rioting. I was afraid they'd blame you, but they didn't. Denton put you on visiscope, and then he cut you off, and they figure he's responsible. And according to my last report, Visiscope International has had more than ten million complaints. Don't worry, Baque. We'll hear from Denton soon enough, and the guilds, too."

"The guilds? Why the guilds?"

"The Tunesmiths' Guild will be damned furious about your dropping the Coms. The Lyric Writers' Guild will go along with them on account of the Coms and because you're using music without words. The Performers' Guild already has it in for you because not many of its members can play worth a damn, and of course it'll support the other guilds. By tomorrow morning, Baque, you'll be the most popular man in the Solar System, and the sponsors, and the visiscope people, and the guilds are going to hate your guts. I'm giving you a twenty-four-hour bodyguard. Miss Manning, too. I want both of you to come out of this alive."

"Do you really think Denton would—"

"Denton would."

The next morning the Performers' Guild blacklisted Lankey's and ordered all the musicians, including Baque, to sever relations. Rose and the other singers joined Baque in respectfully declining, and they found themselves blacklisted before noon. Lankey called in an attorney, the most sinister, furtive, disreputable-looking individual Baque had ever seen.

"They're supposed to give us a week's notice," Lankey said, "and another week if we decide to appeal. I'll sue them for five million."

The Commissioner of Public Safety called, and on his heels came the Health Commissioner and the Liquor Commissioner. All three conferred briefly with Lankey and departed grim-faced.

"Denton's moving too late," Lankey said gleefully. "I got to all of them a week ago and recorded our conversations. They don't dare take any action."

A riot broke out in front of Lankey's that night. Lankey had his own riot squad ready for action, and the customers never noticed the disturbance. Lankey's informants estimated that more than fifty million complaints had been received by Visiscope International, and a dozen governmental agencies had scheduled investigations. Anti-Com demonstrations began to errupt spontaneously, and five hundred visiscope screens were smashed in Manhattan restaurants.

Lankey's finished its first week unmolested, entertaining capacity crowds daily. Reservations were pouring in from as far away as Pluto, where a returning space detachment voted to spend its first night of leave at Lankey's. Baque sent to Berlin for a multichordist to understudy him, and Lankey hoped by the end of the month to have the restaurant open twenty-four hours a day.

At the beginning of the second week, Lankey told Baque, "We've got Denton licked. I've countered every move he's made, and now we're going to make a few moves. You're going on visiscope again. I'm making application today. We're a legitimate business, and we've got as much right to buy time as anyone else. If he won't give it to us, I'll sue. But he won't dare refuse."

"Where do you get the money for this?" Baque asked.

Lankey grinned. "I saved it up—a little of it. Mostly I've had help from people who don't like Denton."

Denton didn't refuse. Baque did an Earth-wide program direct from Lankey's, with Marigold Manning introducing him. He omitted only the Sex Music.

Quitting time at Lankey's. Baque was in his dressing room, wearily changing. Lankey had already left for an early-morning conference with his attorney. They were speculating on Denton's next move.

Baque was uneasy. He was, he told himself, only a dumb musician. He didn't understand legal problems or the tangled web of connections and influence that Lankey negotiated so easily. He knew James Denton was evil incarnate, and he also knew that Denton had enough money to buy Lankey a thousand times over, or to buy the murder of anyone who got in his way. What was he waiting for? Given enough time, Baque might deliver a deathblow to the entire institution of Coms. Surely Denton would know that.

So what *was* he waiting for?

The door burst open, and Marigold Manning stumbled in half undressed, her pale face the bleached whiteness of her plastic breast cups. She slammed the door and leaned against it, sobs shaking her body.

"Jimmy," she gasped. "I got a note from Carol—that's his secretary. She was a good friend of mine. She says Jimmy's bribed our guards, and they're going to kill us on the way home this morning. Or let Jimmy's men kill us."

"I'll call Lankey," Baque said. "There's nothing to worry about."

"No! If they suspect anything they won't wait. We won't have a chance."

"Then we'll just wait until Lankey gets back."

"Do you think it's safe to wait? They know we're getting ready to leave."

Baque sat down heavily. It was the sort of move he expected Denton to make. Lankey picked his men carefully, he knew, but Denton had enough money to buy any man. And yet—

"Maybe it's a trap. Maybe that note's a fake."

"No. I saw that fat little snake Hulsey talking with one of your guards last night, and I knew then that Jimmy was up to something."

"What do you want to do?" Baque asked.

"Could we go out the back way?"

"I don't know. We'd have to get past at least one guard."

"Couldn't we try?"

Baque hesitated. She was frightened—she was sick with fright —but she knew far more about this sort of thing than he did, and she knew James Denton. Without her help he'd never have got out of the Visiscope International building.

"If you think that's the thing to do, we'll try it."

"I'll have to finish changing."

"Go ahead. Let me know when you're ready."

She opened the door a crack and looked out cautiously. "No. You come with me."

Minutes later, Baque and Miss Manning walked leisurely along the corridor at the back of the building, nodded to the two guards on duty there, and with a sudden movement were through the door. Running. A shout of surprise came from behind them, but no one followed. They dashed frantically down an alley, turned off, reached another intersection, and hesitated.

"The conveyer is that way," she gasped. "If we can reach the conveyer—"

"Let's go!"

They ran on, hand in hand. Far ahead of them the alley opened onto a street. Baque glanced anxiously upward for air cars and saw none. Exactly where they were he did not know.

"Are we—being followed?" she asked.

"I don't think so," Baque panted. "There aren't any air cars, and I didn't see anyone behind us when we stopped."

"Then we got away!"

A man stepped abruptly out of the dawn shadows thirty feet ahead. As they halted, stricken dumb with panic, he walked slowly toward them. A hat was pulled low over his face, but there was no mistaking the smile. James Denton.

"Good morning, Beautiful," he said. "Visiscope International hasn't been the same without your lovely presence. And a good morning to you, Mr. Baque."

They stood silently, Miss Manning's hand clutching Baque's arm, her nails cutting through his shirt and into his flesh. He did not move.

"I thought you'd fall for that little gag, Beautiful. I thought you'd be just frightened enough, by now, to fall for it. I have every exit blocked, but I'm grateful to you for picking this one. Very grateful. I like to settle a double cross in person."

Suddenly he whirled on Baque, his voice an angry snarl. "Get going, Baque. It isn't your turn. I have other plans for you."

Baque stood rooted to the damp pavement.

"Move, Baque, before I change my mind."

Miss Manning released his arm. Her voice was a choking whisper. "Go!"

"Baque!" Denton snarled.

"Go, quickly!" she whispered again.

Baque took two hesitant steps.

"Run!" Denton shouted.

Baque ran. Behind him there was the evil crack of a gun, a scream, and silence. Baque faltered, saw Denton looking after him, and ran on.

"So I'm a coward," Baque said.

"No, Baque." Lankey shook his head slowly. "You're a brave man, or you wouldn't have got into this. Trying something there would have been foolishness, not bravery. It's my fault, for thinking he'd move first against the restaurant. I owe Denton something for this, and I'm a man who pays his debts."

A troubled frown creased Lankey's ugly face. He looked perplexedly at Baque. "She was a brave and beautiful woman, Baque," he said, absently caressing his flat nose. "But I wonder why Denton let you go."

The air of tragedy that hung heavily over Lankey's that night did not affect its customers. They gave Baque a thunderous ovation as he moved toward the multichord. As he paused for a halfhearted acknowledgment, three policemen closed in on him.

"Erlin Baque?"

"That's right."

"You're under arrest."

Baque faced them grimly. "What's the charge?" he asked.

"Murder."

The murder of Marigold Manning.

Lankey pressed his mournful face against the bars and talked unhurriedly. "They have some witnesses," he said. "Honest witnesses, who saw you run out of that alley. They have several dishonest witnesses who claim they saw you fire the shot. One of them is your friend Hulsey, who just happened to be taking an early-morning stroll along that alley—or so he'll testify. Denton would probably spend a million to convict you, but he won't have to. He won't even have to bribe the jury. The case against you is that good."

"What about the gun?" Baque asked.

"They'll have a witness who'll claim he sold it to you."

Baque nodded. Things were out of his hands, now. He'd worked for a cause that no one understood—perhaps he hadn't understood himself what he was trying to do. And he'd lost.

"What happens next?" he asked.

Lankey shook his head sadly. "I'm not one to hold back bad news. It means life. They're going to send you to the Ganymede rock pits for life."

"I see," Baque said. He added anxiously, "You're going to carry on?"

"Just what were you trying to do, Baque? You weren't only working for Lankey's. I couldn't figure it out, but I went along with you because I like you. And I like your music. What was it?"

"I don't know. Music, I suppose. People listening to music. Getting rid of the Coms, or some of them. Perhaps if I'd known what I wanted to do—"

"Yes. Yes, I think I understand. Lankey's will carry on, Baque, as long as I have any breath left, and I'm not just being noble.

Business is tremendous. That new multichord player isn't bad at all. He's nothing like you were, but there'll never be another one like you. We could be sold out for the next five years if we wanted to book reservations that far ahead. The other restaurants are doing away with visiscope and trying to imitate us, but we have a big head start. We'll carry on the way you had things set up, and your one-third still stands. I'll have it put in trust for you. You'll be a wealthy man when you get back."

"When I get back!"

"Well—a life sentence doesn't necessarily mean life. See that you behave yourself."

"Val?"

"She'll be taken care of. I'll give her a job of some kind to keep her occupied."

"Maybe I can send you music for the restaurant," Baque said. "I should have plenty of time."

"I'm afraid not. It's music they want to keep you away from. So—no writing of music. And they won't let you near a multichord. They think you could hypnotize the guards and turn all the prisoners loose."

"Would they—let me have my record collection?"

"I'm afraid not."

"I see. Well, if that's the way it is—"

"It is. Now I owe Denton two debts."

The unemotional Lankey had tears in his eyes as he turned away.

The jury deliberated for eight minutes and brought in a verdict of guilty. Baque was sentenced to life imprisonment. There was some editorial grumbling on visiscope, because life in the Ganymede rock pits was frequently a very short life.

And there was a swelling undertone of whispering among the little people that the verdict had been bought and paid for by the sponsors, by visiscope. Erlin Baque was framed, it was said, because he gave the people music.

And on the day Baque left for Ganymede, announcement was made of a public exhibition, by H. Vail, multichordist, and B. Johnson, violinist. Admission one dollar.

Lankey collected evidence with painstaking care, rebribed one of the bribed witnesses, and petitioned for a new trial. The petition was denied, and the long years limped past.

The New York Symphony Orchestra was organized, with twenty members. One of James Denton's plush air cars crashed, and he was instantly killed. An unfortunate accident. A millionaire who once heard Erlin Baque play on visiscope endowed a dozen conservatories of music. They were to be called the Baque Conservatories, but a musical historian who had never heard of Baque got the name changed to Bach.

Lankey died, and a son-in-law carried on his efforts as a family trust. A subscription was launched to build a new hall for the New York Symphony, which now numbered forty members. The project gathered force like an avalanche, and a site was finally chosen in Ohio, where the hall would be within easier commuting distance of all parts of the North American continent. Beethoven Hall was erected, seating forty thousand people. The first concert series was fully subscribed forty-eight hours after tickets went on sale.

Opera was given on visiscope for the first time in two hundred years. An opera house was built on the Ohio site, and then an art institute. The Center grew, first by private subscription and then under governmental sponsorship. Lankey's son-in-law died, and a nephew took over the management of Lankey's—and the campaign to free Erlin Baque. Thirty years passed, and then forty.

And forty-nine years, seven months and nineteen days after Baque received his life sentence, he was paroled. He still owned a third interest in Manhattan's most prosperous restaurant, and the profits that had accrued over the years made him an extremely wealthy man. He was ninety-six years old.

* * *

Another capacity crowd at Beethoven Hall. Vacationists from all parts of the Solar System, music lovers who commuted for the concerts, old people who had retired to the Center, young people on educational excursions, forty thousand of them, stirred restlessly and searched the wings for the conductor. Applause thundered down from the twelve balconies as he strode forward.

Erlin Baque sat in his permanent seat at the rear of the main floor. He adjusted his binoculars and peered at the orchestra, wondering again what a contrabassoon sounded like. His bitterness he had left behind on Ganymede. His life at the Center was an unending revelation of miracles.

Of course no one remembered Erlin Baque, tunesmith and murderer. Whole generations of people could not even remember the Coms. And yet Baque felt that he had accomplished all of this just as assuredly as though he had built this building—built the Center—with his own hands. He spread his hands before him, hands deformed by the years in the rock pits, fingers and tips of fingers crushed off, his body maimed by cascading rocks. He had no regrets. He had done his work well.

Two ushers stood in the aisle behind him. One jerked a thumb in his direction and whispered, "Now *there's* a character for you. Comes to every concert. Never misses one. And he just sits there in the back row watching people. They say he was one of the old tunesmiths, years and years ago."

"Maybe he likes music," the other said.

"Naw. Those old tunesmiths never knew anything about music. Besides—he's deaf."

(*Introduction*)

For two years I taught a creative writing course at a nearby state hospital for the mentally ill. It may or may not reflect on my teaching ability when I say that I learned more than my students, though not about writing.

One afternoon my class ran overtime, and I found myself locked in the building. A staff member happened along and opened the door for me; and then, as I started to leave, she asked, "May I see your ground card?"

She had mistaken me for a patient, and that points up a common problem at mental hospitals: How do you tell the doctors and staff members (and, in my case, the volunteer workers) from the patients?

In William Seabrook's classic account of life in a mental institution, *Asylum,* he describes a dance where one rule was strictly enforced: patients could not dance with other patients. Almost every dancing couple consisted of a patient and a staff member, and one might suppose that with the problem thus simplified one could pick out the patients with a high degree of accuracy. Seabrook could not even attain the fifty per cent that the law of averages would seem to guarantee. On his first ten tries he guessed wrong seven times.

"Another fox trot began and I tried to improve my average. There were several I was sure I couldn't be wrong on—a microcephalic, giggling hatchet-faced blonde with her hair bobbed like Joan of Arc, an open-mouthed young man with adenoids and steel-rimmed spectacles who looked like the village idiot after he had set fire to the barn in a way-down-east melodrama, and an elated, screen-conscious young creature with Diesel engine eyes who labored under the hallucination that she was Greta Garbo.

"I indicated them discreetly to Miss Pine, and said that at any rate anybody could recognize them as patients.

" 'Yeah,' she said, 'well, you'd better not let them hear you say so. The first is a graduate nurse from Bellevue, the man is a student nurse planning to be a psychiatrist, and your Garbo is a superintendent in the diet kitchen.' "*

Add one more ingredient, Shakespeare's famous lines from *As You Like It:* All the world's a stage, and all the men and women merely

* William Seabrook, *Asylum.* Copyright © 1935 by Harcourt, Brace & Co.

players. They have their exits and their entrances; and one man in his time plays many parts.

Editor Horace Gold interpreted this perfectly when he published the story: "There was one thing wrong with all the world being a stage . . . so many grudging people had to be bit players and stage-hands!"

2

LEADING MAN

He wandered aimlessly down the long corridor, opening doors and closing them, feeling a growing frustration as each room stretched its yawning opulence before him. He was hungry and he wanted food. He wanted to find a single fireplace where no fire crackled cheerfully. He wanted to find one door that failed to open at his touch. He knew that his every move was being watched, and he wanted something to happen; but most of all he wanted food.

He tried another door, thrusting it open impatiently, and froze with his hand on the doorknob.

A man stepped forward, plump, elderly, silver hair crowning his solemn face. His black coat made a most amusing, bulging V over his white shirt. He bowed humbly. "Did you ring, sir?"

"I don't think so. Did you hear me ring?"

"No, sir."

"Then I didn't ring."

He backed away and closed the door firmly. "I'll count doors," he told himself. "That should do it."

He moved on down the corridor, his feet sinking noiselessly into the plush piles of the carpet. "One!" He slammed open a door and glanced in at the flickering fire. He moved on. "Two!" he shouted. "Three!" He was approaching the end of the corridor. He threw open another door. "Four!"

The silver-haired man stood before him, bowing humbly. "Did you ring, sir?"

He gazed thoughtfully at the bulging V and pointed a finger. "You—are—a—butler."

"Yes, sir."

"I didn't ring."

He closed the door quickly and hurried on. "Five!"

At the end of the corridor he paused to look out of the multi-paned window and saw only his own face reflected back at him. He turned angrily and started back down the opposite side of the corridor, savagely opening and slamming doors.

"Six! Seven!"

The butler's face was blandly innocent. "Did you ring, sir?"

"No!" He slammed the door, pushed it open again. "Did you *hear* me ring?"

"No, sir."

"I didn't ring."

He stood for a moment by the closed door, scratching an itching ear thoughtfully. He was beginning to wonder if some fumbling director had given his cast the wrong briefing. It had been known to happen.

"Eight!"

The ninth door opened before he reached it and the butler stepped forward. "Breakfast is served in the Green Room, sir. The Duchess is waiting."

"Oh." He took three quick strides along the corridor, hesitated, and turned back. "You're sure it's the Green Room?"

"Yes, sir. If you would be so good as to follow me, sir—"

Keeping his eyes on the sedate blackness of the butler's broad back, he followed meekly.

As they entered the Green Room, the Duchess scrambled to her feet—a bit ungracefully, he thought—and hurried toward him, her flowing gown lightly brushing the carpet. He winced when her dry lips touched his cheek.

"Good morning, dear," she said. There was a brittle eagerness in her bright voice.

"Morning," he said curtly.

She returned to her chair, and the butler escorted him to the other end of the long table and seated him. He glowered distastefully at his egg cup.

"Ham?" he asked hopefully.

"I'm sorry, sir, but the doctor—your stomach, you know."

"I'm *hungry!*"

"Would you like two eggs, sir?"

Sadly he reached for a spoon and jabbed at the egg.

The Duchess was picking delicately at her breakfast. He watched her curiously, wondering where he had seen her before. Joan of Arc? No, that girl'd had a thinner face. A thinner figure, too. The Duchess was actually good-looking. Cleopatra —that was it, but he hadn't been Julius Caesar for more than a month. Odd that she would still be around.

She glanced up at him, and his searching gaze triggered her face into an instant smile. "Did you sleep well, dear? I hope the speech isn't worrying you."

He dropped his spoon, and it clattered dully. "Speech?"

"You have just three days left, and Parliament will be in a frightful stew if you don't have it ready. You *will* work on it this morning, won't you, dear?"

The butler whisked away his egg cup and returned it with another egg. He looked around for the salt and saw none. "Salt?" he asked.

"I'm sorry, sir, but your doctor—"

"Damn the doctor! I'll get another doctor! I haven't had a decent meal since Waterloo!"

He jabbed furiously with his spoon. He'd have to be someone healthy soon, he told himself, or he'd starve to death.

The Duchess carefully got to her feet—she was obviously uneasy about her train. A pity, he thought, that they hadn't given her time to practice.

"You will excuse me, won't you, dear?" she asked. "I must go over the household accounts. I've been putting it off for days. I'll be in the West Sewing Room."

He fed himself a large mouthful of egg and waved her away.

"James," she said to the butler, "see that the Duke is settled in the library as soon as he's finished breakfast. Do work hard on the speech, won't you, dear?"

He watched her approvingly as she swept out of the room. She had a very good figure. She'd even had a good figure as Cleopatra, and there wasn't any place for padding in *that* costume.

He turned to the butler. "Another egg?"

"Sorry, sir, but your doctor—"

He shattered the egg cup on the floor and then followed the butler down the long corridor to the library.

He sat for some time before the polished expanse of desk, doubtfully eying the pile of scented paper that lay in front of him. He was hungry. Damn, but he was hungry! He wondered what he should do next. He glanced at the ring that circled the small finger of his left hand—a large gold ring with 1319 engraved on it in tiny numbers. He rubbed it futilely. Finally he seized a quill and scribbled a few lines.

The door opened almost before he touched the bell. "You rang, sir?"

"About this speech. Want to ask your opinion about something."

"Certainly, sir."

"Beginning of a speech is very important, you know. Should catch the attention right from the first word. Universal appeal and all that sort of thing."

"I understand, sir."

"Wonder if you'd give me your opinion of this beginning."

"With pleasure, sir."

He cleared his throat and bellowed, "Now is the time—" He glanced up. The butler stood watching him attentively, alert interest in his grave face. "Do you think it might go better with more emphasis on the 'now'?"

"Why don't you try it that way, sir?"

"Mmm—yes. *Now* is the time—"

"A decided improvement, sir."

"Thank you. Please don't interrupt until I've finished." He got to his feet, paced back and forth briefly, and struck a heroic pose. "*Now* is the time for *all* good men to come to the aid of their party." He glanced at the butler. "What do you think?"

"A most moving beginning, sir."

"Think it'll do?"

"I'm sure of it, sir."

"Tell me, James, just what is this speech supposed to be about?"

"The Spanish crisis, sir. The entire nation is waiting to hear what the Duke of Wellington will have to say about it."

"Spanish crisis? Spain? Is that in Africa?"

"No, sir. In Europe. It's *close* to Africa."

"I was sure it was. I think, James, that I'd like to have the Duchess hear this beginning."

"Certainly, sir. I'm sure she'll be delighted."

He followed the butler, chuckling quietly to himself as James resolutely took the wrong turning and led him down the long corridor to the end of the east wing. James opened a door, glanced in, and turned to him blankly.

"I'm sorry, sir. I thought she said the East Sewing Room."

They marched back along the corridor to the west wing. The Duchess was seated at the far end of the spacious room, talking quietly with a neatly dressed middle-aged woman. That would be the housekeeper, he told himself. Had he seen her somewhere before? He couldn't recall. He noted their heaving bosoms with amusement, wondering where they'd been that they had to dash back with such haste.

"I have a beginning for my speech," he said. "I want you to hear it."

"I'd be delighted, dear."

He paced about nervously.

"Go right ahead, dear," she said soothingly. "Just pretend I'm not here."

"*Now* is the time," he thundered, "for *all* good men to come to the aid of their party."

"Wonderful, dear. Is there more?"

"No. That's—that's as far as I got."

"I'm sure Parliament will be delighted. You go right back and finish it."

As he stood staring at her she got to her feet and backed away anxiously. The butler stepped forward and placed a firm hand on his arm.

"Where's my harem?" he muttered.

"Your—harem, sir?" the butler said, containing his amazement superbly.

"Where's my harem?" he shouted. "Just because the Duke of Wellington invites me—what did you do with my harem?"

The Duchess and the housekeeper scurried out of the room in near panic.

"You've embarrassed the ladies, Your Excellency," the butler said. "Naturally the Duke couldn't permit your harem *here*—politics, you know. But if you'll come with me, I'll be glad to take you."

He permitted himself to be led away. With the butler's plodding assistance he attired himself in robes and a turban, awkwardly mounted a camel that awaited him at the front door, and rode off through the park with an escort dashingly mounted on prancing Arabian horses.

On the far side of the park they came to a tent village. The last tents were just going up, and the turbaned workers were perspiring in the crisp fall air.

A rotund, turbaned figure darted from the nearest tent, robes trailing, sank to his knees and pressed his forehead to the ground. "All awaits your pleasure, Excellency."

"Arise," he commanded. "I expect to eat well today. My favorite dishes."

"It is arranged. Will you honor your wives with your presence?"

"Later. The ride was long. I need rest."

He followed the bowing figure into the largest of the tents. "My favorite dishes, mind you," he said sharply.

"It is arranged, Excellency."

He stretched out on a pile of rugs and closed his eyes. Music drifted in from the tent that adjoined his. Pleasantly exotic, it almost made him forget the hunger that seethed within him. He listened until he lost himself in sleep.

It was afternoon when he awoke. His hunger brought him off the rugs with a bellow. Attendants hurried in, and immediately the music started.

"I will watch my wives dance while I eat," he announced.

He strode haughtily into the adjoining tent and seated himself on a rug-decked dais. An attendant humbly placed food before him. The music grew louder and the scantily clad girls began writhing about with immodest abandon.

He tasted the warm, watery wine, grimaced, and forced himself to drink deeply. Then he plunged his fingers into a sickly-looking stew, brought out a piece of meat, tasted it, spat it out.

"In Allah's name, what is this?"

"Your favorite dish, Excellency. Camel stew. Would you like a larger portion?"

He took another piece of meat and worked his teeth futilely on its rubbery texture. "This camel was old before its time," he snarled.

"It is the old camels that Allah blesses with flavor."

He chewed energetically and forced some pieces of meat down his throat. To his surprise, they stayed down. Still ravenously hungry, he waved the food away and turned his attention to the dancing girls.

He recognized several of them. A lusty-looking brunette had been Madame Pompadour the last time he was Louis XV. He also saw a former Queen Elizabeth and a former Josephine, and suddenly he noticed, sitting demurely in a far corner, his late Duchess.

She did have a good figure, and the filmy dancing-girl costume suited it perfectly—much more so than had her Cleopatra costume. She wasn't the queenly type, he told himself.

Leaning forward, he summoned her with a commanding gesture. She moved toward him with obvious reluctance, sank to her knees at his feet, and blushed furiously as he drew her up beside him.

"More music!" he called. "Louder!"

The twangy, whining notes crescendoed to an ear-straining blast, and the dancers whirled faster. With a sudden impulse he picked up the girl and carried her into the next tent. Attendants fled in discreet panic as he placed her gently on the rugs and began covering her with passionate caresses and kisses. The deft way she plucked the hypodermic syringe from her brief costume delighted him. He pretended not to notice, even when she plunged it into his arm. He counted ten slowly and began to relax. In a few minutes he was feigning sleep, and she carefully covered him with a rug and tiptoed away.

A rotund, turbaned figure, alias James the butler, met the girl as she came out of the tent. "Everything all right, Dr. Rogers?" he asked.

"I gave him a hypo," she said. "He was getting pretty worked up. He should be out for several hours."

"It'll do him good. It's usually a strain on them when they switch characters so quickly. Too bad. For a few minutes I thought he really would come up with a speech. It would have been interesting, getting a Parliament together and letting him deliver it."

"Yes. Maybe we pressed him too hard on that speech. Responsibility always makes them regress if they aren't ready for it."

"Don't I know it! We had Twelve ninety-six ready to cross the Delaware last week, and the strain of making that decision regressed him all the way back to toy soldiers. He hasn't come out of it yet. But Thirteen-nineteen—I thought he was coming along nicely. He was magnificent yesterday at the Battle of Waterloo. Today he seemed confused, as though his being the Duke of Wellington was our idea instead of his. I don't think the speech was wholly responsible."

"We can't do anything at all until we see what he is when he wakes up. Going to leave the tents standing?"

"We might as well. We may get another call for them."

"I have to change and file my report. Have the others left?"

"Oh, yes. They left the minute you were—abducted."

He helped her roll an air car out of a tent. She took off, and five minutes later she brought it in for a landing in the spacious Central Administration parking lot.

Most of the harem girls had already changed when she reached the dressing room. They were trimly attired in crisp white coats and white skirts, and except for several who were having aching legs massaged, their mien was strictly professional.

"Stell," a husky blonde called, "what happened there? I

thought Thirteen-nineteen was the Duke of Wellington today."

"Sudden regress," Dr. Rogers said, peeling off her dancing costume. "Right in the middle of preparing a speech for Parliament, he started shouting for his harem. I'm afraid he nearly cracked."

"He *would* pick a time when I'm on call. How'd you make out? Was he impetuous?"

"Very. I hypoed him."

"Good girl. I was glad when he carried you out. Another five minutes of dancing—hello!"

A sedate middle-aged woman—1319 would have recognized her as the Duke of Wellington's housekeeper—dashed in and peered about nervously. "Emergency! Harem requested for Seven thirty-eight."

"Oh, my God!" the blonde groaned.

The patter of conversation in the room cut off abruptly.

"Who is it for?"

"Twice in one day? What next!"

"Are they giving Seven thirty-eight hormones? It was only day before yesterday—"

"You should complain!" the blonde snapped. "You're not his favorite. I'm still black and blue from the last time. If that lecherous old buzzard tries to paw me today—"

"Don't forget your hypo!"

"I won't. I know darn well I'll need it."

The wardrobe attendant was moving among them and passing out the dancing-girl costumes. The girls struggled into them.

"What was Seven thirty-eight doing?"

"He was a college professor today. Teaching Einstein's Theory of Relativity to undergraduates. They say it was really weird."

"One of his students probably showed him too much leg, and bang, he wanted a harem. That's all it would take."

The middle-aged woman was counting confusedly. "Dr. Rogers, are you available?"

"Afraid not," Dr. Rogers said, buttoning her white coat. "I have to file my report on Thirteen-nineteen."

"Hurry it up, girls. The air cars are waiting. We've already sent the camel for him."

"Dr. Zerbon left the tents up," Dr. Rogers said. "But Thirteen-nineteen is still asleep there."

"He's been moved back to his permanent quarters. Better put that in your report. Dr. Cameron, will you take charge?"

"You just bet I will," the blonde said. "I'll make a fuss over him right from the start, and maybe we can cut the dancing short. My legs won't take much more."

Chattering irritably, they trooped out to the air cars.

Dr. Rogers left the dressing room, stepped into the hallway, and rode the conveyer to her office in Wing M—the male division. She shared the office with a taciturn young male doctor who seemed half afraid of her. He was seated glumly behind his desk staring at a report form, and he did not look up when she entered.

"Good afternoon, Dr. Karl," she said primly.

"Oh. Good afternoon, Dr. Rogers."

She sat down, dialed 1319, and a record card dropped onto her desk. She studied it and then snapped her fingers. "I *knew* I'd seen him somewhere. He was Julius Caesar. That was my first week. I was Cleopatra, and I was scared stiff."

"How long ago was that?" Dr. Karl asked.

"More than a month ago."

"They must like your work. Not many of us stay that long."

"It's more likely that I haven't progressed rapidly enough to be promoted," she said dryly.

She penned another entry onto the card and sat back looking at it thoughtfully. "I wonder if he'll ever be cured. He's not so old and he really seems like a nice person. But he's been here six months and he keeps building up and regressing."

"The directors know what they're doing. If he was hopeless, they wouldn't have him here."

"The patients really have it soft, don't they? Look here. He decided he was Napoleon, so we gave him a luscious Josephine and a court. He went off to fight the Battle of Austerlitz and we rounded up an army for him. Then he made himself Duke of Wellington and beat his former self at Waterloo. Today he wanted a harem and we gave him one. Seems as though you have to be insane to have any fun out of life."

He winced. "Hush! Not that word—we have no insane patients here. They merely suffer mental delusions."

"They don't suffer anything—they enjoy every minute of it. Think of the money it must cost to run this place."

"These patients aren't ordinary people," Dr. Karl said slowly. "They have talents our civilization needs. They're worth saving at any cost."

"So I've been told, but how many do we save? I haven't heard of a single cure since I've been here. We staff members come and go, but the patients stay on."

He shrugged. "It's a new dimension in mental therapy. We can't expect miracles from every experiment." He glanced at his watch and got to his feet. "I'll have to run. Women's Division has a Helen of Troy today, and I'm drafted for a battle scene."

"Just you wait," she said. "You'll end up envying the patients, too."

He called over his shoulder, "I've envied them since the day I arrived."

She carried 1319's card down to Central Administration and asked about her next assignment. Dr. Barnstall, the personnel director, peered at her inquiringly, eyes serious behind his thick glasses.

"You look depressed."

"Maybe I am. I'm beginning to envy the patients."

"That's nothing to worry about. It happens to most staff members sooner or later."

"Is that why staff personnel is changed so often? I've wondered."

"That's part of the reason. Are you serious about that? Envying the patients?"

"I suppose so. It seems as though we have to jump to satisfy every little whim they have, and they haven't a worry in the world, and yet we never seem to get anywhere with them. They're always regressing."

He smiled. "Take the rest of the afternoon off. I'll keep you assigned to Thirteen-nineteen, and it'll be evening now before he picks up a new direction. Or would you rather have a change?"

"Oh, no. I don't mind Thirteen-nineteen."

"Fine. His next role is likely to require something entirely different."

"That would be nice," she said. "I didn't care for the duchess role."

She walked across the sunlit park toward her quarters. The sound of rippling water reached her from a spacious, circular building, and she paused to peer through a one-way observation port.

The calm Pacific Ocean stretched before her to a watery horizon. Six men lounged on a battered *Kon Tiki*, nonchalantly floating it toward a distant and invisible Pacific island. One was a patient; the other five were staff members, laboring mightily to stay in character.

She sighed. "The patients have all the fun," she said to herself, and she hurried toward her quarters.

1319 lay on a cot in his quarters and tried to think about something that would not suggest food. Or eating. If he could have one decent meal, he thought, he might survive. But it would have to come soon.

It was evening, and there had been considerable activity outside his door. He waited impatiently until the noise faded into the distance. Still feigning sleep in case someone was scanning him, he turned over, slowly edged a blanket over his head, and clicked a microscopic switch on his ring.

"Jones reporting," he said softly.

The ring squeaked back at him. "One moment, please." Then a male voice rasped, "Nice work, Jones. That was a clever switch you pulled."

"Glad you think so," Jones said. "I could see that the Wellington line was taking us nowhere. But you never know what to expect from these people. They come up with the damnedest things. Have you ever tasted camel stew?"

"Can't say that I have."

"May Allah spare you that pleasure. Where did they get the stuff? Are we missing a camel?"

"Not that I know of. I'll have someone check."

"They carry realism too far. Which reminds me of something else. I want the reference librarian shot. Where is he getting that information about the alleged weak stomachs of historical personages? I'm *starving*."

"I'll speak to him. You came up with some fine acting today. You deserve a bonus."

"May I have it in steaks?"

"You'll be Romeo when you wake up. Give it a good play."

"Sure. And by the way—"

"What's the matter?"

"If it turns out that Romeo has a bad stomach or a passion for raw vegetables, I'm resigning."

He clicked off the radio, turned over abruptly, and rolled off the cot. Seconds later the door burst open and an attendant hurried in. Pushing himself into a sitting position, 1319 mumbled groggily.

"Did you sleep well, Excellency?" the attendant said. "Do you wish to visit your harem?"

"What harem?" 1319 demanded. "Where's Juliet?"

The attendant took a step backward. "Juliet?"

"I have a date with Juliet. Can't be late. Got to watch out for those Capulets, too. Where's my sword?"

The attendant unwound the turban from 1319's head. "Of course. You'll have to dress first, and then I'll take you to Friar Laurence. I'll be back as soon as I make the arrangements."

1319 suppressed a chuckle. He'd caught them flatfooted. Suddenly his ring tingled his finger, and he pressed it to his ear.

"Make this good, now," the rasping voice said. "Rogers will be your Juliet, and I think we're going to pull her out of it."

1319 risked a question. He moved the ring and whispered through clenched teeth, "Who's Rogers?"

"Your Duchess. The girl in the harem. That trick you pulled was just what she needed. She's been here over a month, with almost no progress, and we've been worried about her. She's finally starting to think. Now if you can get her personally involved as Juliet—she has a brilliant mind, and insanity is too much of a luxury for people like that. Give it a good play."

The attendant came hurrying back. "Just follow me," he said.

Half lost in his own thoughts, 1319 stumbled after him. Where'd the story take place? Venice? Or was it Verona? Either way there should be some good seafood. He could do with a thick filet.

(Introduction)

For all of the thousands of years that man has condescended to accept the fact that he is, irrefutably, an animal, he has stubbornly searched for that illusive quality that nevertheless makes him unique —makes him man.

So he has called himself a political animal (Aristotle); a social animal (Seneca); a reasoning animal (Seneca); the only animal that knows nothing and can learn nothing without being taught (Pliny); a more perfect animal (Napoleon); the only animal that laughs and weeps (Hazlitt); an intellectual animal (Hazlitt); a tool-using animal (Carlyle); and so on, the list can be as long as one chooses to make it, but it should be noted that as man learned more and more about animals, the differences became more and more tenuous.

Now man has another rival, the machine, and his concern as to whether he himself is or might become a machine is less recent in origin than one would suppose. Burns wondered whether man was a piece of machinery; Colton, whether man was a mere breathing part of that machinery by which he works. Thoreau stated that men become the tools of their tools; Oscar Wilde declared that the real evil of machinery was in making men themselves machines. Nietzsche maintained that what we know of man today is limited precisely by the extent to which we have regarded him as a machine.

And Science Fiction has already pondered what might happen if a computer began to reason, "I think, therefore I am."

One can but wonder whether future philosophers will strain to see man as the unique machine where past philosophers strove to see him as the unique animal: the political machine, the social machine, the reasoning machine, the only machine that knows nothing and can learn nothing without being taught, the more perfect machine, the intellectual machine, and so on.

As with our increasing knowledge of animals, the increasingly awesome capabilities of machines make man's uniqueness more and more tenuous. Man has already lost his distinction as an artistic, a creative machine—machines now compose music and write stories.

There is one glimmer of hope: there are machines that tell jokes, but as yet there is no machine that has a sense of humor. One may perforce be clinging to a feeble reed, but one can still confidently expect man to triumph in the end simply because he, and he alone, is able not merely to laugh, but to laugh at himself.

3

SPARE THE ROD

Professor Oswald J. Perkins was the last person I wanted to meet that morning, so naturally I walked through the door of the post office and found him standing directly in front of me with his hand extended. I either had to accept the hand or turn and run, so I shook it, and inquired after his health, and asked him if he thought the hot weather would last and how his daughter was getting along with her allergy shots and how the grandson at M.I.T. was making out and whether the weather forecast had said anything about rain.

In four minutes I'd exhausted every conversational cliché I could think of, and I was beginning to feel embarrassed. At that moment Postmaster Schantz came to my rescue. He stuck his head through the stamp window and bellowed, "It's a damned dirty shame!"

The professor's thin lips twisted into a faintly ironic smile, and his long, white hair rippled as he shook his head. "Machines have been putting men out of work ever since men started making machines," he said. "Most of the men find other jobs, and everyone profits because the machines produce more. Do things better, too. Any time a machine can do my job better than I can do it, I'll cheerfully retire. But they haven't built that machine yet, and I don't think they ever will."

We went into a spontaneous huddle around the stamp window. I looked past the postmaster, and through the rear window of the post office I could see an air car lifting slowly. Its bright red, white and blue stripes glistened in the early morning sun-light. Young Bill Wade was at the controls, leaving on his rural delivery route. I made a mental note to ride along with him some day and do a story about him. The farmers all admire young Bill. They say he can hit a mail funnel from five hundred feet.

"I just had a talk with Sam Beyers," I said to the professor. "He's taking a full-page ad in Sunday's *Gazette*. He's announc-ing that his robot now has more than eighty violin students and that all of them are making six months' progress with every lesson. He told me confidentially that in another week you won't have a student left."

"I know two students he'll have left," the postmaster growled. "I'm not having my grandchildren taking no violin lessons from no robot."

"That's nice of you," Professor Perkins murmured. "But Sam Beyers isn't far wrong, you know. This morning I had twenty-four students. When I get home, there'll be three or four can-cellations, and then I'll have maybe twenty. Another week and I'll be down to your two grandchildren. Why not? Why should anyone pay for something he can get free."

"Sam Beyers is a crook," the postmaster said to me. "You shouldn't take his advertising."

"Sam isn't a bad guy," I said. "I don't like what he's doing with that robot, but as long as there's nothing improper in his advertising, I can't refuse it."

The postmaster shook his head gloomily. "Maybe if the pro-fessor would advertise—"

"I offered him free space," I said. "He wouldn't take it."

"It isn't necessary," the professor said. "In another week, Beyers will have almost all of my students. In a month or so, I'll start getting them back. I can wait. Did my music come in?"

He stretched out long, graceful fingers for the slender package of music.

I picked up the *Gazette's* mail and thumbed through it to see how many checks might be enclosed before I hurried off after the professor. He was standing at the edge of Waterville Park watching a game of scooter ball.

As we looked, one of the boys got the ball squarely in his sights and scored a direct hit. It looked like a triple mark. In fact, it looked as if the ball would carry all the way to the river. It didn't—the wind held it up—but it would have made the river on the first bounce if it hadn't been for a nervy little red-headed boundaryman on a red scooter. He rode straight for the water, executed as neat a skid as I've ever seen right on the edge of the bank, and netted the ball. He had it jammed in his launcher by the time he'd completed the skid, and he laid a perfect shot right on the central bag. The rider was out by three lengths.

"Neat play," I said.

"That Pinky Jones is a live one," Professor Perkins agreed.

"Student of yours?" I asked.

The professor grinned. "He was up until last week. I almost feel sorry for the robot. Pinky tries to play with the violin up-side down. He files the strings so they break during the lesson. One day he comes with a cricket inside his violin. He has it trained somehow so it chirps when he wants it to. 'Professor,' he says, 'something's wrong with my violin. It makes the fun-niest sounds.' He goes through the motions with the bow and the cricket chirps. 'That's easily corrected,' I say. 'An extra twenty minutes a day on the exercises.' That's the last time he brings the cricket." He laughed. "Yes, I almost feel sorry for the robot."

"You don't seem to realize how serious this Beyers thing is," I said.

"Of course I realize it's serious. I'm losing money, and I can't afford to lose money. But people will soon find out that a robot can't give violin lessons. Does a machine know when a student needs maybe a little more padding on the shoulder? Does it know when a student needs a heavier bow? Does it know what student needs to be coaxed and what one needs a kick in the pants? Does it make the student know the difference between a nicely played phrase and one that isn't? No. No machine can do the thousand things any good violin teacher has to do. Peo-ple will find that out soon enough, and the Beyers robot will go back to the factory."

"I think you're wrong," I said. "As long as Beyers is giving the lessons free, people will send their children to him. What have they got to lose? Long before they become dissatisfied with the robot, you'll have got tired waiting and moved. Just what is Beyers up to, anyway?"

The professor smiled and said nothing.

"I can tell you what I think he's trying to do," I said. "He'll give free lessons until he's forced you to leave, and then he can charge whatever he wants. Students will have to pay it or lose all the time and money they've already invested in their music education. He'll charge double what you charge for lessons. He'll have to, to get back his investment in that robot. Those things are expensive."

The professor looked amused. "So you think Sam Beyers is after a profit."

"It isn't like Sam," I admitted. "He came up the hard way himself and he's always been pretty square. I know back nine or ten years ago, when Hardson's appliance store was going broke, Sam loaned him money to try and keep him in business. Sam said business thrives on competition. Hardson went broke anyway, but Sam helped him as much as he could. That's why I don't understand this at all. But how else can you figure it?"

We turned together and walked slowly along Main Street. I watched an air car settle down in front of Warren's Feed Store. A burly farmer hurried in, and a moment later a robot rumbled out with half a dozen bags of feed. One of the Warren boys directed it from the doorway as it loaded the feed into the air car.

Half a block down the street we came to Beyers, Inc. Beyers sells a little of everything, but until lately most of his business had been in atomic appliances and machinery. This morning he had a new, glaring red sign in the window: ALL KINDS OF ROBOTS. In the rooms above the store was the new Beyers School of Music. And the robot violin teacher.

As we passed the store, the door opened and a girl tripped out gaily. Her long, golden curls fluttered after her as she ran. She wasn't more than ten, but already a womanly loveliness was blended with angelic, childish mischief in her glowing face.

It was Sam's daughter, Sharon, and she darted past us laughing merrily. Then she glanced over her shoulder and came to a sudden stop.

"Hello, Sharon," the professor called.

She turned sullenly, her eyes on the professor. Slowly, deliberately, she stuck out her tongue.

"You shouldn't do that, Sharon," I said. "It isn't polite."

She stuck out her tongue at me, and then she dashed away.

"Now what brought that on?" I asked.

"I'm not very popular with the Beyers family," the professor said.

If any other kid in Waterville had behaved that way, I'd have had a few words with the parents. Speaking to Sam Beyers about Sharon would have wasted my time and also made me an enemy. He worshiped the kid. She was pretty and smart and talented and probably a great comfort to him after the way his son turned out to be a dunce, and all she really needed was a good spanking. She'd never get it from her father.

We stopped suddenly as the bright tones of a violin drifted down to us. The professor pulled on my arm, and we moved away from Beyers, Inc., past the fancy façade of the Waterville Café (Air Car Parking in the Rear—Visit Our Roof Gardens for Gala Evening Entertainment), and paused to stare unseeing at the glamorous young ladies' frocks in the window of Terrestrial Styles, Ltd., Waterville Branch.

"Beethoven," Professor Perkins said, his smooth, ageless face taut with excitement. "Sonata in C Minor, Opus Thirty, Number Two."

"I know," I told him. "You made me play it, once."

He nodded. "This robot merits some respect. Few teachers know the violin's historical repertory well enough to be aware of the existence of such a forgotten masterpiece."

"The robot plays well," I remarked.

The professor looked at me quickly. "Do you think so?"

"It also plays like a robot," I said.

There was something grimly mechanical in its indifference to technical barriers, in its rhythmic severity, in its scorning of emotional values. The robot's students would sound like machines, every one of them, and unfortunately the good people of Waterville and environs would never know the difference. Nor would they care if they did know—the finer points of musical taste and expression meant nothing to them as long as their grubby offspring *played*.

We crossed the street and took up a position in the doorway of Saylor's Pharmacy, where we could hear better, and we stood there listening to the dazzling thread of violin music that came drifting down with the sunlight. The robot played one excerpt after another, and I recognized a passage from an old concerto by Alban Berg and some modern pieces by Morglitz. The professor listened intently and said nothing.

The music stopped precisely on the half-hour. A moment later the street door of the Beyers School of Music was flung open violently. Jeffery Gadman, aged eleven, charged out, flung himself onto the waiting scooter, and putted away toward the park and the game of scooter ball.

"Now that's odd," I said. "I didn't hear *him* playing once."

The professor smiled. "You haven't seen the robot in action or heard how it works? I thought not. The robot does not play the violin. It can't play the violin. It only assists the student."

I stared at him.

"Yes," he said. "What you heard was young Mr. Gadman playing. Three weeks ago he does not even play the scales smoothly. He does not even play a nice little folk song and stay in tune. Then the robot gives him two, maybe three lessons, and he plays Beethoven and Berg and Morglitz like a mature artist. The robot is a wonderful thing, don't you think?"

He laughed and patted me gently on the back and hurried away.

I went back to the *Gazette* and locked myself in my private office and settled down to have a good worry. The professor didn't seem greatly concerned about robot competition, but as editor of the only newspaper in the county, I knew the people.

And I knew we were going to lose the professor.

Sam Beyers had plenty of money. There wasn't any limit to the time he could go on giving free lessons, but there was a limit to the time the professor could sit around waiting for his students to come back to him. Eventually he'd have to go where he could earn money teaching.

Waterville needed the professor. He was our last remaining defender of culture. He'd come to Waterville twenty years before to escape the high-pressure life led by artists in the big cities. At the time it must have seemed like an unpromising place for a music teacher, but the professor was young—in his early forties—and he had plenty of drive and enthusiasm. He finally got across the idea that art was not something to be housed in a museum or experienced as a kind of passive shower bath from visiscope. The average person could learn to create or re-create art for himself.

"Kids don't get any physical benefit from *watching* scooter ball," he would say. "If you want to enjoy the spiritual benefits of art, you have to participate. You can't just watch it from the sidelines."

People understood that kind of talk, and Professor Perkins built up a big class of students. When they were advanced enough he started an orchestra, and he conducted it himself, without pay. If sections needed help for a concert, he brought professional musicians out from the city and paid them himself. He gave several recitals a year, and he had his students in regular recitals. He hired the best professional accompanists he could find to help out, and naturally he had to pay them. I knew that his savings couldn't amount to much. He'd invested all of his money in culture for Waterville.

These concerts and recitals were *events*. Everyone in the area had at least one relative on the program, and everyone came—admission free, of course. And it didn't stop there. The professor made arrangements for a couple of young artists to spend their summers in Waterville giving inexpensive art lessons to anyone interested. I couldn't guess what that cost him. When my father died and I took over the *Gazette*, the professor had me sponsoring story contests and poetry contests and essay contests and running the winners in the *Gazette*. At least that didn't cost him anything—I put up the prizes myself.

But the idea was the same: Don't watch from the sidelines,

have a go at it yourself. With the professor pushing it for twenty years, that philosophy really took hold. We had everything from wood-carving clubs to oil-painting clubs, from poetry-writing clubs to musical-composition clubs. And the professor was the sponsor and guardian angel of each and every one. Almost every kid who'd grown up during the past twenty years had studied a musical instrument at one time or another, and so had a lot of the adults. The professor had become a local institution. Everyone loved him, especially the kids.

It was hard to believe that people would throw him over for Sam Beyers's robot after the contribution he had made. I suppose the robot had the same appeal as the new kitchen or farming gadget that everyone rushes to buy. There's something intriguing about a robot that can give music lessons.

And the lessons were free, and would be until Beyers got rid of the professor. That was bad enough, but if the robot actually could take one of the professor's beginners and have him playing Beethoven and Berg and Morglitz after two or three lessons . . .

If there was a way to help the professor, I couldn't see it. After moping about for most of the morning, I decided to have another talk with him.

He lived in a small house located on the edge of town and remote enough from the immediate neighbors so that the music lessons wouldn't bother them. It also had room for him to exercise his talents as a horticulturist. In the summer his yard was knee-deep in flowers.

His daughter Hilda met me at the door. There were wrinkles in her plump face that I hadn't seen before, and her mouth drooped mournfully. The professor's life had seemed comfortably secure, and suddenly everything was falling apart.

"He's out in the garden," she said. "You sit down and I'll call him."

I preferred to pace the floor while I waited. In most homes this would have been the living room, but the professor had made it his studio. It was attractively furnished, with pictures of composers on the walls, and a framed page of that odd-looking medieval music, and photographs of orchestras the professor had played in. It was the only room in the house that was air-conditioned. After his investments in Waterville's culture, the professor hadn't much money left for physical comforts.

He was surprised to see me but as eagerly hospitable as ever. Hilda faced him glumly before he could speak. "Mrs. Anderson called," she said. "Carol—"

"Ah, yes. Carol goes to Beyers and the robot gives her lessons free. Today she has troubles with the little exercises, and tomorrow she plays a Morglitz concerto without mistakes." He winked at me. "The robot is a wonderful thing, eh, Johnnie? How many does that leave us? Twenty-two?"

"Twenty-one," Hilda said. "You forgot about Susan Zimmer. Or didn't I tell you?"

"You didn't. But it's quite all right. Well, Johnnie? What brings you to see an obsolete musician?"

We sat side by side on the sofa, and Hilda brought us coffee and a small plate of cakes. We sipped coffee and munched cakes, with me trying to think of what to say and the professor waiting politely.

"What do you know about Beyers's robot?" I asked finally.

"Enough to know what is wrong with it," he said. "I've seen similar robots demonstrated in New York. I know about the experiments that have been made with them. Beyers's robot may be an improved model, but they all have the same basic defect."

"How do they work?" I asked. "You see—I'm trying to put my finger on something I could use in the paper. In an editorial, perhaps."

He smiled. "You keep on trying, don't you. Never say die, where there's life there's hope, the game isn't over until the last violin student is out." He got up and helped himself to another cup of coffee. "Beyers says I'm a selfish old fogy standing in the way of progress, but he's wrong. There's a place for machines— even in art there's a place—but the machine can't ever replace the artist. It can assist him. It can stimulate him. It can relieve him of mechanical labor. It *can't* supply imagination and feeling. Those have to come from the artist.

"Take the music-writer. The composer plays, and the music-writer writes down what he is playing. The machine doesn't compose, but it relieves the composer of the drudgery of making notes on paper, and it permits him to compose without shattering his thread of inspiration every few notes so he can write something down before he forgets it. It's an invaluable machine. Writers and poets have the word-selector. The machine doesn't choose the word, it merely reminds the writer of the possibilities. There are the theater amplifiers. No machine can make emotional expression out of a series of words—to a machine all words are equal—but the amplifiers can deliver the actor's natural voice to the people in the rear so he doesn't have to shout when he should be whispering."

"How can a machine stimulate?" I asked.

"You've heard of the composing machines?"

"I thought they were a joke."

"They were as long as they were designed to follow a system. The music they wrote was perfectly correct and horribly dull and naïve. Then someone built a machine that had no system at all. What it produced was absolute chaos, but scattered through that chaos were magnificent tonal effects that the machine happened onto by accident. It took a great artist to understand those effects and use them properly. The last and greatest compositions of Morglitz were inspired by the random beauties he found in composing-machine chaos."

"Then where does the robot violin teacher come in?" I asked.

"It doesn't. With the robot teacher, the machine becomes the artist, and the artist becomes the machine. It's difficult to explain. Consider that robot Warren's Feed Store uses to carry and load bags of grain. Supposing that instead of carrying that grain, the machine merely strengthened a man's spine so he could carry larger loads himself. That's what the robot teacher does. It gives the student proficiency without understanding and without ability. He can carry a bigger load while the machine is helping him, but without the machine he'll be worse off than he was before the robot lessons started."

"I still don't understand what the robot does," I said.

"The robot is a big box with a mass of tentacles that attach to the student. It tells the student when his violin is in tune. It places his fingers and arms in the correct position. The position is perfect, because the robot won't let it be anything else. The student can't play out of tune, or play a wrong note, because there's a tentacle on each finger and the robot won't let the student put a finger in the wrong place.

"The robot flashes the music on a screen, and the student knows just what he's playing because each measure lights up as he gets to it and disappears after he plays it. If he bothers to watch the screen, he knows. If he doesn't watch it, it doesn't make any difference. The robot won't let him make a mistake. I saw a robot demonstrated with young children who were frightened to death of it. It ignored their crying and went right ahead making them play."

"That sounds bad," I said. "I'd think all kids would hate being taught that way."

"Actually, the robot doesn't teach anything. All it does is use the student like an instrument. The robot's student can't play without the robot any more than a violin can play by itself. A man in New York did a research project. He started one group of students with a violin teacher and another group with a robot. At the end of two years the teacher's students were coming along nicely, and the robot's students couldn't play a thing. Except with the robot, of course. They could play anything with the robot."

"What if we were to do a research project like that in Waterville?"

The professor shook his head. "There isn't time. If I gave lessons for nothing I could get my students back, or get some new students, but it would take too long to prove anything."

"Is there any chance that the robot might be harmful?"

"Unless it's used by an expert, it might be, and Beyers hasn't got an expert. Muscles have to be strengthened gradually. It certainly isn't good to force a young person's fingers to play difficult music before they're ready for it. There was a composer named Schumann. Nineteenth century. You probably haven't heard of him. He was a pianist, and he built a gadget to exercise a finger he thought was weak. It ruined his career as a performer."

"Was he an important composer?" I asked.

"He was fairly important."

Suddenly I was feeling much better. "Now that's something I can use. It makes good material for an editorial. 'Is the Robot Harming Our Children?' That'll make people sit up and take notice."

He shook his head sadly. "People never stay sitting up very long. Too uncomfortable. No, Johnnie. You'd need a lot of research data and a lot of time."

I got up and paced the floor again. Hilda came in and cleared away the coffee things, and then she came back to the doorway and stood there wringing her hands.

"What do you expect me to do?" I demanded finally. "Just stand around and watch while Beyers wrecks everything you've accomplished in Waterville?"

"Just be patient," he said. "A machine cannot replace the artist. Remember that. And a teacher—a good teacher—is an artist."

"How did Beyers ever happen to buy that robot in the first place?"

The professor smiled sadly. "You know what he thinks of his daughter. She's the smartest kid in town. She writes stories and poems, and she's won first prize in the last two contests you sponsored. She dances as though gravity doesn't exist. She acts in plays. He figures she ought to be a whiz at music, too, and he sends her to me for violin lessons. I send her home again. She's a lovely girl, and she's bright and talented, but she's also tone-deaf.

"Beyers thinks I insulted him. I explain that a girl who can't hear the difference between one note and another is wasting time and money if she takes music lessons, and he says her being tone-deaf has nothing to do with it, and anyway she isn't, and he'll show me I'm wrong if it's the last thing he ever does. So he orders the robot to give Sharon violin lessons, and while he's at it he gives free lessons to everyone and tries to take all of my students."

"Beyers would naturally hate anyone who suggested that Sharon wasn't perfect in every respect," I agreed. "But why didn't you just go ahead and give her the lessons? It'd be his money that'd be wasted."

"I try to be an honest man, Johnnie. There are lots of things the girl can do well. It wouldn't be healthy for her to try something she's physically incapable of doing."

"Well, I'm glad you're so sure things will work out all right. I wish I could be as confident. Even so I'd like to help them along a little—speed them up."

He looked thoughtful. "There's only one way, I think, to speed them up. The robot would have to give me a violin lesson, and Beyers would never let me near the thing."

"Just what did you have in mind?" I asked him.

He shook his head without answering.

"If all you want is a lesson, I can arrange that easily. Beyers will have to give it to you. He's been advertising free lessons for anyone."

"He wouldn't accept me."

"If he doesn't, he's guilty of fraudulent advertising. Here, let me call him."

I went over to the visiphone and cut off the visual transmitter. Then I put through the call and got Beyers.

"I suppose you're having trouble reading that ad," he said, laughing. "I should have had it typed."

"No trouble," I said. "I just wanted to make an appointment with that robot of yours. I have a new student for it."

"Hey—that's great!" he said. He'd been trying to interest me in the robot—he thought I hadn't given it the publicity it deserved. "Send him over—there's time open right now."

"I'll bring him myself," I said. I cut the connection and told the professor, "Let's go!"

He picked up his violin. I was feeling nervous before we got outside the door, and it didn't help any when the professor had to stop eleven times before we reached the street to show me his pet flowers.

We panted our way up the stairway to the Beyers School of Music, and at the top we entered a small, comfortably furnished waiting room. On the wall was a large color photo of Sharon Beyers, looking lovely and doll-like in her dancing costume. On the opposite wall was a charcoal drawing of Sharon, beautifully done by one of the professor's young summer artists. On the other walls were smaller photos of Sharon. If Beyers ever had a picture made of his teen-aged son, Wilbur, I never saw it. He probably kept it in the stock room.

I walked over and touched a button. A moment later footsteps came banging up the stairway and Wilbur burst into the room. If life were a five-card game, Wilbur would be the unfortunate type who had to get along with three. He wasn't quite ugly enough to be repulsive, and he wasn't quite intelligent enough to appear normal. He grinned at me, and then he saw the professor and froze.

"What's he doing here?" he yelped.

"I've come to take a lesson," the professor said peacefully. "Mr. Cranton made an appointment for me."

There's nothing wrong with Wilbur's instincts. He was instantly, belligerently suspicious; but it took him a while to think of the next question, and when it came it wasn't especially brilliant. "What's the big idea?"

"The idea," I said, "is that the professor is here to take a lesson."

"He ain't no student!"

"One is never too old to learn," the professor said cheerfully. "Don't they teach you that in school? No? Such a shame. You'll be as old as I am, some day, and you should remember that. When a man stops learning he's already dead. So is a robot, when it stops learning."

"I won't give you a lesson."

"Not you," the professor said. "The robot. The robot gives me the lesson."

Wilbur glared at him, groping deeply for words and not finding them. "I better get Pa," he said finally.

His footsteps went slamming back down the stairway. He slammed back up a moment later and waited at the top. Sam Beyers came up the stairway slowly. He was a slight, quiet-looking man with graying hair and a carefully trimmed mustache. He had a pleasant-looking face and usually he wore a friendly smile; but he wasn't smiling, and there was nothing pleasant in the glance he threw at the professor.

He turned on me. "What's Perkins doing here?"

"You told me to bring him over for a lesson. I brought him, and let's have the lesson."

"He can give himself lessons. Out of here, both of you."

He fully intended to eject us bodily if we wouldn't leave, or at least to make a good try at it. His face was white, with a dull, red touch of anger in his cheeks. His hands were trembling. I felt sorry for him, and I wondered if those who love too much invariably end by hating too much.

I turned to the professor. "If he wants to violate the law, that's his business. Let's look up Tom Silvers and have him draw up a couple of affidavits for the District Attorney."

Beyers squared his shoulders and said icily, "I'll run this business any way I want to run it."

"No, you won't," I told him. "For three weeks you've been advertising free lessons for *anyone.* If you refuse to give the professor a lesson, that makes it fraudulent advertising. Check that with your own attorney."

He was slowly regaining control of himself. The red was gone from his cheeks, but the pasty-white color that remained was no improvement. He sat down heavily and glared at the professor. "What are you after?"

"Music lessons," the professor said.

"If he thinks the robot is a good thing, maybe he'll retire," I said. "Then you'd get all of his students."

"I'll get all of his students anyway," Beyers said.

"No you won't," I said. "You'll lose what you have when people start wondering why you refused to give him a lesson."

Beyers's color was almost back to normal. He studied the professor slyly and said, half to himself, "You know—that really might not be a bad idea. If the robot can give Perkins lessons, people will know it can give anyone lessons." He jerked erect. "Give him a lesson, Wilbur. I want to watch this myself."

Wilbur led the way into the next room, the sanctuary of the robot, and the rest of us trailed along. The professor got out his violin and approached his rival calmly. The robot stood in the center of the room, an impressive edifice of glistening metal and plastic. The multitude of metallic tentacles hung limply at its sides. On its back was a large control panel; on its front was a darkened screen and a row of inset signal lights.

I glanced sideways at Beyers. He'd lost interest in the proceedings already—he'd seated himself in the corner and was staring across the room at a full-length photo of Sharon. I thought to myself, in a few more years that girl will be a beauty, and woe to any young man who tries to court her!

Wilbur bustled about nervously, measuring the professor and fussing with the dials on the back of the robot. He adjusted the screen to the professor's eye level and moved him forward until his shoes slipped into recesses in a protrusion of the robot's base. Then he ducked behind the robot.

"Beginner?" he giggled.

"Anything you like," the professor said.

"We'll call you advanced," Wilbur announced. He threw a switch, and the robot hummed quietly. The word TUNE flashed onto the screen.

The professor scornfully plucked his strings, one at a time, and a green light flashed as each tone sounded. Wilbur stood staring at the robot.

"Wow!" he exclaimed. "Most of the kids take ten minutes to get green on that!"

"I believe you," the professor told him.

Music flashed on the screen, but he made no motion to raise his violin to playing position. The tentacles suddenly encircled him. As I watched in amazement, the robot gently positioned the violin for him, eased his elbows to the proper angle and raised his bow. The violin tone filled the room, a brittle, mechanical tone. I knew it was not the professor playing.

He called out above the music, "I am completely relaxed. I do nothing at all, and still the robot makes me play. You see, Johnnie?"

"Incredible!" I breathed.

Sam Beyers chuckled quietly.

"Now I play myself," the professor said. Instantly the tone was warm and expressive. "Now the robot relaxes. But supposing I try to make a mistake. There, you see? No mistake. And this *fortissimo* passage—supposing I try to play *pianissimo*. And I can't—you see? If I relax, the robot puts the necessary pressure on the bow."

"Incredible," I said again.

The music flowed on to the end of the exercise. Sometimes it was the professor I heard, sometimes the robot, and the professor kept up a running comment on what was happening. Then the tentacles dropped away, the screen went blank, and the word TUNE appeared. The professor stepped back.

Wilbur Beyers giggled proudly. Sam Beyers walked over and started to place his hand on the professor's shoulder. Then he changed his mind. His smile appeared to be normal, but there was a vindictive gleam in his eyes.

"Are you willing to admit that my robot can teach you a few things?" he asked.

"But certainly! It's already given me an idea or two. I'm not satisfied with the response, though. Would you mind if I change strings?"

"Of course not. Go right ahead."

As the professor took new strings from his violin case, voices drifted in from the waiting room. Mrs. Karl Anderson stuck her blonde head through the door. "Is it time for Carol's lesson? Oh!" She stared at the professor.

"Bring Carol in, Mrs. Anderson," the professor said. "She has her lesson as soon as I finish mine." He turned to Wilbur. "Right?"

"Right," Wilbur giggled. He winked at Carol, and that young lady blushed and scurried over to seat herself very primly beside her mother.

"It won't take much longer," the professor said. "I'll try maybe one more exercise. Does it have something difficult?"

"Sure," Wilbur said. "I'll give you something good and hard. It's pretty good stuff. I was playing it myself yesterday."

The professor moved back to the robot, took his position, and plucked his strings. The green lights flashed and the music appeared.

"Ah!" the professor said. "Paganini. So you play Paganini, Wilbur. That's wonderful!"

"Never had a lesson in my life, except from the robot."

"You don't say!"

"Sharon plays Paganini, too," Beyers blurted.

The professor smiled but said nothing—the tentacles were already embracing him. I leaned forward, waiting to see which would do the playing—the professor or the robot.

It was neither. After the first few notes even Sam Beyers realized that something was wrong. He bounded to his feet and raced across the room. The sounds limped on, distorted beyond any resemblance to music. Red lights crackled on and off. The robot's faint hum became louder. Wilbur buried his face in the control panel, mouth agape.

"Something's wrong," Beyers said. "What'd you do, Wilbur?"

"Nothing—there's nothing wrong here," Wilbur gasped.

The hum became rumbling thunder punctuated with thuds. As the violin labored on, the robot produced a shuddering vibration that shook the room. A thin ribbon of smoke curled from its base.

"Turn it off!" Beyers shouted.

Wilbur reached for the switch—too late. The robot's lights went off, the screen went blank, and the tentacles released the professor and drooped downward, shaken by an occasional spasm.

"What happened?" the professor asked innocently.

I glanced at him and saw him working hard to suppress a grin.

Beyers ignored the question. "Wilbur," he snapped, "get Ed up here to take a look at this thing."

Wilbur scampered away. Smoke continued to pour from the base of the robot, and Beyers went from room to room opening all the windows.

"Doesn't Carol get her lesson?" Mrs. Anderson asked him.

"I don't know," Beyers said. "We'll have to wait until Ed— Here he is. Ed, what's got into this thing?"

Ed shrugged his massive shoulders, dropped a box of tools onto the floor, and went to work on the robot's backplate.

Beyers bent over him, watching. "Ed's really handy with robots," he said. "He can fix just about anything."

Ed twisted off the plate, flashed a light into the opening, and whistled. "Can't fix that," he said. "What happened? This thing's really burned out."

"What's that?" Beyers demanded incredulously. "You can't fix it?"

"Have to send it back to the factory. Needs a whole new unit in there."

"Doesn't Carol get her lesson?" Mrs. Anderson demanded.

Beyers gestured helplessly. "I guess not. As soon as I get it fixed, I'll let you know."

"Well, I like that!" she said indignantly. "How is Carol going to learn to play if she can't depend on her teacher? Professor, can you give her a lesson today?"

"You call Hilda," the professor said. "She makes the appointments."

"Now just a minute," Beyers protested. "It'll only take a few days."

Mrs. Anderson stared him down. "The professor charges for his lessons," she said, "but at least he's dependable."

"That's right, Mrs. Anderson," the professor said. "I take cold shots and allergy shots and vitamin pills, and now and then maybe I have a sprained ankle or a cut finger. But never yet have I missed a lesson because of a blown fuse."

Mrs. Anderson left with Carol firmly in tow. I started after her and waited in the doorway for the professor, who had gone over to pat Wilbur on the back consolingly.

"Such a pity, Wilbur. Maybe you wore the robot out playing too much Paganini. You let me know when you get it fixed and I'll finish my lesson."

Sam Beyers reared back and pointed a trembling finger. "You're responsible for this, Perkins. I don't know what you did, but I'm going to find out, and then I'll sue you for everything you've got. I know it isn't much, but I'll sue you for it!"

"Mr. Beyers," the professor said gently, "I'll give you some friendly advice. Send the robot back and forget about it. It's a wonderful machine, but it can never be a music teacher. I've been playing for nearly sixty years and teaching for fifty, and I know. Robot or human being, there can be no violin teacher without a sense of humor. Shall we go, Johnnie?"

We went down the stairway and walked along Main Street. The professor was smiling faintly and humming a little tune. If I hadn't been so curious, I could have done some singing myself.

"All right," I said, when I couldn't stand it any longer. "Just how did you manage that?"

"Tricks, Johnnie. In fifty years of teaching the violin to children, I've learned tricks no robot will ever know. I even remember a few tricks from the time when I was a little boy."

"That I can believe," I said. "What particular trick did you pull on the robot?"

"I studied at a conservatory when I was young. Boys will play pranks, you know, and one day they played a prank on me. I was to perform a little solo in a recital, and just before I went on they took my violin and switched all the strings around. The strings have been in the same order on the violin probably from the time violins were first made—from lowest to highest, G,D,A,E. The boys switched my strings around and put the highest where the lowest should have been, and the lowest in between somewhere, and when they got through none of the strings was where it was supposed to be.

"As soon as I got onstage and started to tune I knew what they'd done, but there I was—already in front of the audience. The piece I was to play wasn't difficult, so I tried to go ahead. I couldn't even play the first measure! I stopped and made a little speech explaining what had happened, and I changed the strings back to where they belonged. The audience enjoyed it, and I got a lot of applause, and afterward the boys took up a collection and bought me a little medal for courage under duress. I still have it."

"Then when you put on new strings—"

"I changed them around. Instead of G,D,A,E, I made them E,A,D,G. A human being is the most adaptable thing there is, but not even an expert human musician could adapt to that. The robot didn't have a chance. Its instruments told it the strings were in tune, but wherever it directed my fingers, the wrong notes came out. All it could do was break down. Maybe I cost Beyers a lot of money, but I'm not really sorry. The robot isn't good for the students. With it doing everything for them, they could never learn."

"Oh, it won't cost Beyers anything," I said. "He's too clever for that. He'll have a guarantee on the thing, and probably he only bought it on approval. But he'll get the robot fixed and try again, and he certainly won't give you another chance to mess it up."

"It doesn't matter," the professor said. "All I really did was speed things up a little. It would have happened anyway, sooner or later. The boys will have their little tricks, and it would have been the filed strings, or someone with vaseline on the bow, the way you did once—no, I haven't forgotten—or a violin with the sound post removed, or the strings in all different kinds of wrong order, and the robot would have gone back to the factory. If the boys run out of tricks, I can always make a little whisper to one of Beyers's students. 'What would happen if you did this?' The robot won't have to go back to the factory many times before the parents get disgusted with it. A violin teacher—"

"I know," I said. "A violin teacher has to have a sense of humor."

He stopped and grabbed my arm. "Johnnie, we rushed things too much. We should have waited."

"How's that?" I asked. "What's the matter?"

He looked at me slyly, his eyes sparkling, his face wrinkled into a mischievous smile—the smile of a small boy who's been bad and knows he won't be spanked. Suddenly he had me feeling chagrined about all the worrying I'd wasted. The professor was a match for any robot and he knew it. He hoped Beyers would get the thing fixed so he could have another crack at it. I could imagine him getting together with some of his boys and saying, "This time we'll try—" No wonder the kids loved him!

He turned away and shook his head sadly. "We should have waited. I'd give anything to know what the robot would have done with Pinky Jones's trained cricket."

(*Introduction*)

Erlin Baque, in "The Tunesmith," read a description of Greek ethos in an ancient book about music. Paul Henry Láng's *Music in Western Civilization* (which in Erlin Baque's time will be an ancient book) explains ethos like this: "According to their writers the will can be decisively influenced by music in three ways. It can spur to action; it can lead to the strengthening of the whole being, just as it can undermine mental balance; and finally, it is capable of suspending entirely the normal will power, so as to render the doer unconscious of his acts."*

Orpheus is said to have moved rocks and trees with his music, but even apart from the Orpheus myth it is evident that the ancient Greeks were obsessed with the power of music, and their comments about it have fascinated students of music and music history ever since. (Until the twentieth century, the Greek musical instrument, the aulos, was erroneously thought to be a type of flute—actually it was a double oboe with a strident, piercing tone similar to that of a bagpipe—and professors of Greek were fond of pointing out to their awed students that the soft, ethereal tones of the flute could drive the sensitive Greeks to frenzy and were even employed for martial music, whereas modern man is so degenerate that an entire Wagnerian symphony orchestra fails to move him.)

Were the Greeks really that susceptible to music (or was their music really that powerful?)? Láng says, wisely, "According to their writers . . ." What their writers said about music may have borne no more similarity to its actual effects than today's patent medicine ads bear to the actual effects of the nostrums they describe. Future archaeologists may be as hard put to explain the alleged potency of a certain mouthwash as we are to explain Greek ethos.

And yet—would writers such as Plato and Aristotle have spoken at such length and with such precision about ethos if it were entirely theoretical?

When, as a young student of music history, I had my turn at attempting to make sense of this subject, I found to my amazement that musical scholars tended to formulate their own theories and then ignore any part of the Greek testimony that was not in agreement.

* Paul Henry Láng, *Music in Western Civilization*. Copyright © 1941 by W. W. Norton.

When I wandered somewhat afield from the usual musicological sources, I discovered that there was also an ethos of the rhythm and subject matter of Greek poetry, apparently as unknown to musical scholars as the numerous commentaries on the ethos of musical scales and rhythms were unknown to scholars of Greek literature. Music is music, and literature is literature, and as far as I was able to determine the scholars of the twain had never met. I was left wondering to what extent the classic Greek concept of ethos could have been based upon music *and* poetry: upon song. I'm still wondering.

But I feel that Plato would have understood perfectly the potency of a song that could fire a wandering orphan with an irrepressible yearning for home. On a somewhat lower level the urge might even be understood—just a little—by those contemporary couples who wax nostalgic over a trite bit of nonsense known to them—privately—as "our song."

4

Prologue

Harg stooped low, pushed the skin aside, and stepped through the narrow opening into his smoke-filled hut. His wife, Onga, straightened up from the clay stove, pushed the stringy black hair back from her face, and looked at him anxiously.

"What'd the sky-man want?"

"He says Zerg must have a party."

She gazed at him blankly. "What's a party?"

"It's eating things, mostly."

She paled and walked toward him with small, frightened steps. "They think we don't give Zerg enough to eat? Is that why they take him?"

"No. It's—" He gestured helplessly. "I don't know what it is. Like a Star Festival, maybe, but with just us. And there are to be gifts, the sky-man said. We must make joy."

"Joy!" she moaned. She sank to the floor, and sobs shook her frail body. Finally she controlled her grief and stared up at him, eyes wide with horror. "They take Zerg, and we must make joy?"

He turned away and stood peering through a window slot. "The sky-man said he would send the things—the party things. We must make the party at the dawn, and then we must take Zerg to the River."

She did not answer. After a time he turned and bent over her and gently raised her to her feet. "At the dawn—" he began.

"We will make the party. I do not know how, but we will

make it. We will take Zerg to the River because we must. But we will not make joy." There was savage determination in her face, and Harg, who had no conception of beauty, thought her beautiful.

An ominous rumbling sounded in the distance, and Harg whirled and hurried to a window slot. One of the sky-men's strange things-that-crawl came rocking down the path from the River. He watched it with mouth agape as it swirled along, sending clouds of dust high into the air. It veered suddenly and roared straight toward the hut. Harg stood his ground fearsomely, but Onga fled moaning toward the mat where little Rirga lay sleeping. The thing-that-crawls slowed with a clanking of tracks and came to a halt by the hut.

There was only one of the sky-men riding in it, and he jumped down and looked about. Harg stooped through the door and approached him humbly.

"Harg?" the sky-man said, speaking so strangely that Harg almost failed to recognize his name.

"Yes. Harg."

The sky-man turned, picked up a box, and set it at Harg's feet. And another, and still a third. "Par-ty," he said, mouthing the word strangely. "For par-ty."

"I understand," Harg said. "We will make the party."

The sky-man nodded, vaulted aboard his thing-that-crawls, and thundered away toward the River. Dust whirled about Harg, choking him, but he stood his ground until the sky-man had vanished over a distant hill. Then he turned slowly and carried the boxes into the hut. He placed them in a corner, stacking them carefully, and neither he nor Onga touched them again. When Zerg came strutting in waving an ornt he had caught, radiant with the frank pride of his three summers, he approached the boxes curiously, and Onga shouted him away.

They arose in darkness, and when the first dim light of dawn touched the top of one-tree hill, they awoke Zerg and his sister and made the party.

One box, the heaviest, contained food—delicious smoked meats, and bread, and a cake with awesome patterns traced upon it in color. They superstitiously held back from the cake and might never have tasted it had not one of Zerg's greedy little hands snaked out and broken off a large piece. After that they devoured it, smacking their lips over the sweet, melting texture. They ate the meat and bread, but the other contents of the box were odd, circular objects that Harg's puzzled fingers found no way to open.

The other boxes contained gifts. For Onga there was cloth, lengths and lengths of it, so finely woven and brightly colored that she regarded it openmouthed and sat fingering it until they had finished making the party. There was a doll for Rirga, a life-sized sky-baby doll that frightened her, and she would do no more than toddle up to it and touch it quickly before she scurried away. There was a knife for Harg, long, glimmering and sharp, and a hatchet, and fish hooks of the kind that the sky-men used with such wonderful fortune. For Zerg there were clothes that made him a sad little miniature sky-man, and they would have laughed had they been making joy.

And there was a tiny thing-that-crawls, with a tiny sky-man riding in it, and when Zerg handled it with his curious, prodding fingers it suddenly emitted a loud, grinding noise. He dropped it, and they all stared in amazement as it crawled away across the packed dirt floor of the hut.

Satisfied that they had made the party, they put all except Zerg's gifts back into the boxes and started off on the long, faltering walk to the River, with Zerg wearing his sky-man clothes and clutching the still-grinding thing-that-crawls.

At the River they skirted the mud huts of the natives and went to the shining, round-roofed huts that the sky-men had made. There were other families there, all with a child of Zerg's summers, and they huddled together in a long, strange hut while the children were undressed and sky-men and sky-women in white looked at them and handled strange, glimmering objects. Then they were outside by a towering thing-from-the-sky, and a sky-man was telling them quietly that they must make their farewell with Zerg.

Zerg, seeing tears in his mother's eyes, wept frantically, and

Onga proudly wiped away her tears, and Zerg's, and firmly pushed him away.

There was weeping in other families, and Buga, who had had three daughters born to her in a miraculous birth, fell to the ground and rolled hysterically in the dust because the sky-men were taking all three.

An anguish of fright shook little Zerg when he reached the thing-from-the-sky. He shrieked and kicked wildly as he was carried up the steep metal slope, and when he reached the top a sky-lady in white picked him up and lifted him kindly for a last look at his family. And when he continued to scream and kick she took his hand and moved it up and down in a final, pathetic gesture before she disappeared with him into the yawning opening.

When the last struggling child had made its sobbing, wailing trip up the slope, the opening was closed. The sky-men moved them back to the edge of the meadow. Fire flashed around the thing-from-the-sky, and thunder roared, and it lifted upward until it became a shining speck and disappeared.

Harg and Onga plodded slowly homeward. Onga walked with her eyes on the rippling dust, and Harg halted, now and then, to gaze futilely up into the sky. Onga clutched the sleeping Rirga tightly in her arms, and she knew that both Rirga and the child that stirred within her would make that frightening journey into the unknown.

And she sobbed soundlessly, "What do they do with them? *What do they do with them?*"

I

Thomas Jefferson Sandler III looked out of his window on the ninety-eighth floor of the Terra-Central Hotel and saw the planet Earth at close range for the first time in fifteen years. He'd had his feet on genuine terra firma the night before, at the space port, and he'd flown from the port to the hotel—but that was a different Earth. An artificial Earth. A planet or a woman, he thought, never looks the same by daylight.

He swept his gaze over the welter of towers and spires that

glittered brightly in the early-morning sunlight, watched the precisely stratified air traffic, and leaned forward to peer at the scurrying microbes in the street below.

"Earth," he said softly, and strained his eyes at the horizon. The city stretched as far as he could see, and farther. Galaxia, the greatest city on Earth. The greatest city in the galaxy. Its site had once been a desert, the guidebooks said; and now it was a garden spot, a prime tourists' attraction and the holy city of cities for businessmen and politicians.

"Capital of the galaxy," he murmured, and turned his gaze to the glistening white government buildings and green parks that stretched across the heart of Galaxia in an unbroken chain. He'd heard violent protests in the most distant parts of the galaxy about having a capital planet in such an out-of-the-way-sector, but that didn't concern him. They could move it four galaxies away, for all he cared.

"Home," he said, and repeated the word doubtfully. That was why he was here. That was the reason for his long trek across the light years, to see Earth again. To see his home. And he stood looking out at the snowy puffs of cloud and the delicate blue sky and felt an overwhelming surge of disillusionment. Why should this planet be home to him? He turned away from the window and sang softly, mouthing the words in disgust.

> "Home is that place
> In deepest space
> Where memories burn.
> Home is a sigh
> For a color of sky,
> And a will to return."

He ended by cheerfully damning the planet Earth and adding a few choice curses for little Marty Worrel.

He'd run into Marty on a dozen worlds, or fifty, or a hundred. It seemed that everywhere he went he met Marty Worrel—if he happened into a dive that was cheap enough, and dirty enough, and illegal enough. Worrel was a man Sandler's age, with a wrinkled, ageless face and an insatiable thirst for alcohol.

Inveterate wanderer of the galaxy, man of superb, hopelessly squandered talents, brilliant exponent of disillusionment, disgustingly enslaved alcoholic—that was little Marty. He could have been a genius at almost anything he chose to work at, but all he ever worked at was a bottle.

Sandler had last encountered Worrel on Kranil, and the shabby little fellow had managed to stay sober long enough to write a song. Or perhaps he'd tossed it off in a state of exhilarated intoxication. The facts of Worrel's activities were always hard to come by.

But he had written the song, and Sandler had met Worrel in a tough spacers' hangout near the Kranil City port and heard a slatternly bar girl give the song its first public performance. "Homing Song," Worrel had called it, and like most of Worrel's conversation the words were sometimes immortal poetry and sometimes nonsense, but the melody was a haunting, soaring masterpiece of poignant emotion. It entwined itself into Sandler's consciousness and defied eviction. Even if it had not he couldn't have forgotten it, because it swept across the galaxy on hyperdrive, and everywhere Sandler went he heard it. Even on Earth—he'd heard it the night before, in the hotel's Martian Room, sung with enticing gestures by a tall, sedate-looking blonde.

It was the song that brought Sandler to Earth. Its words had pounded away at him, home . . . home . . . home, and its melody had tormented him, and finally he had signed on a run across half the galaxy to Earth. To home. And he had arrived only to learn that he had no home, and the bitter realization pained and frustrated him.

He was Pilot First Class T. Sandler, and his brightest memories were the blur of unidentified stars and the sweeping emptiness of space—meaning everywhere or nowhere—and he didn't give a spacer's damn where he went. Or as he'd heard another spacer put it, home was the nearest planet with a breathable atmosphere.

Sandler dropped into a chair and visiphoned the space port. He reported to Inter-galactic Transport and gave his name and code number. "I want the first assignment that'll get me off this damned planet," he said.

The dispatcher chuckled, did some checking, and said, "You're stuck here for forty-eight hours. That's the best I can do."

"I'll take it," Sandler said.

He walked back to the window and looked out at the soft blue sky of Earth. "And as long as I'm here," he told himself, "I might as well have a good look at it. I certainly won't be coming home again."

The hackie leaped in front of him as he came out of the hotel, gripped his lapel, and babbled with pathetic, well-rehearsed enthusiasm. "Ground tour? See everything you want to see. Stop anytime you want and look around. Can't do that on an air tour. I'm an expert, I am. I can show you anything in Galaxia worth seeing. Make a day of it and see all the sights. What d'ya say, mister? Reasonable rates. Three credits an hour and you get a personally guided tour."

"Let's go," Sandler said.

The hackie ceremoniously escorted him to a shabby ground car, got him seated, and took his place in front. He beamed with triumph. "Yes, sir. Where to first, sir?"

"Just drive around," Sandler said.

"Ever been in Galaxia before?"

"Can't remember. Probably was here when I was a kid."

"Then you come from Earth."

"Originally, yes."

The hackie seemed vaguely disappointed, as though he might have to curb his enthusiasm somewhat in describing Earth's wonders to a native Earthling. "Well, then," he said. They were gliding smoothly along Vega Boulevard toward Government Circle, where two dozen stellar boulevards converged. "Art Institute, Galactic Museum of Natural History—they got stuff there that gives you nightmares for weeks. Then there are all the government buildings. Congress isn't in session, but they take visitors through the House of Congress on tours. Then there's the Museum of Space Travel—"

"That might be interesting. Let's try that one."

The hackie nodded, and their speed picked up somewhat. Sandler leaned back against the worn cushions and idly watched the buildings flow past him: elegant shops, towering luxury hotels, the sprawling office buildings from which galaxy-wide businesses were directed, occasionally behind a high wall and park-like blur of greenery the Earth residence of a galactic multi-billionaire or the official residence of a cabinet minister.

They made a three-quarter circuit of Government Circle, passed the vast House of Congress, and started up the spacious parkway called Government Mall.

"Shorter this way," the hackie said.

Sandler doubted it, but he made no protest. The mall was beautiful. Flowering trees from a hundred planets, or perhaps a thousand, dotted the sweep of sparkling green grass. The splendid government buildings stood at regular intervals, each in a style of architecture native to a planet of the Galactic Federation, each surrounded by a small park landscaped with such specimens of that planet's flora as lavish care could keep flourishing on Earth.

They drove down Government Mall for a mile and turned right onto Luna Avenue, and Sandler raised his eyes from a cluster of purple-leaved shrubs to glimpse briefly the façade of the government building they were passing. The shock of recognition jolted him.

"Stop!" he shouted.

The hackie glanced around at the traffic and wailed, "*Can't* stop *here!*"

"That building—back there, the one on the right. Can we stop anywhere close to it?"

"Should be able to."

They turned off, followed a curving drive, and entered a two-level parking pavilion—lower level, ground cars; upper level, air cars.

"What building is this?" Sandler asked.

The hackie consulted a map. "The Ministry of Public Welfare."

Puzzled, Sandler reached for the map. "Never knew there was such a thing," he said.

He wondered what memory he could have of this building. Could he have seen a similar structure on another world—its native world? If so, why should a passing glimpse of it startle him so?

"I want to look around," he said, opening the door. Uneasiness flickered in the hackie's face, and Sandler grinned and handed him a ten-credit note. "There's pay for two hours with a nice tip. We haven't been out half an hour. If I'm back any time during the next hour and a half, I'll expect to find you waiting."

The hackie's head bobbed. "Right." He took a newspaper from the storage compartment.

Sandler stepped onto an escalator and rode up to the air car level. The building was enormous, a three-quarter circle stretching its arms about the parking pavilion. It was undistinguished in every way except one. Its windows were the darnedest things Sandler had ever seen.

Only he had seen them—somewhere.

They were circular, but each circle was punched in at the top by a stabbing indentation. Sandler said aloud, "Like sticking your finger into an arnel cake." And then, startled, "What the hell is an arnel cake?"

A passer-by spun around and regarded him strangely, and Sandler strode away and rode the moving ramp into the building. It seemed to be nothing more or less than a vast office building. Clicking machines could be heard through open doors. To a spacer accustomed to a different mechanical breed, they were alien machines, and their functions of writing letters, making records, sorting and filing seemed strangely exotic. Occasionally a pretty junior secretary darted out of a room, stepped onto the ramp, and rode away purposefully. Closed doors were marked with a man's name, a fancy title, and the word "Private." Sandler rode from one end of the building to the other and back again. He left the ramp where a glowing sign and an arrow pointed at the auditorium.

He recognized the room as soon as he stepped through the

doorway. He recognized the myriad of globes that hung from the ceiling, dark because the room was not in use, but with planetary markings of a myriad of worlds dimly visible on their exteriors. He recognized the curving plastic front on the control room above the stage. He recognized the plushy seats and the flecks of gold that ran through the rich brown tapestry. He recognized . . .

He moved down the aisle, sat down, and leaned forward. When had it happened? In this life, or in another?

A bloated, bald-headed man—Mr. Minister, they called him —with a loud, sonorous voice that rose and fell in endless gyrations. A nurse with kindly eyes, a warm smile, and a body that had a friendly roundness despite the white stiffness of her dress. A small boy who hid behind the nurse and clung frantically to her skirts. A tall, thin, haughty-looking woman with fur on her dress bending over and staring at the boy and saying, "Aren't his ears a little pointed?" A gruff-looking doctor in a white coat. Other people dashing in and out, a moving blur of faces.

Mr. Minister: "You're an important woman this morning, Mrs. Sandler. You're the five millionth mother to adopt a child through the Ministry of Public Welfare."

Mrs. Sandler: "I still think his ears are pointed."

The Doctor: "No more than yours are."

Mrs. Sandler: "Well, I suppose I'll have to take him. I've waited three years, and I expected to wait two or three years more. He'll have to do. But I hate getting one so old. They always have so many nasty habits that have to be broken—or so I've been told. If one could only get them when they're babies, then they could be brought up properly."

Mr. Minister (horrified): "What's that? You wanted a baby?"

Mrs. Sandler: "Of course I wanted a baby, but I knew I couldn't get one."

Mr. Minister: "If she wanted a baby, why didn't you get her a baby?"

The Doctor: "If she wanted a baby, why didn't she have one herself?"

Mrs. Sandler: "I didn't come here to be insulted!"

Mr. Minister: "Why didn't you get her a baby?"

The Doctor: "There aren't any within light years of here—not for adoption. We tried babies once, and the mortality rate was horrifying. So now we don't take a child until it's two or three."

Mr. Minister: "Well, if that's the way it has to be—we've kept the visiscope men waiting long enough, I guess. These films will be run all over the galaxy, you know. Does the boy know his lines?"

Nurse: "He knows them perfectly."

Mr. Minister: "Say your lines, boy."

The boy: "Won't!"

Mr. Minister (whispering): "Now get this, brat. We're going in there in front of the cameras, and you're going to do exactly what the nurse has told you, or I'll bat your ears off! That better be clear!"

Eyes half-closed, Sandler stared vacantly at the stage. Had he really stood there as a boy and chanted his lines like a very small robot? Had he ridden the hall ramp beside the tall, unfriendly woman, cringing at the coldness of her hand on his? Had he stood in the parking pavilion beside the shining air car and looked back at the building's odd windows and thought, "Like sticking your finger into an arnel cake?"

A song unwound itself slowly in his mind, a lament of saddened beauty that had brought him halfway across the galaxy, home to Earth where he had no home.

> Home is a sigh
> For a color of sky,
> And a will to return.

"For a color of sky," he mused. Not the pale blue sky of Earth, nor the infinite shades of blue and lavender and green and yellow and red that he had seen in his tireless treks across space. A blue sky that was not blue. A touch of green in the sunset, a touch of pink at the dawn and bright promise of the day to come.

He rode the ramp to the end of the hallway and stopped at an information desk. The young lady in charge smiled encouragingly, and Sandler said, "I have a problem. I was an adopted child, and I'd like to find out who my real parents were and where I come from."

Her smile faded. "You were adopted through the Ministry of Public Welfare?"

"Yes. Right here in this building."

"We only discuss these cases with the adopting parents."

"They're both dead."

"I see. Would you fill out this card, please?"

She dropped the card into a slot, and less than a minute later it flipped out of a delivery chute. Stamped across its face in bright red letters were the words, "File Negative."

"Evidently no such records were kept," the girl said. "Sorry."

II

The blonde had finished her song, and she was moving about the Martian Room, chatting with the guests and acting as an informal hostess. Sandler sat at an out-of-the-way table half concealed behind a bushy, fern-like plant, and the blonde walked past without seeing him, glanced back, and turned toward his table.

"You look lonely," she said, sliding into the opposite chair.

Sandler smiled. The music was playing softly in the background, some of the exotic plants gave off pleasing scents, and he had just finished a delicious terrestrial steak. But if the baffling emptiness he felt could be called loneliness, she was right.

"You're a spacer, aren't you?"

"Yep. Here today, light years away tomorrow. A poor insurance risk, a poor matrimonial risk, and in the eyes of the politicians, a generally poor citizen."

"According to the politicians, you aren't a good citizen unless you vote the right way."

"Maybe that's it. I'm always in space on Election Day. Have some desert with me?"

"That's nice of you, but no, thank you. I'll have some coffee, though, if you don't mind."

Sandler touched a button and gave the order. Seconds later a server rolled across the room and gently attached itself to his table.

Sandler served the coffee. While they drank it he studied the girl, and she met his gaze effortlessly and without embarrassment. She was considerably older than he'd thought—thirty, at least. Her blonde hair had darkish overtones that suggested it might be natural and a brilliant, almost bluish sheen that denied it. He tossed the problem aside. A man could go crazy speculating about a woman's hair.

"I heard you sing that song last night," he said. "Do you like it?"

"Everyone likes it. I sing it four or five times a night."

"It's an idiotic song," Sandler said. "Some of the words are nonsense."

"The words are beautiful."

Sandler chanted in a mocking singsong, "Home is a light across the night of love enshrined. Home is the smart of tears and a heart of faith left behind. Explain that, please."

"Feelings can't be explained. You've never had a home."

"You're right. I haven't. I can hardly remember my life before I was adopted—I was too young. I never got along with my foster parents, so I ran away to space when I was sixteen."

"That's odd," she said. She plucked a handkerchief from her bosom, blew her nose loudly, and added, "Dammit!"

"Something wrong?"

"I had a man. Government worker, fairly high up and doing well. We were going to get married and raise a big family. Then this song came along, and all of a sudden he had to go home. Only he didn't have any home. Like you, he was adopted, and he never knew where he came from. But he was determined to go, and off he went. I haven't heard from him since."

"If he was a government worker, maybe he was able to find out where he came from."

"I don't think he even tried. At least, when he left he didn't know where he was going."

"You should have gone with him."

"He wanted me to, but that song does things to me, too. I'm from Earth, from a small town on the other side of the planet, and do you know what I'm going to do? I'm leaving this place at the end of the month and going home. I'm going to buy a little restaurant and marry some local man if there are any available and make a home for as many children as I can have."

"The words are idiotic," Sandler said. "It must be the melody."

"Odd that it doesn't do anything to you. I thought it affected everyone."

"It brought me back to Earth. I thought I was coming home, but this planet isn't home. Not to me. At the Ministry of Public Welfare, today, I tried to find out where I came from. They say they have no record of it."

"They're lying, then. The government has records of everything."

"Are you certain about that?"

"Positive. I haven't lived in Galaxia for ten years without learning a thing or two about the government. Complain to your congressman."

"Congress isn't in session. Besides, spacers don't have congressmen."

"Complain to one of the congressmen-at-large. Tell him you're a traveling salesman, or something."

"I might do that," Sandler said. "Thanks. And good luck with the restaurant. And the large family."

She nodded and moved on to the next table. Sandler waited until he heard her sing the "Homing Song" one more time before he went up to his room.

As a spacer, Sandler considered the popular concepts of night and day to be awkward frames of reference. His living habits were adapted to duty time and free time, and during his free time he slept when he felt like it and generally conducted his life to suit his own convenience.

It irritated him to have his habits imposed upon by such an arbitrary thing as a planet's period of revolution. The dusters—as spacers referred to non-spacers—were always making appointments for times when Sandler preferred to sleep, and offices and stores were only too frequently closed when he felt like transacting business.

When he arrived at the Congressional Office Building he was mildly irked, but in no way surprised, to find no humans present except a score of weary custodians who were charting the routes of their robot cleaners by the flickering lights of control panels. He waited, got into conversation with the clerks as they arrived, and so charmed half a dozen young ladies that appointments with any of fifty congressmen were his for the asking.

Congressman Ringlow, a big, blustery, man-of-the-people type, inclined his shaggy head at Sandler and pointed at a chair. "Mr. Sandler? T. J. Sandler?"

"That's correct."

"Thomas Jefferson Sandler?"

"The third."

"I knew your father."

"My foster father," Sandler said. "I knew him, too—vaguely."

The congressman stiffened. "He was a close friend of mine," he announced haughtily. "I remember talking to him about you just after you ran away. He was very disappointed with you."

"We disappointed each other."

"Yes. Well, I suppose there are two sides to any disagreement. What can I do for you?"

"I was at the Ministry of Public Welfare, yesterday, trying to find out a few things. Such as where I came from originally and who my real parents are. I was told that no record was kept of this information."

"I can understand your wanting to know, but I can't very well help you if there's no record."

"I've been reliably informed—" He smiled, remembering the singer's confident assertion. "I've been reliably informed that the government always keeps records. I feel that I'm entitled to that information, and I resent being lied to."

The congressman stiffened again. "Here! That's rather strong language."

"I'm beginning to feel rather strongly about this."

The congressman got to his feet and strode to the window. "Your father—foster father—was a decent person," he said thoughtfully, speaking with his back to Sandler. "I think he'd have wanted you to have that information if you wanted it. I'll see what I can do."

"Thank you. You can reach me at the Terra-Central Hotel. Or leave a message there if I'm not in."

The message was waiting when Sandler got back to the hotel. Congressman Ringlow had checked with the Ministry of Public Welfare. No records had been kept on the background of a child placed for adoption by the ministry. This was a long-established governmental policy, pursued in the best interest of all concerned. The congressman expressed his regrets.

Sandler took an air cab out to the space port, reported at the offices of Interplanetary Transport, and presented his resignation. He collected his back pay and pay for accumulated leave time, and withdrew his retirement and savings funds. He converted most of this small fortune into Inter-galactic travelers' checks, which could be cashed anywhere in the galaxy with no identification other than a reasonable number of fingers to match the ten fingerprints on each check.

From the space port he flew directly to the Ministry of Public Welfare. He demanded a personal interview with the minister. After a series of awkward interviews with underlings, during which he became increasingly adamant, he obtained an appointment with the third assistant to the fourth sub-minister. He was shown into the office of a long-faced young man who squinted timidly at Sandler through bulging contact lenses. His pale countenance had a comical look of near-fright.

"It seems," he said shyly, examining a piece of paper, "that you made a certain inquiry at the information desk yesterday."

"I did."

"You did not accept the information that was furnished. You went to Congressman Ringlow and asked him to obtain further information for you."

"I did."

"And you still aren't convinced that we don't have the information you want."

"I am not. Until I am convinced, you're going to continue to hear from me."

"I have this for you," the official said. "It's a photograph of your record card. This card represents the ministry's complete record on any adoption case. You will find here all the information that is available with regard to your background. We've had so many queries of late—many quite as persistent as yours—that we've decided to supply similar photographs to any person requesting one."

Sandler took the photograph and glanced over it quickly: Medical report on the child, description, fingerprints, report on the foster parents, notes on follow-up investigations. A crisp notation on his running away at the age of (approximately) sixteen. End of record.

"Satisfied now?" the official asked hopefully.

"I'll be perfectly satisfied after I've compared this with the original."

"I'm afraid that's impossible. No unauthorized person can be permitted—"

Sandler's hand was in his pocket. He moved it slowly and revealed the bulging muzzle of a flame pistol. The official's eyes widened and his throat made gurgling noises.

Sandler spoke softly. "You have a master file screen on the wall. I'd hate to have to use this. At such close range there wouldn't be much left of you but your head and two legs. It would probably make me sick. Are you going to dial the file number, or shall I?"

"There's nothing there you don't already have."

"Then there can't be any harm in showing it to me. Photographs are very easily tampered with, and I don't like this blank space in the upper right corner. Dial."

The official dialed. In his nervousness he got the wrong card and had to dial again. Sandler made a quick comparison and turned, grinning triumphantly. "Just alike, you say? Look in the right-hand corner. 'Source One eighty-seven.' What does that mean?"

The official quickly darkened the screen. "I haven't the faintest idea."

"It refers to the world of my origin, doesn't it?"

"I don't know." He looked at the flame pistol and added, "It might."

"There'll be a list of planetary sources somewhere. Where is it?"

"I don't know. The ministry hasn't handled any adoptions for years, and I don't know anything about them."

Sandler decided to believe him. "Why all the secrecy about this?"

"I don't make policy. I just follow orders."

"A lucky thing for you." He pocketed the pistol. "Now listen —I'm not going to tell anyone where I got this information as long as you don't mention it. If you make a complaint, I'll say I bribed you for it. Is that clear?"

"Certainly."

"Get away from your desk."

Sandler found the recorder and erased their conversation. "If anyone asks you," he said, "you forgot to turn it on. I thank you for your cooperation."

He rode the ramp back to the parking lot. No alarm sounded. A few minutes later he was back at his hotel. He rented a private pool, floated lazily in the water staring at the brilliant designs in the tiled ceiling, and sang lustily. "From far I come, a drifting scum upon the void. No home have I, no world to cry, nor asteroid."

He wanted to go home. He was going home. The far-reaching, all-powerful, omniscient galactic government was stubbornly opposed to his so much as knowing where that home might be. He formulated several crucial questions, and he began to make plans to shake some satisfactory answers out of responsible officials. By the neck, if necessary.

III

The blonde sang a different song in the Martian Room that night, and afterward she stopped at Sandler's table and said glumly, "Heard the news?"

"What news is that?"

"Ministry of Public Welfare. Censorship Department. The 'Homing Song' is bad for public morale. Further performances prohibited."

"How could that song harm anyone?"

"It couldn't, unless it's bad to make people want to go home. And since it isn't, I figure there's something about it that might harm the government."

Sandler nodded thoughtfully. It was of a pattern, along with the ministry's refusal to give him the information he wanted. "What would happen if you sang the song?" he asked.

"It would cost me a month's pay, at least. I could even get into trouble for telling you this. The censorship is supposed to be kept confidential. The government seems to think the song will run off and hide if professional performers stop singing it."

"That's ridiculous. Everyone in the galaxy knows it by this time."

"Try that argument on a governmental edict."

"What would happen if the public demanded the song? I mean, supposing your audience started calling for it the next time you're on?"

"I still couldn't sing it. But it would be fun!"

"We'll try it and see what happens."

As she moved onto the stage for her next song, he called out, " 'Homing Song'!"

A murmur of approval rippled about the room. The blonde ignored it, and as she started her song, Sandler called out again. The other guests began to chant, " 'Homing Song'!" and drowned out the music.

Sandler sat back to enjoy the confusion, felt a firm hand on his shoulder, and found himself staring at the credentials of a government public investigator. He paid his check and followed along meekly.

Outside the door he faced the burly officer and demanded, "What's the charge?"

"Disturbing the peace. Endangering public morale."

"You'll have some fun proving that, fellow, with everyone in the place doing the same thing."

"I'll prove it." He patted his pocket. "I have a recording. You started the disturbance."

"If you can convince a judge that it was a disturbance."

At Police Central Sandler was registered and passed along to the night court. The white-haired judge listened to the charges, had the evidence played, and questioned the investigator incredulously.

"You say the Censorship Department has prohibited this song, but the public has not been informed. The defendant certainly could not have known that he was asking the singer to do something unlawful. There is no indication that the hotel guests or its management regarded his actions as a public disturbance. The evidence points to the contrary." He paused. "I doubt that the courts will uphold the censorship order against the 'Homing Song,' but I see no need to concern myself with that question now. Case dismissed."

"I intend to appeal the dismissal," the investigator said haughtily.

"The law states that you may make such an appeal at your discretion. I shall schedule a hearing for ten tomorrow morning before Judge Corming, and I recommend that in the meantime you give some consideration to the meaning of the word 'discretion.'"

As a final insult to the investigator, he fixed bond at ten credits. Sandler posted the bond, caught a ground cab, and then dismissed it two blocks from the station. He strolled slowly along Vega Boulevard and several times stopped to look cautiously behind him.

The investigator's presence in the Martian Room had been no accident. His arrest on the flimsiest of pretexts had been no accident. The government wanted him out of the way, and if

Judge Corming refused to cooperate the case would be appealed further, or the police would fabricate new charges. If he didn't want to spend the next few years trying to break rocks with a light hammer on a low-gravity satellite, he'd have to move cautiously.

He heard strains of music, entered a small café, downed two drinks, and lost his newly acquired caution. He turned to the musicians and shouted, " 'Homing Song'!"

A near riot followed, but Sandler did not wait to see the outcome. He hurried off into the night, taking his patronage to another café, and to a stylish restaurant, and to a smoke-filled tavern, and with identical results. By the time he got back to his hotel, two dozen eating and drinking places along Vega Boulevard were rocking to the chant, " 'Homing Song'!", police cars were swooping down from all directions, and Sandler was in a mildly intoxicated condition.

From his hotel room window, he looked down at the clusters of police cars and tried to make out what was happening. Above him the sky was clear, the stars bright and coldly distant.

"Somewhere out there is where I belong," he told himself. "And I'm going there. It may be only a dump of a planet, but it's mine."

> A moonlet drear
> With atmosphere
> Is sacred ground.
> The barren loam
> Of any home
> Is flower-crowned.

An air car darted across the face of the hotel building, slowed abruptly, and dropped past his window. He threw himself to the floor as a heavy flame gun burned the air above him, wrecked his bed, and bored into the far wall. He dove for his baggage and came up with his own pistol, but the air car was already out of sight.

The hotel manager charged in a few minutes later, surveyed the damage, and stood fretfully wringing his hands.

"I think," Sandler said calmly, "that someone doesn't like me. It might be better for both the hotel and myself if I were to check out."

The manager agreed enthusiastically.

Traveling a tortuously meandering route, Sandler checked in at a shabby spacers' hotel near the port. He registered under an assumed name, paid for one night in advance, and settled into his cramped room to make plans.

He had no intention of placing himself in the hands of the police a second time, and when he failed to appear in court he would be a bona fide fugitive from justice. The government would begin searching for him openly. His photo would be circulated, transportation agencies would be notified, and port officials alerted. His situation would grow more perilous by the minute. Whatever he did had to be done quickly.

At dawn he carried his belongings to the port. He left them in a rented locker, descended to a lower level, and at a dispenser bought a handful of tokens for the only anonymous means of transportation in Galaxia—the overburdened pneumatic underground railroad. The masses facetiously referred to it as the air train.

Sandler changed trains five times and rode to the end of the line in a distant part of Galaxia. In a public visiphone booth, he hung his coat over the visual transmitter and made four calls.

A distinguished Galaxia attorney: "My dear sir, we might be able to establish your right to information about your parents and the planet of your origin, but what good would that do if government officials were to swear under oath that no record of this information exists? You'd win your point without gaining a thing."

The editor of a leading opposition newspaper: "We're always happy to embarrass the administration, but we don't want to embarrass it *that* much. The Department of Censorship would close us. I advise you to get away from Earth while you're still healthy."

A prominent visiscope commentator: "The less I know about this, the better I'll like it."

An opposition congressman: "Your case isn't the first I've heard about. Sure, we could stir things up a bit. But it wouldn't help you, and the Expansionist Party would spend a billion to defeat me next election. My advice: Forget it!"

Sandler checked both viviscope and the newspapers and found no mention of the disturbances over the "Homing Song." He wondered if the government would be satisfied if he quietly faded away. At a minimum there would be a galaxy-wide Confidential on him. Never again would he be able to use his own name or land openly on a planet without undergoing continuous and humiliating harassment.

"And since I'm into it that far," he told himself, "I might as well go all the way. I think I'll have a quiet talk with this Minister of Public Welfare."

But he could visualize that august individual shaking his head mockingly and saying, "Sorry. We have no records. No records at all. Be very happy to help you if I could. I knew your foster father. But without records—"

There were drugs, talk pills and anti-hib sprays and truth serums in a multitude of types, each with complicated medical and investigative uses. None of them were available to casual purchasers, no questions asked.

Sandler prowled the streets until he found a doctor's office. He intentionally avoided looking at the name, concentrating on the faded word "Psychiatrist," as he climbed the worn stairway. He emerged in a hallway that reeked of a strange mixture of odors, most indefinable and probably unmentionable. On the street level there had been a pawnbroker's establishment. On the floors above were dwelling units. He could hear squalling children and snarling mothers. This was the reverse side of the polished, gem-like capital of the galaxy. The night side. The foul, indescribable slum side.

The consultation room was jammed with the slovenly dregs of humanity: The aged, the infirm, the addicts, the alcoholics, all shabbily dressed, all waiting with dumbly inexpressive faces for the forces of healing to probe their crumbling minds.

Sandler turned aside and edged his way along the filthy hallway. Again avoiding the doctor's name, he pressed his ear to a door.

". . . Mrs. Schultz," a shrill male voice said. "Then I'll see you Tuesday at eleven."

Shuffling footsteps. A door opening. The shrill voice asking, "Who's next?" And then, as the visiphone gong chimed musically, "Just a moment, please."

The door closed. The visiphone mumbled inaudibly. The shrill voice piped, "What's that you say? Oh, pills! Yes, as soon as I can get there."

Footsteps moved urgently about the room and suddenly approached the door. Sandler stepped back as the lock clicked and raised his flame pistol. The doctor halted with the door half-opened, his wrinkled face transfixed with amazement. Sandler pushed through and closed the door after him as the doctor backed away.

The doctor cackled mockingly. "I don't suppose, young man, that you've called for professional assistance."

"I want to buy something," Sandler said.

"You've come to the wrong place. I'm a psychiatrist. I don't kept addictive drugs in my office. If I did, in this neighborhood, it'd be broken into ten times a night."

"I don't want addictive drugs," Sandler said.

"I have an emergency. A man has been injured in a street brawl. They call a psychiatrist to treat a bump on the head—but then, there aren't any other doctors in this neighborhood. Please state your business quickly."

He was a mere wisp of a man, gaunt, the pink of his head radiant beneath his sparse white hair. Sandler remembered the riff-raff in the waiting room and regarded him with admiration. He was a real doctor, a doctor who lived only to serve.

He said firmly, "I want a hypodermic syringe and a maximum dose of truth serum."

The doctor scrutinized him with professional interest. "You don't look like a bad man."

"I'm a wronged man," Sandler said wearily. "I've harmed no one, I've violated no law, but the police are looking for me and an agency of the government has tried to murder me. I ask you in the name of justice to sell me what I want and forget about it."

"The police have truth serum," the doctor said. "I might forget, but could you?"

"I've done everything I could to protect you. I don't know your name. I'm a stranger in Galaxia, and once I leave your office I'll never be able to find my way back here."

"Even so, it would be safer for me to report it. Tomorrow—supposing I report it tomorrow?"

Sandler nodded.

"Well, then—I can't sell the things to you. Look." He got out a hypodermic syringe and filled it. "I'm ready for my next patient. And I get an emergency call, and in my hurry I forget to lock the door. I'm an old man, and I won't miss the thing until tomorrow. So?"

Sandler stepped aside, and the doctor hurried away. He grabbed the syringe and slipped a hundred-credit note into the doctor's desk. From the general character of his practice, Sandler thought he might need the money.

Sandler hurried down the stairs, saw the doctor tottering along the street, and turned in the opposite direction.

IV

The official residence of Jan Vildson, the Minister of Public Welfare, occupied a choice location at the intersection of Centaurian and Solar Avenues. Its grounds were enclosed on three sides by a towering, vine-covered wall. On the fourth was a tall commercial building, its wall windowless to the eighth story.

Sandler had circled the place a dozen times during the afternoon, gaping like an awed tourist while he made his plans. He'd expended a small fortune in air cab fares, riding back and forth to catch a passing glimpse of the mansion. He had prowled the neighborhood to set up alternate escape routes.

But he felt more determined than confident as he stood on Centaurian Avenue and watched the ground cab speed away. It was shortly before midnight, but the artificial "moons" that dotted the sky over Galaxia bathed the spacious avenue in light.

He shouldered his heavy bag and hurried toward the minister's residence.

He reached the wall and crouched there under a steady whir of air traffic, seeking a shadow where there was none. From his bag he took a heavy, triangular-shaped building stone and tossed it so that its looping trajectory just cleared the wall. Then he raced along the street, tossing stones as he ran and hoping that at least one of them would trigger the mansion's alarm system. As he turned onto Solar Avenue he could hear a gong booming faintly, far away. He ran frantically, reached the far corner of the wall, and hauled himself up on the clinging vines.

On the other side he slid to the ground and sprinted for the cover of weird-looking, spiral-leaved shrubs. Men were dashing about at the other end of the grounds, and their shouts reached him faintly. He heard the excited yelp of a dog. Crouching, he ran from shrub to shrub and finally hurled himself into the tall, sprawling density of a flower bed. The flowers were of some exotic species, and they were in full bloom. The heavy sweet scent overpowered and stifled him, and he lay gasping for breath.

The alarm continued to sound. More men arrived, and a squadron of patrol cars swooped down and landed in an open space near the mansion. Sandler kept his head down, sank his fingers into the rich, moist soil, and waited.

His racing pulse counted off the minutes. Then the alarm stopped suddenly. Two of the searchers came trudging back and met a third man near the gate.

"Some idiot threw stones over the wall," one of them said.

The patrol cars lifted gracefully, one at a time, circled, and moved off in formation. Other men came straggling back in twos and threes. There was more grumbling conversation as they disappeared around the corner of the mansion.

A sentry resumed his plodding circuit of the grounds. With his head raised cautiously above the flowers, Sandler timed his movements and began planning a route of approach.

His first sprint carried him across twenty feet of open lawn to the cover of a large tree. He moved in spurts separated by maddening intervals of crouched waiting. After forty minutes of cautious maneuvering he was huddled in the scant shadow of a flowering bush studying a balcony that extended out over an artistically landscaped terrace. At one side, flowering vines wove their way up a metal framework. Sandler watched the sentry and waited.

The sentry moved out of sight behind the building. Sandler ran, leaped, and hauled himself up the vines. Thorns stabbed at him, ripping his hands and clothing. He stumbled across the balcony and tried the door. It opened easily. He stepped through, closed it silently, and squinted into the darkness.

Suddenly a beam of light struck him full in the face, blinding him. "All right, Fritz. See if he's armed," a crisp voice said.

Sandler closed his eyes and stood with fists clenched. Hands moved expertly over his body, spun him around roughly, and removed his pistol. The room lights came on, and Sandler saw three men watching him alertly. Two of them had flame pistols leveled unwaveringly at his stomach.

The crisp voice spoke again. "You're a patient man, friend. But then—so am I. I've been watching you for the last half-hour." He turned to the others. "I can handle him. I'll call you if I need you."

The door closed behind them, and he gestured with his pistol. "Now, then. You will sit down there and place your hands on the table. Right. Jan Vildson is my name. Minister of Public Welfare. And you are Thomas Jefferson Sandler. What can I do for you?"

The minister was an elderly man, but swarthy, robust-looking, and without a touch of gray in his black hair. He looked a youthful sixty-five and could have been fifteen years older.

"You surprise me," Sandler said boldly. "You hardly look like a scoundrel."

"I was thinking the same about you, young man. I've known you for longer than you think. I knew your adopted father well. He had high hopes for you. On your performance of the past two days I'd say you were quite capable of fulfilling his hopes. You show a commendable determination. It's a pity you squander it on trivialities."

"If my objective is so trivial," Sandler said, "why is the government going to such extremes to make me fail?"

The minister seated himself on the opposite side of the wide table and laid his pistol in front of him. "Trivial or not, your objective is certainly futile. The information you want was destroyed years ago—long before I became Minister of Public Welfare."

"The planet of my origin is clearly indicated on my record card."

"The planet's *number* is indicated. The number refers to a list of several hundred planets from which orphan children were taken for adoption. The number has no meaning without that list, and all copies of the list have been destroyed."

"Why was the list destroyed?"

The minister shook his head slowly. "Perhaps for the most noble of reasons, perhaps for stupid bureaucratic expediency, perhaps for criminal reasons—though I don't know what they could have been. It doesn't matter. We can't undo it now, we can't undestroy something that's been destroyed. I'm sincere, and everyone else has been sincere, in telling you to forget the whole business."

He paused, and Sandler waited silently.

"Now here is what I suggest," the minister went on. "You're in trouble, but it isn't serious trouble. I believe I can arrange to keep the whole affair quiet. I'll see that you get to the port and onto an outgoing ship. There will be no police report on your performance of this evening. After all, you are the son of an old friend. What do you say?"

"Will you answer a few questions?"

"Gladly, if I have the answers."

"The Department of Public Censorship is under your control, isn't it?"

"It is."

"Why have you banned performances of the 'Homing Song'?"

The minister looked puzzled. "The 'Homing Song'? Banned?"

"Bad for public morale. Or so your censors say."

"I've heard the song. Who hasn't? But I don't recall anything —*banned*, you say? I'll have to look into that."

"Banned without public notice. I was arrested for asking a professional performer to sing it."

The minister shook his head perplexedly.

"What government official gave the order to have me murdered?" Sandler asked. "Was it you?"

The minister slowly rose to his feet. "Murdered? Someone ordered you murdered?"

"I was fired on from an air car. Fortunately I ducked in time, but it made a mess of my hotel room."

The minister dropped back into his chair. "That's not true," he protested. "It can't be true."

Sandler dove across the table and seized the pistol. He regained his seat, breathing heavily, and held the weapon under the table. "If your men check up, you'll tell them everything is under control."

The minister had a hurt expression on his face. "You tricked me. I've tried to be nice to you, Sandler. I've given you every consideration—"

"Shut up!" Sandler snapped. "I'm a nobody, and I don't expect special consideration. However important my foster father may have been, I'm a nobody. All I want to do is go home. Why is the Federation Government determined to do anything in its power, legal and illegal, up to and including murder, to keep me from doing that? Why would it prefer me dead rather than answer questions about my home planet?"

"You shouldn't make such reckless accusations. Why would the government want to kill you?"

"No one outside the government cares what I do. I haven't any other enemies, and it isn't coincidence that my arrest and the attempted murder came immediately after I started these inquiries. Now—the planet's number is One eighty-seven. What is it, and where is it?"

"I told you the truth. To the best of my knowledge, there isn't a copy of that list in existence."

Sandler loosened his shirt and gripped the hypodermic syringe he had taped to his arm. "I've had enough of your kind of truth. Now I want my kind. Bare your arm, please."

The minister straightened up in alarm. "What's that you have?"

"Truth serum. I mean you no harm, but I'm going to have the truth if I have to kill you to get it."

"You don't believe me?" the minister croaked, his frightened eyes focused on the needle. "Think of it. Old T. J.'s son calling me a liar. Do you know, Sandler, I held you on my lap when you weren't more than six years old?"

The screen on the far wall flickered to life. One of the minister's guards glanced at them suspiciously. "Everything all right, sir?"

Sandler's hand tensed on the pistol.

"Everything's all right," the minister said weakly. The screen darkened.

Sandler rounded the table and stood waiting. "Bare your arm," he ordered.

"That's dangerous," the minister protested. He looked at Sandler's face, shrugged, and slipped out of his coat. "If that's all that will satisfy you—"

He rolled up his sleeve, and Sandler inexpertly jabbed the needle into his arm. He walked back to his chair and tossed the syringe under the table.

He watched the minister anxiously, wishing he'd got more information from the doctor. He hadn't any idea how much time the serum might require to take effect. The minister leaned back in his chair, eyes closed, breathing deeply.

Finally Sandler asked, "What is planet One eighty-seven?"

"Don't—know. List—destroyed."

"Who would have a copy of the list?"

"Destroyed—long ago."

"Why was the list destroyed?"

The minister doubled up suddenly, clutching both hands to his heart. His breath came in whistling gasps, his face was white and taut, and his teeth were clenched in searing agony. Sandler dashed around the table and bent over him in alarm.

He remembered belatedly that he had casually asked the doctor for a maximum dose of truth serum—and that a maximum dose might be too much for a man of eighty. It was too much. The minister was dying.

Sandler hurried to the balcony and looked out across the grounds. The sentry was not in sight. He slid quickly to the ground and ran. There was no time to worry about taking cover. He reached the wall and was going over the top when a light flashed in the balcony's open door. At the same time the alarm gong boomed urgently.

Sandler drove himself in merciless, headlong flight for two long blocks to an air train station. He hurtled down the moving escalator stairs, thrust a token into the turnstile, and pushed through, glancing anxiously at the clock. He had spent an hour, that afternoon, memorizing train schedules. He was waiting on the right platform twenty-five seconds later when a train glided smoothly to a stop. He boarded it, transferred at the next station, and rode the trains until dawn, leaving a meandering, criss-crossing trail through subterranean Galaxia.

He spent the day in a squalid hotel, and that evening he wove another meandering trail out to the port. He collected his belongings, and with the wile of a veteran spacer stowed away on a lumbering ore freighter that lifted at midnight for Mars. The freighter's crew smuggled him past Mars Customs, and he bought forged identity papers and shipped as a common spacer on a ship outward bound from the Solar System.

He stood in an observation port for a last, contemptuous look at Earth—a brittle spark thrown off by a shrinking sun.

V

Thomas Jefferson Sandler III drifted slowly across the galaxy, a derelict caught in weirdly eccentric currents. He shipped as a spacer when he found a post. He stowed away. Once he joined a hopeful group of immigrants in their cramped quarters. He piloted a cargo of smuggled gold from Lamruth to Emmoy. On Kilfton he was recognized, and he killed two guards in escaping.

Or perhaps they recovered. He never heard what happened to them, or cared.

Twice he encountered Marty Worrel, but he cautiously kept

his distance. The little musician had a pronounced talent for fomenting disturbances—as on Hillan, where he got up on a table in a crowded tavern and sang his "Homing Song." Sandler made a hurried exit before the police appeared. He could not risk being associated with any kind of disturbance.

He drifted on, moving always outward from Earth, following the long axis of the galaxy. In Sector 187 he invaded the private residence of the Sector Commissioner, thinking that the number on his identification card might refer to sector rather than to planet. The commissioner persisted in his declarations of ignorance with Sandler's fingers about his throat. Sandler left him unconscious, stowed away once more, and drifted onward. He waylaid a dozen sector Chiefs of Public Welfare. He attempted to bribe government officials, and he threatened them with violence and sudden death, and he learned nothing.

The months drifted by and became years. Sandler moved from planet to planet, searching for a color of sky, for anything that would match his few blurred recollections of home. Hot worlds and cold, wet worlds and dry, he studied them hopefully from an observation port, wandered their surfaces until disillusion seized him, and then left without a backward glance.

Three years after leaving Earth, he stood staring at the dingy, gray face of one more planet as his ship flashed downward, and he felt depressed. Usually a new planet offered some hope, but not this one. Twisting clouds of dust erupted and slowly spread their heavy film across its surface. It was Stanruth: barren, lifeless, waterless world, but a world rich in minerals, so there was a colony, and there were humans who sought wealth, and found it or failed to find it, and fled homeward. No one would call Stanruth "home."

"But then—who can say?" Sandler muttered. Some day, perhaps children born on that blighted planet might see it as a place of beauty.

> The barren loam
> Of any home
> Is flower-crowned.

To Sandler, it was no more than a steppingstone that he must touch in passing. It was one strange world of many in the weary fabric of his existence, of his coming and going, of his hiding, of his seeking and not finding.

The ship landed, and he tensed himself for the inevitable customs inspection. His handsome, young-looking face had undergone transformation. He had scarred it hideously. His head was shaven bald. He wore a bushy, uncouth beard. His body was a weird gallery of spacer tattoos. But he knew that sooner or later a sharp-eyed official would recognize him and his search would be over.

He passed through customs almost unnoticed and moved on into the stark, treeless town. The building stones were fused sand. Sand drifted everywhere, and even the feet of a slow-moving pedestrian stirred up clouds of dust.

Sandler entered a squalid tavern, where a tumbler of water cost a credit and a bottle of good whisky was only a rumor at any price. He glanced about the smoke-filled interior and saw, huddled in a dark corner, a familiar figure: that little man of enormous talent and small worth, Marty Worrel.

Worrel's apparent sobriety intrigued Sandler, and he slid onto a fused-sand bench across the table from him and said, "Hello."

Worrel stared without a spark of recognition. "Do I know you?"

Sandler leaned forward and whispered, "From far I come, a drifting scum upon the void."

Worrel winced and glanced about cautiously. "Whoever you are," he said, "you've changed."

"You haven't changed. I thought that song would make you a billionaire with a big estate and a dozen air cars. I suppose someone stole it from you. You've been wearing the same suit for the last four years. It doesn't even look as though you've had it off."

"Clothes," Worrel said disgustedly. "Rags to hide the body's immodesty. The soul fashions its own raiment." He signaled for drinks and waved Sandler's money away. "I *am* a billionaire. A millionaire, anyway. Someone copyrighted that song for me. I didn't even know about it. I have money in the banks of half the planets of the galaxy. And what's money? The dowry of evil.

The prop of tyranny. The strangling nourishment of greed. It corrodes the soul. It buys a woman's honor and a man's integrity. It lays waste to the body and stifles happiness. We are wanderers all, we puny humans, seeking wealth to buy the unattainable. You want money? I'll give you money. Hell, I'll give it all to you."

He slumped forward, spilling his expensive whisky, and sobbed brokenly with his face buried in his hands.

Sandler straightened up in alarm. "You're drunk," he said disgustedly.

"I'm always drunk. What else is there? One must be either drunk or sober, and I'm drunk. Money can buy *that*. Money buys whisky and whisky benumbs the senses and benumbed senses crave whisky and whisky requires money and money buys whisky and whisky benumbs the senses—"

He sobbed again and began to sing, in a cracked, nasal voice. "Home is that place in deepest space where memories burn."

Sandler leaned over and slapped Worrel's face. Worrel's head snapped back, and he shook himself, stared oddly at Sandler for a moment, and signaled for another drink. "What are you doing here?" he asked.

"Seeking the unattainable. Without money."

"You are a wise man. A wise, noble, generous, virtuous, deserving, admirable, good, worthy, unculpable—" He paused and squinted doubtfully. "What did you say your name was?"

"I didn't," Sandler said.

"No-Name. It's best that way. A name is but a label applied at birth through the connivance of dishonorable parents. I like you, No-Name. What did you say you were seeking?"

Sandler glanced about them cautiously. More spacers had come in, and the place rocked with their boisterous laughter. Bartenders and serving girls were rushing about frantically. The dingy corner was ignored, but Sandler leaned forward and said in a whisper, "Home."

Worrel paused with his glass in mid-air, face pale, manner unaccountably sober. "We must talk," he said. He drained his glass and screamed, "Bottle of whisky!" A serving girl hurried

over. Worrel paid her and gripped Sandler's arm. "Come. We must talk."

He led Sandler from the tavern and along the dusty street. They entered a shabby, sand-eroded rooming house and climbed three flights of stairs to Worrel's room. It was virtually unfurnished. The bed was a pile of filthy blankets in one corner. In another corner was a pile of empty bottles. A bench of fused sand stood against one wall. Powdery dust covered everything.

Worrel seated Sandler on the bench, dashed out again, and returned with a pair of tumblers. He poured the drinks with trembling fingers and squatted on the floor.

"Tell me," he said. "Tell me everything."

Sandler sketched out the story of his frustrated efforts to find his home planet, carefully omitting any hint of criminal activity.

"But you did find the number of your planet," Worrel said excitedly. "What is it?"

"One eighty-seven."

Worrel got slowly to his feet. He fumbled in an inside pocket, produced a card, and handed it to Sandler: A photograph of a Ministry of Public Welfare record card concerning a child identified as Marty Worrel. And this photograph was complete. In the upper right corner Sandler read, "Source: 187."

Worrel snatched the card and stood in front of Sandler, body tense, eyes gleaming, his small, wrinkled face alight with tremendous excitement. "Brother!" he whispered.

Sandler nodded slowly. "I suppose I could be your brother."

"And we have a sister. Come!"

He gripped Sandler's arm, hurried him down a flight of stairs, and rushed him into a room on the floor below. This room was neatly furnished, tidy, almost free from dust. Its sole occupant was a young woman, who started up and hastily draped a robe over her bare limbs as they entered.

"Another one!" Worrel called. "Another One eighty-seven."

"No!" she exclaimed. She stared wide-eyed at Sandler, disbelief showing in her lovely face. "You look—well, so old for a space-orphan."

"Space-orphan?" Sandler echoed.

"From far we come, a drifting scum upon the void," Worrel

chanted. "Space-orphans are we, and space-orphans we shall ever be. Cast us adrift in time, wrap us gently in the empty shroud of space, and lull us to sleep with the clanging music of the spheres. No one cares, and nothing else matters. Home is a moonlet drear with atmosphere, and who gives a damn whether the homeless breathe or not?" He waved his bottle. "Let's drink to One eighty-seven, somewhere on the bottom side of nowhere."

"You're drunk again, Marty," the girl sighed.

"I'm drunk *yet*," he corrected. "Oh. Introductions. Miriam, this is No-Name. No-Name, this is Miriam." He thrust his head forward and looked inquiringly at Sandler. "You're sure you haven't got a name?"

"My adopted name is Thomas Jefferson Sandler."

"So that's who you are. I remember. You're a pilot. You've changed. Your own mother wouldn't recognize you." He laughed shrilly. "That's a joke. Your own mother—"

"How did you find out you were both from One eighty-seven?" Sandler asked.

"Bribery. Cost me fifty thousand. That's another use for money. It adapts itself to any dishonorable purpose."

Miriam was still watching Sandler with frank suspicion. "Marty, are you sure he's—I mean, he looks so *old*."

"He's a fugitive from injustice," Worrel said. "That ages one. On the other hand, how *do* I know you came from One eighty-seven?"

The girl turned her back to them and whirled around suddenly with a small pistol in her hand. "We can't afford to take chances," she said sharply. "Prove it!"

Sandler moved over to the wall and sat down on a bench. "My papers are forged," he said. "I'm wanted on every planet in the galaxy for murder, attempted murder, assault on highly placed officials, smuggling, flouting of customs regulations, unlawful flight to avoid whatever charges may have been placed against me, and an odd assortment of other things. I had a photo of my record card, but I lost it long ago. What proof do you want?"

She hesitated. "Can you remember anything at all about home?"

"A color of sky," Sandler said slowly, "that I can't describe, but if I saw it I think I'd know. I've tried many times to remember, but it's all so vague. A mud hut, with narrow slits in the walls. A small boy hurrying proudly home carrying an ornt by the tail. A mother who is a shapeless figure without features, and who is also wonderful. A father who helps a small hand grip a spear that is much longer than the boy. An arnel cake. Not much, is it?"

The pistol disappeared. Miriam threw herself on him, gripped him tightly, and kissed him profusely.

"One of us," Worrel said and chanted loudly. "Three space-orphans are we. Three space-orphans we be. Two are you and one is me. I am a minority." He sat down on the floor and tipped up the bottle.

"Stop it, Marty," Miriam pleaded. "Maybe he has some ideas. Maybe we can plan."

Worrel got up abruptly. "Plan," he said. "You have a plan?"

"No," Sandler said. "I'm just drifting. I've killed one man and possibly more, and I've nearly choked several men to death, and all I can find out is that no one knows. One eighty-seven is just a number. We'd be as well off not to know it. Better off, maybe."

Worrel seemed oddly sober again. "I know a man," he said. "Commissioner of Sector Fifteen thirty-one. He's an old man, he's been around a long time, and he knows something about the space-orphans. He goes around looking for them and asking them questions. Me he won't talk to. Me he laughs at. You're a man of action. He won't laugh at you."

"I'll see him," Sandler said. "Who is he?"

"Name's Novin. Commissioner Novin. On Pronna."

"Then I'll go to Pronna."

"We'll all go to Pronna," Worrel said. "We'll leave today."

"There may not be a ship."

"There'll be a ship. I'll buy a ship with my filthy, filthy money. When we find One eighty-seven, I'll buy the planet and throw the Federation off. I'll buy a space fleet and demolish Earth. I'll buy paradise and populate it with space-orphans. What sector do you suppose paradise is in? Is that another number no one remembers?" He sat down again and tilted the bottle.

VI

Worrel bought a ship, a rusted space-worn freighter, but Sandler had to qualify for a pilot's license under his assumed name, and it was a week before they could leave Stanruth. They made slow, plodding progress, stopping off at a dozen planets for Worrel to convert his bank accounts into cash.

On New Miloma they traded their freighter and half a million credits for a sleek space yacht that Worrel renamed, privately, the 187. On Calmus they waited several days while Worrel completed complicated arrangements to withdraw some money from banks across half the galaxy. They landed on Filline for still more financial transactions and found the police waiting.

"Thomas Jefferson Sandler," the young captain said cheerfully. "The Galactic Bureau of Investigation has been wanting you badly for a long time."

"Sure," Sandler said. "How'd you locate me?"

"You made the mistake of qualifying—or should I say, requalifying—for a pilot's license. Your fingerprints went all the way to Earth, and eventually someone got around to making cross-checks. He was most pleasantly surprised. All of you are under arrest."

Worrel, caught in one of his rare moments of sobriety, turned on Sandler in panic. "Why'd you do it?" he hissed. "You didn't need a license. We could have sneaked off Stanruth and no one would have noticed."

"They always notice," Sandler said wearily. "Then all three of us would have been fugitives. This way it's only me." He turned to the captain. "Why bother these people? They didn't know who I was. They just hired a pilot."

"They'll have every opportunity to prove their innocence."

Sandler was flown out into the open country to a small, walled prison. He was treated with politeness and consideration. His cell was comfortable, his food excellent, and he was given fresh clothing. He shaved off his beard and began to feel better.

Through the months and years he had known that this day would arrive, and he faced it almost with a sensation of home-

coming. Ahead of him lay more futile quests, to Pronna, to other planets; and more futile interviews with officials who could not or would not talk; and more violence and more hiding. The drifting scum, the space-orphan, was better off returned to the void.

An elderly, dignified lawyer called on him that afternoon and brought the welcome news that Worrel and Miriam had been released. Worrel had hired him. He went over the file of charges with Sandler, growing increasingly gloomy at each successive item, and finally he recommended that Sandler plead insanity.

"They'll hold you for psych-treatment if you bring it off," he said, "but that's better than death. The death penalty is still revived for special cases—about one a century—and I think they're going to make a special case out of you."

"Thanks," Sandler said dryly. "I'll think it over."

But he was determined that there would be no insanity plea for Thomas Jefferson Sandler III. He wanted the entire sordid story of his career in crime aired in open court. The government could eliminate Sandler, but it couldn't eliminate the sensational publicity that attended a criminal trial.

Or couldn't it? Instead of a trial it could easily arrange a convenient accident on the long trip back to Earth, and there wouldn't be a thing that Sandler could do about that.

He went to bed, drifted off into a peaceful sleep, and was awakened in the dim hours of early morning by an urgent whisper.

"Sandler!"

He leaped to his feet. The cell door stood open, and Marty Worrel was in the corridor prodding a guard with a flame pistol.

"Quick!" Worrel hissed.

Barefooted, half dressed, Sandler took Worrel's pistol and hurried the guard on ahead of him. They found Miriam holding a pair of guards at pistol point near the entrance. With quick, deadly motions Sandler clubbed them into unconsciousness.

"Can we make the ship?" he demanded.

"We can try," Worrel said. "We've got an air car hidden outside."

"Let's go!"

They sprinted across the brightly lighted yard to the prison gate. The gate stood ajar, and a dead guard was crumpled in the guardhouse, his face gruesome even in the shadows.

They moved through the gate and were running across the glaring patch of light that surrounded the walls when a guard saw them. A shout rang out, and a heavy flame rifle burned the air above their heads.

"It's in a clearing in the woods," Miriam gasped.

The flame rifle fired again and missed. They were running in darkness, but Sandler knew they had only seconds before the rolling meadow would be lighted. The shadows of trees loomed far ahead of them. They stumbled across the slight depression of a water course, and Sandler guided them along it.

"It gives us some cover," he panted. "We'd better spread out. Running together we're too good a target. Miriam first."

They separated, running in single file along the water course. Trees loomed ahead of them.

The flame rifle snapped again, slicing between Sandler and Worrel. Sandler stopped, fired carefully, and heard a cry. He fired again, and shouts of alarm sounded behind him. "Slowed them down," he thought, and ran on.

Lights glowed suddenly, bathing the meadow in naked brilliance. Beams from a dozen rifles crackled about them. Miriam's piercing scream cut across the night, and Sandler flung himself to the ground and methodically cut down the silhouetted pursuers. He moved on a moment later and found Miriam bending over Worrel's prostrate figure.

"Go on," Worrel whispered urgently. "Don't worry about me. Go on!"

Without a word Sandler picked up the little musician and led Miriam into the safety of the trees. He carried Worrel gently, ignoring the gushing blood and the gaping emptiness that had been his right side.

They reached the air car. Sandler carefully placed Worrel on a seat, and Miriam bent over him with tears in her eyes as Sandler took the controls.

"No good at this sort of thing," Worrel whispered. "Gun in my hand scares me stiff. See what my filthy money brings me?

Sordid end of a sordid beginning. One less glob of scum on the troubled face of time."

"Don't talk," Miriam pleaded.

"You should have left me there," Sandler said bitterly. "You two hadn't done anything wrong. You could have kept on looking. Now you'll be hunted along with me."

Worrel's words were pain-wracked sobs. "Needed you. Couldn't pull it off ourselves. I don't count, except for money. You two will make it."

Sandler brushed his hand across his wet eyes and lied bravely. "Nonsense. You'll make it."

"Sordid end of a sordid beginning." Worrel lurched forward. "If you make it—if you find One eighty-seven—take my ashes with you. Promise!"

"You'll make it right along with us," Sandler said.

"Promise!"

"Of course. But you'll make it."

Marty Worrel was dead when they reached the space port. They landed by their ship, and Sandler raced up the ramp with Worrel's dead body, wrenched open the sealed air lock, and hurried to the controls. Police cars were swarming down on the port, and they lifted just as officers and guards were fanning out to approach the ship.

Sandler busied himself for hours with a complex, zigzag course that would evade detection. Finally he relaxed and turned to Miriam.

"Maybe they don't know you were involved in that mess. I can drop you off somewhere, and you can find a new identity for yourself. The longer you're with me, the less chance you'll have."

She shook her head. "Pronna. Marty would have wanted it that way."

"Yes," he said. "I suppose so." He took her hand and stroked it gently. She attracted him as no woman had ever attracted him, and yet—

"You're a brave woman," he said, and added quickly, to be quite safe, "sister."

She smiled wanly. "No. You're a brave man. Maybe a little reckless, but brave."

They slipped in on the night side of Pronna and landed in a forest clearing. For an exorbitant fee a village mortician cremated Marty Worrel's body and asked no questions. Miriam found lodgings in the village, and Sandler turned most of Worrel's money over to her.

"If I don't come back," he said, "forget about the ship. Forget about One eighty-seven. Forget about me. Go off to the other side of the galaxy and make a new life for yourself."

"You'll come back," she said. "And I'll be waiting."

It took Sandler three days to make his way halfway around the planet to the capital city. It took him only twenty minutes, under the cover of darkness, to make his way into the sector commissioner's sprawling residence. His fiendish efficiency amused him. "Getting to be an expert at this sort of thing," he told himself grimly.

He cornered a frightened servant, got detailed information about the house, and left the servant in a closet, bound and gagged. He found the commissioner's bedroom, awoke the old man, and blinded him with a light.

"I mean no harm to you or anyone else," he said softly. "I want information."

"You pick an irregular way asking for it," the commissioner said testily. "Can we sit down and talk peacefully, or do you have to blind me?"

Sandler turned his light aside, locked the door, and flipped on the room lights. The commissioner stopped rubbing his eyes and studied Sandler curiously. He was a small man, with a grotesquely wrinkled face and a shining bald head, but there was lively alertness, almost humor, in his dark eyes.

"Thomas Jefferson Sandler," he chuckled. "I've been averaging one bulletin a month on you for years. I suppose I should have expected this." He got to his feet and ceremoniously indicated a chair. "Please be seated. And put the gun away. I know you mean well, but I can't help thinking those things are known to go off accidently."

Sandler pocketed his pistol, seated himself, and watched

alertly while the commissioner slipped into a robe. He took the chair opposite Sandler and smiled at him benevolently.

"You interest me, Thomas Jefferson Sandler. I'm pleased that you took the trouble to call on me."

"Planet One eighty-seven," Sandler said. "What is it and where is it?"

The commissioner shook his head. "I don't know. I believe I can safely say that no one knows. Such records as were kept were all in the files of the Ministry of Public Welfare on Earth, and my confidential information is that they were destroyed years ago."

"I've heard so many lies," Sandler said wearily. "How do I know you're telling the truth?"

Commissioner Novin held up his hand. "No truth serum, please. On my word as a sector commissioner, and a galactic citizen, and a fellow human being, that is the truth."

"I've learned that violence doesn't really solve anything, so I'll believe you. I'll offer you my thanks and apologies and leave."

"Oh, don't go," the commissioner exclaimed. "I don't know about planet One eighty-seven, but I may be able to help you. As I said, you interest me. By profession I'm a psychologist, and I've been following your career carefully. I've also studied the problem of what you probably call the space-orphans. I have my ways of finding out things, and I know somewhat more about the matter than the authorities on Earth. My position out here places me much closer to the problem. Sit down, please, and I'll tell you what I know."

Suspecting a trap, hand clutching the pistol in his pocket, Sandler sat down.

"I believe some background information is in order," Commissioner Novin said. "Among us humans, fads are peculiar things. Sometimes they are mildly eccentric, and sometimes they reach the point of absolute mania. At the present time, for example, large families are something of a fad among the wealthy. One measure of a man's success in life is the number of children he has. It is also a measure of a woman's adequacy as a wife. The fad is a mild one, treated somewhat humorously but nevertheless sincerely. Perhaps you've encountered it yourself."

"In recent years I've had very little social contact with wealthy families," Sandler said dryly.

"I consider this fad to be a direct reaction to a fad of roughly twenty to forty years ago in which women considered it a very real stigma to bear even one child. That fad did reach the point of mania and resulted in a craze for adopted children. Fortunately for the human race it was a passing thing, and it never touched the lower classes at all. It was not even pursued by a majority of the upper classes, but only by a small, closely knit, socially select group that centered in the Earth sector. The unfortunate consequences resulted from the fact that the group had financial and political influence all out of proportion to its numbers.

"The craze for adopted children quickly exhausted the supply, and political pressures resulted. The Ministry of Public Welfare set up a special department and began to search the galaxy for children available for adoption. And it encountered a stubborn obstacle. The well-organized, civilized planets had their own laws concerning such children, and they flatly refused to permit meddling by the Ministry of Public Welfare. The situation grew more critical, and the political pressure became enormous. And finally a solution was found. Do you mind if I smoke?"

Sandler shook his head. The commissioner produced a bulging cigar from the pocket of his gown, lit it, and waved it at Sandler, who was listening intently.

"The solution," the commissioner said, "was simple. The Federation is constantly expanding and constantly discovering new, inhabited planets. The people of many of those planets have at best a primitive civilization. A high percentage of them could be termed 'savages.' We don't need to go into the conflicting migration and evolution theories which try to account for the presence of humans on these newly discovered planets. The point is, humans are constantly being discovered and many of them are living under rather primitive conditions. Where there were no obvious difficulties, such as distinctive racial characteristics or an apparent low level of intelligence, children from these planets were—taken."

"Stolen?" Sandler gasped.

"If you like. 'Appropriated' is a more apt term, with the government proceeding as though it had a legal right to such action. The children were transported to Earth, educated to the normal level of a civilized child of their age, and distributed to the adoption crazed wealthy."

"Inhuman!" Sandler muttered.

"Decidedly. I was, for a time, local administrator on one of those planets, and one day a converted battle cruiser dropped down on us with a skeleton detachment of pediatricians and nurses and orders from highest authority. They processed the native children carefully, picked out a shipload, and left." He pointed his cigar at Sandler. "They did it kindly, I suppose, but never as long as I live will I forget the plight of those unfortunate parents. Ships dropped in periodically as long as I remained on that planet."

"Inhuman," Sandler muttered again.

"Governments frequently tend to become inhuman. So do laws. The Federation Government is a huge, complicated, impersonal thing. Supposing a need for a certain metal develops. The government locates a planet rich in that metal that has a primitive population and literally strips it. Later, when the planet develops a technology and its own need for the metal, the supply is exhausted. This stripping of a helpless planet of its natural resources was called 'colonial exploitation' by the ancients. It was done frequently, and it's still being done."

He blew a cloud of smoke in the general direction of the ceiling and said slowly, looking intently at Sandler and weighing every word, "In the eyes of the government, those children were just another natural resource, there for the taking."

Sandler managed to control his anger and keep his voice steady. "Up until now I've regretted the murders I've had to commit. But no longer."

"Ah! But those you murdered were in no way responsible for the crime. The craze for adopted children waned long ago, and eventually government officials began to foresee unfortunate long-range consequences. The exploitation was halted, but that did not eradicate its terrible impact on native populations. Some native parents, after being deprived of one child after another, stopped having children. And today, some of those planets are almost depopulated."

A violent pounding shook the door, and Sandler leaped to his feet. The servant babbled hysterically, and the commissioner shouted, "All right. Go to bed. I'll tell the police myself in the morning."

Sandler took a deep breath and resumed his seat. "That still doesn't explain all the secrecy over this."

"Politics," the commissioner said. "Sordid politics. The Expansionist Party has been in power for more than a hundred and seventy-five years. It intends to remain in power indefinitely. Its margin has always been comfortable but never overwhelming, and now some of these exploited planets are approaching the point where they must be given full membership in the Federation. The Expansionist Party must admit them, because to refuse would be to abandon its own principles. It would certainly lead to defeat. On the other hand, if all the details of that miserable exploitation were made public, the opposition would certainly control those new planets, and a good many of the old planets would turn against the Expansionists. A party in power for a hundred and seventy-five years becomes firmly entrenched. It develops ways of silencing criticism. It permits opposition—it has to—but only up to a point. So the adoption scandal has been suppressed, and the Expansionists will go to any extreme to keep it that way."

"Even murder," Sandler said. "You may not believe it, but my career in crime started back on Earth when the government tried to have me murdered."

"Not the government. The Expansionist Party. What you were doing couldn't have harmed the government."

"I'm grateful for your information. Now I'm able to understand why I'm a space-orphan, but that doesn't help me to find planet One eighty-seven."

"This might," the commissioner said. "The Expansionist Party has already been defeated. It doesn't realize it, yet, but the next election, or the one after that, will bring us a new government. A number of those planets are in my sector, and during the past few years—in fact, ever since that odd 'Homing Song' went around the galaxy—space-orphans have been coming home by the thousands. They've dropped everything, wherever they were, and come home. Some even left wives or husbands and children."

"How did they know where their homes were?" Sandler demanded.

"As a psychologist, I find that question intriguing. How *did* they know? I've talked with many of them, and they did not even go so far as to discover their planet numbers. They simply decided to come home. On the other hand, others, such as you, have searched widely about the galaxy without a glimmer of an idea as to where their home planet might be. Can you account for that?"

Sandler shook his head.

The commissioner discarded his shrunken cigar and lit another. "I have a theory," he said. "I give it to you for what it's worth and wish you luck. It is a well-known fact that many animals have a kind of homing instinct. So do many primitive peoples. Few civilized peoples retain any of it. The space-orphans are not far removed from primitiveness, and evidently they retain that homing instinct. With sufficient motivation, and the song gave them that motivation, they got themselves ships, and said, in effect, let's go that way, and went home."

"Across *space?*" Sandler said incredulously. "That's impossible!"

"Of course it is. Any intelligent, civilized man realizes that, but the fact remains that they've been coming by the thousands and tens of thousands."

"I can't believe it."

"No. That's why you interest me. Lose a primitive human, and his instinct takes him home. Lose a civilized man, and he looks around for a map or a chart. You're a trained pilot and navigator, and you know far too much about space travel to attempt to rely on instinct for anything. You consult a star chart, and you make complicated mathematical computations, and you know they will take you where you want to go. But if you can't find your destination on a chart, if your objective is some vague entity like 'home,' you're completely frustrated. Your homing instinct has been civilized out of you."

Sandler said, "Yes . . . yes . . ." And he thought about Marty Worrel. Worrel the wanderer. Sandler the wanderer. If the theory were even remotely correct, the wanderers had carried their defeat within them. Worrel's foster father had been a space line executive, and Marty had been traveling almost since he was adopted. He'd even had rudimentary training in stellar navigation. Like Sandler, he'd been civilized.

But there was Miriam. Would she have found her way home if she hadn't burdened herself with Worrel and Sandler?

Sandler got up wearily, raising with him the crushing burden of wasted years and wasted lives. "I'm grateful," he said. "If anyone back there on Earth had been decent enough—"

The commissioner raised a hand. "I know you're no criminal. As I said, I saw it happen, and I'll never forget it."

"If I'm able, I'll test your theory."

"Please let me know how you make out."

"If it's at all possible, I will."

The commissioner ushered Sandler through the silent house and stopped once to open a safe and stuff a bundle of currency into his hand. "It might be best if the police think a common thief was here tonight," he said. "I'll give you a couple of hours' start before I call them."

Solemnly Sandler shook the commissioner's hand.

Three days and a night later, Sandler and Miriam shot spaceward under the cover of darkness. When they reached deep space, Sandler turned to Miriam. "It's up to you, now," he said.

She smiled sadly. "I've always known, but I was afraid to trust myself. It's that way."

VII

Sandler set the ship down into the dawn, into the blue sky that was not blue, into the radiant pink of the promising new day. The planet was called Analon on their charts. They walked down the ramp and stood looking about tremulously as a ground car bounced toward them from the terminal building. A man Sandler's age leaped out and approached them, studying their faces. Suddenly he smiled.

"Welcome home," he said.

Other cars left the terminal and started toward them. "Why did you land here?" the stranger said. "Most of us are putting down in out-of-the-way places. Doesn't do to have this oaf of an administrator know too much. I suppose it doesn't matter now, though."

"Then there are—others?" Sandler asked.

"Enough to scare this administrator if he learned the truth. More than a hundred thousand, and they're still coming. Do you two remember anything? Family names? Places?"

Sandler shook his head, but Miriam said quickly, "My mother's name was Lilga."

"A common name, but we'll do some checking."

The other cars drew up and stopped, and their occupants sat waiting. He chuckled softly. "I have a kind of semi-official position of which the administrator does not approve. I'm head of a settlers' committee, which gives me the right to an exclusive interview before they haul you off for the formalities. Krig is the name, incidentally. We're all adopting our original names if we can find out what they were. And you'll have to learn to speak Analonian, though the old language is already pepped up to the point where you wouldn't recognize it even if you remembered it."

He took their names, descriptions, educational training, and occupations. He inquired about identification marks that might have survived from childhood. He carefully spoke the names of prominent places on Analon to see if they recognized any.

"We'll go into this more thoroughly later on," he said. "We'll do our best to locate your parents if they're still alive, and to help you get together with any brothers or sisters who've returned. The Federation—" He spat the word angrily. "The Federation took all the children in a certain age range. All of them. We estimate that a minimum quarter of a million children were stolen from Analon. Then the Federation pulled out abruptly. Didn't even bother to leave medical or observation teams, but it did leave a lot of alien bacteria, and the population was nearly wiped out. We have a few scores to settle with the Federation. Any day, now, we're going to throw out the administrator and run this planet ourselves."

Krig stepped back and nodded at the waiting officials. "These two have the committee's approval," he called.

A young officer walked toward them waving a folder. "These people aren't settlers," he said.

Krig looked at him coldly. "Of course they're settlers."

"No. They're going back to Earth and settle down to a nice multiple prison sentence. Or worse. Glad you dropped in here, Thomas Jefferson Sandler. This means a promotion for me. Consider yourself under arrest. I've already notified Sector Headquarters to send a ship for you."

"What'd he do?" Krig asked.

"Both of them. The girl is an accomplice, at least. Here—read it yourself. There's six pages."

Krig leafed through the folder, and then he stepped close to Sandler. "Did you really do all of this?"

"I wanted to come home," Sandler said bitterly. "They tried to stop me."

Sympathy touched Krig's face. "We need people like you," he said softly. "It's time we started running this planet our own way. We'll have you out by midnight."

The officer tucked the file under his arm and jerked a thumb toward the ground car. Soldiers closed in on them. Sandler fumbled in his pocket and brought out a small plastic container. He broke the seal and tossed the contents to the searching wind.

"Welcome home, Marty," he whispered.

On a distant planet, the commissioner of Sector 1389 was jerked from a pleasantly sound slumber by the urgently clanging gong of his visiphone. Sleepily he stumbled toward it, listened for a few seconds to the incoherent babbling of a subclerk, and screamed, "Idiot!"

He cut the connection and returned to his bed muttering angrily to himself. "Revolution, indeed!"

The fool should have known that the native population on Analon was practically extinct!

(*Introduction*)

Back in 1939, literary critic Bernard De Voto delivered himself of a memorable blast at Science Fiction. "This besotted nonsense," he wrote, "is from the group of magazines known as the science pulps, which deal with both the World and the Universe of To-morrow and, as our items show, take no great pleasure in either. . . . The science discussed is idiotic beyond any possibility of exaggeration, but the point is that in this kind of fiction the bending of light or Heisenberg's formula is equivalent to the sheriff of the horse opera fanning his gun, the heroine of the sex pulp taking off her dress."*

De Voto's remarks concerning these "paranoid phantasies" may prove to be one of his more lasting observations upon the literary scene, for Science Fiction critics and commentators delight in quoting and requoting the besotted nonsense that is written, from time to time, about Science Fiction. Especially intriguing is the fact that outsiders such as De Voto invariably overlook one of Science Fiction's most striking features as compared with the contemporary so-called Main Stream: the thread of optimism that runs through it even when it depicts man at his worst. As Kingsley Amis remarks in his book *New Maps of Hell*: ". . . if we can imagine *Brave New World* rewritten by Anthony Boucher or Frederik Pohl, we could expect (as well as a little more narrative from time to time) an early scene showing a group of technicians working out a scheme for secretly subjecting all the Beta, Gamma, Delta, and Epsilon embryos to Alpha conditioning, just for a start. And the Savage might die at the hands of Mustapha Mond's police force, but he would never commit suicide."†

Given a group of people in a hole in the ground, the Main Stream apostle of non-heroism describes, with inordinate delight and nauseous detail, those of them who are content to wallow in their filth. The Science Fiction writer is interested in those who are trying to get out.

* Bernard De Voto, "Doom Beyond Jupiter," *Harper's Magazine*, September 1939.
† Kingsley Amis, *New Maps of Hell*. Copyright © 1960 by Kingsley Amis (Ballantine Books).

5

In the center of the table stood a miniature sun. In other places, on other tables, it might have been taken for an ineffectual table lamp, since its battered plastic surface diffused the yellow light feebly. In the board room of Solar Productions, it was a sun.

Bruce Kalder relaxed dreamily and watched the "sun" flicker on and off when the Chairman of the Board thumped on the table. Old Holbertson was powerfully worked up about something, but he talked in such long-winded circles that each subject he touched upon was abandoned before Kalder could properly get a grip on it.

Kalder suppressed a yawn and looked across the table at June Holbertson. "She shouldn't wear low-cut dresses to Board meetings," he thought. He'd intentionally avoided looking at her because he didn't want the other members to think his appointment was due to her influence—which was foolish. They already knew that, and everyone else in the room was watching her. Everyone except old Holbertson.

She smiled faintly and winked at him.

Old Holbertson thumped the table again, paused for a sip of water, and shouted, "Kalder, this is damned serious, and it's your problem. What are you going to do about it?"

Kalder turned slowly and faced the Chairman of the Board. From a condition of easy relaxation he had been slammed into one of stomach-twisting panic. His hands lay paralyzed on the arms of his chair. His dry tongue touched his dry lips and recoiled.

Old Holbertson had talked for perhaps twenty minutes, and Kalder had listened attentively most of that time, and he hadn't any idea as to what problem had the old man so upset. Worse, he'd only started work that morning, and no one had yet explained to him what his job was.

June came to his rescue. "Uncle Emmanuel, this is Bruce's first meeting. Don't you think he should know more about the problem before we ask him to solve it?"

"He's been on the job since this morning, hasn't he?" old Holbertson sputtered. "What's he been doing?"

From the other end of the table Paul Holbertson spoke. "Takes more than three hours for a man to learn his way around this place."

"Bah!" old Holbertson said. "If he doesn't know where the men's room is by this time—"

"I move," Paul Holbertson said, "that we ask Mr. Kalder to have a full report ready for the next meeting."

Seconded and passed. Kalder breathed easily once more, but he did not relax again.

When the meeting broke up, Paul Holbertson crooked a finger at Kalder and June. He said, "My office, I think," escorted them in, and found chairs for them.

"I thought I was going to be fired before I'd learned what all the buttons on my desk mean," Kalder said. "Look—I don't mean to be disrespectful, but I listened as attentively as I could, and I still don't know the problem."

"Emmanuel rambles," Paul said. "Getting old, I'm afraid. He'll retire one of these years, and we'll miss him. Given some alternatives, he's almost infallible in making the right decision. Trouble is, in this case we have no alternatives. We have nothing. The problem is that we're having trouble with our writers. Hence your title—Director of Writer Personnel."

"What sort of trouble are we having?"

Paul Holbertson took a long time getting a cigar lit. He leaned back, stared at the ceiling, and puffed deeply. "They don't write."

He continued slowly, "We have competent men. We know that because of their past performances. We pay the highest rates paid anywhere. We have the best Tank in the industry, and we operate it at peak efficiency. And they don't write. We've always maintained a big inventory and kept more writers than we needed, so we've had a big backlog to draw upon, but the situation has been gradually getting worse for years and now it's approaching the critical point. Our inventory has sagged. We're actually dipping into the rejection files, and even that won't keep us going much longer. To quote Emmanuel, this is damned serious.

"Solar Productions leases four wires, and our contract stipulates that we must run twenty-four one-hour films per day on each wire. That adds up to ninety-six films. We don't have any trouble shooting it. Our organization is absolutely the best. So are our facilities. We could shoot two hundred a day if we had the scripts, but we can't get the scripts."

"There hasn't been any reduction in writing personnel?" Kalder asked.

"Certainly not. We have more writers than we've ever had, and we keep hiring them. We hire some that are hopelessly unqualified just in the hope that they'll produce *something* for us. The quality keeps going down, and the number of scripts turned in drops daily."

"We need an incentive system," Kalder said, speaking with a heroically affected nonchalance. "Let's scrap the writers' contracts, cut their guaranteed wage to the legal minimum, and pay a bonus for each completed script. We can work out a system of extra bonuses for quality."

Paul Holbertson shrugged indifferently and gestured with his cigar. "Everything that obvious was tried long ago. It didn't help. I'll tell you one more thing that won't work. I got the foggy notion that the Tank was involved in some way, so I closed it down for a month. It damned near ruined us. Production dropped almost to zero. Things spurted a little when I opened it up again, but not for long, and production has been dropping ever since. Well—get to work on it, and remember this: No tampering with the Tank, and don't expect the solution to be child-ishly simple. We have some highly capable people on our staff, and none of them have been able to cope with this. The trouble is that we're dealing with writers. I haven't decided whether they're superhuman or subhuman, but I know they aren't functioning normally even when they act normally. The only thing I can do to help you is wish you luck."

"Thank you," Kalder said.

It was an opportunity, but it was also a test. The Holbertsons were a hard-boiled family, and none of its members would experience a twitch of conscience over handing him a problem that had stumped Solar Productions for years. He suspected a conspiracy. Either he would show the family that he was worthy of June, or the family would show June how incompetent he was. It would applaud his success, but no tears would be shed over his failure, and few fingers would be raised to help him. He perhaps should have been grateful that June's father was willing to wish him luck.

"I'd like to talk with some writers," Kalder said.

"So would I," Paul Holbertson said grimly. "If you find out where they're hiding, let me know."

In three days Kalder learned his way about the executive and editorial offices and gained a passing familiarity with the files. On the fourth day he decided to visit the Tank. The company ran a swing train between its offices and its production center, but gainful employment was depriving Kalder of his accustomed daily exercise in tennis and swimming, and he decided to walk.

He ran into trouble immediately. Q tunnel, which was the direct route to the Main, was blocked off. A guard waved him away as he started to enter it. The last of the Q tunnel population was moving out, and Kalder stood aside to let it pass: men, women and children who slouched along absently, each man cradling a TV set preciously in his arms. The women and children carried small bundles of belongings. A few women also carried TV sets—lucky families, to have two!

"What's up?" Kalder asked the guard.

"Radiation seepage," the guard said shortly.

A short distance further on Kalder turned off into a narrow

passageway, thinking he might find his way through to the Main without going all the way to R tunnel. There were numbered doorways along the passage, but few doors. In each room clusters of people sat around TV sets watching intently.

The passage divided, divided again, and gradually became narrower. Whenever two people met they had to edge past each other sideways. Abruptly he left the area of living quarters behind him, and he paused in amazement to contemplate the unfinished walls. He vaguely recalled rumors of a critical housing shortage, and the number of TV sets he had seen in some of the rooms could only mean that several families were living there; and yet this unused space could accommodate dozens of apartments. It only wanted someone to do the digging.

Eventually he found his way through to the Main. The huge, brightly lighted tunnel swarmed with humanity. Government swing trains passed at regular intervals, moving slowly as the tractor drivers shouted people out of the way. Many factory shifts were changing, the men of the new shift reporting with glum faces for their hour's labor. Long, slow-moving lines of women marked the locations of supply depots.

Kalder stepped into the doorway of a medical clinic and stood for a few minutes watching housewives jostle for position in a fresh meat queue. He had passed this way many times, but always blindly and in a swing train or private car. Now it occurred to him that those lower classes politely referred to as *the people* were customers of Solar Productions—his customers— and as such they were important to him.

As he continued to watch he discovered that they were human beings like himself; and in some way that he did not precisely understand, that made them much more important.

At the production center he went to the executives' dining room for an early lunch before he rode the elevator down to the Tank. Barney Fulton, the Tank's manager, was a kindly old man who'd been with Solar in one capacity or another all of his working life. "The boss said you'd be around," he told Kalder. "I'll give you any help I can, but hell, I haven't got any answers."

"I'll have to ask some foolish questions, because all of this is new to me. Now—just what is the Tank?"

"It used to belong to Production," Barney said. "They still use it when they need it, but that's only for the big scenes. Even then the writers kick up a fuss about it. Most of the time the writers have the Tank to themselves, and they're supposed to use it to give them ideas and for research on problems they've encountered in the scripts they're working on. What they actually use it for no one knows, maybe because no one knows how a writer thinks. Jeff Powell, he writes nothing but romances, but when he comes in here he goes on an adventure jag. Maybe that gives him ideas for love stories. Who knows?"

"Maybe you'd better let me look at it," Kalder said doubtfully.

"Sure." Barney strode to the door of his office. "Pete—this is Mr. Kalder, the new vice-president. Take him through the Tank and don't get him killed."

Pete gave Kalder a broad grin and led him away.

They signed in at one of the Tank's entrances and stepped through a doorway into a scene of overwhelming grandeur. One glance at the spaciousness, at the vast, unlimited vistas, took Kalder's breath away. Accustomed all his life to rooms and passageways, he could only stare disbelievingly.

Ahead of them was a tangled jungle. Beyond it a hill rose steeply, and beyond that, other hills. There were glimpses of forests, of distant mountains. Overhead the ceiling arched upward and upward and away to a far distant, brightly lit dome.

"Pretty big, eh?" Pete said proudly.

"It's tremendous," Kalder said.

"We have it on a twenty-four-hour day, meaning we got both day and night. At night we turn off the lights and turn on the stars. We got a moon, too. Come on. We'll have to stay clear of that jungle. They're shooting a jungle scene this afternoon."

They skirted the jungle, climbed a tall hill, and stood looking down on the lovely, still blueness of a lake.

"Where to?" Pete asked.

Kalder consulted his notebook. "I'd like to look around and

see what the place is like. And then—do you know a writer named Walter Donald?"

"Sure. Big fellow, with blond hair. I know all the older ones. Not many of the new ones have been using the Tank."

"I'd like to talk with Donald."

"I'll call in."

Pete went over to a control point to make his call, and he came back shaking his head. "Donald's in the Tank, but they don't know where he is. He probably didn't make any special request. Sometimes a writer just looks around until he finds something that interests him."

"I see," Kalder said. He'd studied the writers' production records with care, and he had a hunch that Donald could give him a clue as to what was wrong. Donald had been the most prolific man on the staff, even though his output had fallen along with that of the others. A month before, his work had suddenly stopped altogether. Kalder tried to get in touch with him and found that he had entered the Tank and stayed there. He had signed in, and he had not signed out. Kalder wanted to know what he was doing.

"Donald has been in here for a month," he said to Pete. "Isn't that a little long to be just looking around?"

"Well," Pete said, "he's a writer."

An elephant trumpeted in the jungle, and a rifle shot rang out. Down on the lake a rowboat came into view rounding a point. Pete handed Kalder his binoculars. "It's Jeff Powell," he said.

Kalder watched the awkward movements of the man rowing the boat. "Where would be a good place to look for Donald?" he asked.

"Couldn't say. If he hasn't asked for anything special, he could be anywhere. It's a big place."

"I think I'd better talk with Barney," Kalder said.

He went to the control point and asked Barney to have his men keep a lookout for Walter Donald. Barney said he'd check with the concessionaires; if Donald had been in the Tank for a month he had to be getting food from somewhere or he was dead.

Kalder returned to the hilltop, sat down in the thick, simulated grass, and watched the man in the boat. Jeff Powell was getting ready to fish. Kalder had seen enough films to vaguely understand the process. In fact, he thought he could have given Powell a few pointers.

After several timid gestures, Powell managed a feeble cast. As his lure hit the water the lake boiled and erupted. Powell knelt in the boat, pole bent double, and battled the monstrous fish.

A trio of shark fins crossed the lake in precise formation and circled the boat. Powell hauled valiantly on his line. The fish sounded, returned to the surface, and suddenly shot away under the boat. Powell spun, lost his balance, and toppled overboard.

"Damn," Pete said. "There he goes again."

Kalder raised his binoculars and watched Powell drown. It was a drawn-out process. He gurgled and threshed, and his pathetic cries were frightening. Finally he sank out of sight.

"Barney said one more time would be the end of it," Pete said. "We're not going to let him near the water again until he learns how to swim. The Board is complaining about our resuscitation bills."

Two men came hurrying along the shore. They splashed into the water, hauled out Powell, and carried him away.

"We ought to leave him be dead," Pete said. "He don't write nothing but romances anyway."

"If he writes anything at all, we need him," Kalder said.

An airplane roared overhead. Kalder watched it curiously, saw a man jump, saw a parachute billow out. The man floated down toward the lake, and the shark fins headed for him the moment he hit the water. He got a raft inflated and pulled himself in just as the sharks made their rush.

Pete chuckled. "If Barney ever put teeth in them sharks, you'd be missing a lot of writers."

Kalder continued to watch the airplane, which cut its motors abruptly and was lowered to the ground behind the trees on the other side of the lake.

Another shot rang out in the jungle. "Ready to move on?"

Pete asked. Kalder got to his feet obediently, and they circled the lake.

At the next control point Kalder called Barney. "Donald is hanging out around Area Five," Barney said. "You can probably see it from where you are. It's the big forest."

"What's he doing there?"

"Don't know. That's where he's been eating. One of the concession men knows him. If you want to find him, tell Pete. He'll help you look."

Beyond the lake they came to a desert. They plodded onward, sinking deeply into loose sand, and in a small ravine they happened on a dying writer. His clothing was ragged, his figure emaciated. He croaked after them, "Water! Water!"

They walked on. "That's Bill Morris," Pete said. "He asked Barney what it felt like to die of thirst, and Barney told him to go out in the desert and find out."

Kalder nodded. Some of the writers used the Tank as a direct source of information. Others seemed to use it as a diversion— Jeff Powell, for example, coming in for adventure but never writing about it. Bill Morris would be getting an excellent idea of what it would be like to die of thirst in a desert, but it seemed to Kalder that there must be quicker ways of discovering what a writer would need to know. Morris certainly had been there for several days, and that was a big investment in time to acquire the background for one short scene in an hour film.

They left the desert and crossed gently rolling farm land. Cattle grazed by a small, meandering stream. Oddly enough, they were real cattle. Never having seen any, Kalder stopped to stare and discovered that they weren't grazing. They were eating cakes of something or other that had been dyed green to match the synthetic grass.

Pete guided Kalder to the right, and they entered the forest. "Area Five," Pete announced. "Shouldn't be hard to find him."

They examined the forest from one end to the other. The large synthetic trees were widely spaced, short synthetic grass covered the ground, and there was no undergrowth. Neither was their any sign of Donald.

They retraced their steps. This time Kalder stopped in a central clearing to examine what looked like an enormous post. He thumped on metal. "What's this?"

"Vent," Pete said. "Or maybe it's an air intake or a solar power inlet. They're all over the place."

"What's inside?"

"Machinery and stuff."

Kalder started around the enormous circumference. Because he was watching the surrounding forest, he was completely surprised when his hand came in contact with a door handle.

He opened the door and staggered backward, hands clasped to his eyes. The vent stretched upward an interminable distance and ended in a blaze of light. It was a moment before Kalder's vision returned to him, and when it did he saw, a couple of feet below the door, a metal grating that spanned the vent. On the grating lay a man.

Pete had caught up with him, and he looked in and exclaimed, "That's Donald!"

It was a big man with blond hair, but his skin was burned black. Kalder said in alarm, "Donald?"

"Leave me alone," Donald said. "Get the hell out of here."

He lay face down on the grating. He was nude, and he did not move when he spoke.

"Maybe he's sick," Pete said. "He don't look so good. Shall we take him out?"

Donald sat up. "Sick?" The dark skin of his face twisted with convulsive bitterness. "You're the sick ones. The dead ones. I'm getting some sunshine. This is one of the few places on this cursed planet where any can be had. Care to join me? Then get out!"

Kalder introduced himself, explaining that he was concerned because Donald had been in the Tank for a month and because he wasn't writing. Would Donald mind telling Kalder what he was trying to do?

"I'm trying to bore myself," Donald said. He lay down again and added, "It isn't easy."

Kalder and Pete withdrew quietly and closed the door. "Where's the nearest exit?" Kalder asked, and Pete obligingly led him away.

That night Kalder sought out his father, to the older man's intense surprise. Dr. Kalder had wanted his son to study medicine. Kalder knew only too well the deadly monotony of the medical profession, and he had no difficulty in finding more amusing ways of spending his time. It was only when he learned that June Holbertson's family sternly disapproved of a young man of twenty-seven who had no occupation or profession that he decided to go to work.

Dr. Kalder was on night duty at a small branch clinic. There were no patients, and he had sent his interns off to bed. "How's the job going?" he asked.

"I don't know," Kalder said. "Tell me, Dad, what's the value of TV?"

The doctor said thoughtfully, "My guess is that without it we'd have a serious situation on our hands in a matter of days, if not hours. Maybe a revolution. Why?"

"Tell me why," Kalder said. The doctor regarded him perplexedly, and he quickly added, "I just want to hear someone talk about it."

Dr. Kalder sighed. "So you're discouraged already. You'll have to learn to apply yourself, Bruce. What will happen to the human race if you youngsters shirk your responsibilities? When the big move comes there won't be enough educated and professional people to keep things going."

"TV," Kalder reminded him. "Why?"

"It's rather obvious, isn't it? Most people have nothing to do. It keeps them occupied."

"It seems to me that there's lots of things people could be doing. We keep hearing about the housing shortage. I saw a mob of people moving out of Q tunnel over in Section Twenty-seven. I don't know where they went unless they moved in with friends and relatives. People have all that time to watch TV. Why doesn't someone put a few of them to digging out more living space?"

"It's been tried," the doctor said. "They won't do it. That's what brought on the last riot. That was seven—no, eight years ago."

"Why won't they do it?"

"They're satisfied the way things are. The four hours of work a week they accept, because it's always been that way. As long as we're able to feed and clothe them, and they're healthy, and they have fifteen films to choose from every hour, they're satisfied. They won't demand more, but they won't take less! Oh, they'd like better quarters and less crowding if someone else would make it possible, but as for doing it themselves—why, the men grumble about that four hours a week, and the women grumble about the time they spend away from TV waiting to buy their supplies."

"I see," Kalder said. He got to his feet. "How many doctors will we have thirty years from now?"

"Enough for the present situation. Health is pretty much under control down here."

"Supposing we were able to go back to the surface?"

"Then we wouldn't have enough of anything."

"I wish someone had spelled this out to me ten years ago."

"I tried, Bruce. I tried my best. Maybe I didn't spell very well."

"Maybe I didn't listen very well," Kalder said.

Before he returned to his own plush quarters in the Bachelor's Club of Section 317—the section of the wealthy—he walked around for a long time in a maze of passageways, looking through doorways at the flickering TV sets.

Paul Holbertson bent over the graphs and traced a configuration thoughtfully. "Mmm, yes. We didn't try this. Getting anywhere?"

June leaned forward anxiously, her hands clasped.

"I can state the problem," Kalder said.

"The problem is that they're not writing."

"No. That's merely a result. The problem is that they've lost interest in their subject matter, and they're regaining their contact with reality."

Paul Holbertson grinned slyly. He said to June, "You'll have to keep this boy away from the library."

"I've done very little reading," Kalder said, "but I've done a lot of talking with writers. With a recorder. Listen."

The voice was Walter Donald's—bitter, accusative. "I shall write no more comedies about pirate ships. Or the private lives of queens. Or romances about knights in armor. Or adventures in space. God, what a laugh that is—man in space, when he can't even get out of a hole in the ground! We're drugging the people and ourselves with stories of things that aren't and can't be. I'm beginning to doubt that they ever were. Those things I can't write, and I won't. What I can write I don't know."

Kalder touched the switch. The president of Solar Productions said soberly, "I knew the problem was serious, but I had no idea—are they all like that?"

"Either they are or they soon will be. Are our competitors having the same trouble?"

"Naturally they don't tell us their troubles, but I'm certain that they are. Only yesterday I suggested to Roger Atley that we might be willing to give up one of our wires so we could concentrate on quality productions. He begged me not to think of such a thing, which means that the government would have a tough time finding a replacement. Where do we go from here?"

"There are two possible approaches. Either we renew their interest in their subject matter, or we find new subject matter that they *are* interested in. By the way, I won't be ready to face the Board tomorrow."

"I don't think it'll be necessary. Leave the graphs with me. I'm especially interested in your comparison of scripts produced with hours spent in the Tank. Obviously the Tank helps production up to a point, and too many writers are using it beyond that point. Wouldn't it solve the problem if we limited writers to eight hours a week?"

"No, but if the Board needs something to talk about you can suggest that. I'll have definite recommendations ready for the next meeting."

June took his arm as they went out, and in the corridor he placed an affectionate kiss on her forehead and one considerably more affectionate on her lips.

"Going to save the family business?" she asked.

"Is it that bad?"

"Every hour on the hour we have to have four new films

ready. One comedy, one romance, one adventure and one miscellaneous. That's ninety-six deadlines to meet every day. We've had to sneak an old film in now and then just to pad things out, but people have terribly long memories and we're taking a frightful risk. Yes, it's that bad."

"I'm afraid you're wrong," Kalder said. "Things are much worse than that."

In spite of the fact that there were different writers there, or writers doing different things, the Tank always seemed the same. The one unchanging element was Walter Donald, who was in his usual place in the Area Five vent.

Kalder prodded him with his foot. "I have a problem," he said. "I need your help."

Donald rolled over onto his back. The pattern of the grate was deeply impressed upon his dark skin.

"Will you help me?" Kalder asked.

Donald did not look up. "What kind of problem?"

"I'm trying to get a script written. It's about a writer. He and his family live in a small room over in Section Four ninety-five. He's the only writer that lives there, and all the other men are factory workers. This writer's family can't understand why his work takes so much time. The other men work for an hour, and then they come home and watch TV with their families. The writer works long hours and has to spend days in the Tank looking for ideas. He earns good wages and his family can have luxuries the other families can't afford, but his children just can't understand why he's never home to watch TV with them. I can't think of a way to end it. Can you help me out?"

Donald said flatly, "Nuts. Didn't you ever read the Code? They'd never film a thing like that."

"Of course they would if I could get it written. The question is, could you write it? I realize you've never done anything like that, and if you don't think you can handle it just say the word. I'll ask someone else."

Donald sat up. He stared dully at Kalder, his scowl wrinkling dark lines in his dark forehead. The sunlight had bleached his hair to a startling whiteness. He said, "I know the Code forward and backward. I could get fired for wasting time on something like that."

"I'm taking the responsibility," Kalder said. "Could you write it?"

"I don't know." Donald pushed himself to his feet and climbed out of the vent. "A writer, you say. How many children?"

"That's up to you. How many children do you have?"

"Three. Three children. They want him to watch TV with them, you say. But he hates TV because he writes scripts for TV, so whenever they turn it on—"

He pulled on his clothing and wandered away muttering to himself.

At the edge of the forest Kalder found Jeff Powell lying on his back staring up at a tree. Kalder sat down beside him, and Powell spoke without looking at him.

"In the autumn, the leaves turn color. Nature paints a masterpiece in the forest. By and by the leaves fall to the ground. If I wait here long enough, do you suppose these leaves will change color and fall?"

"Those leaves are phony," Kalder said. "They'll never change."

Powell winced and regarded Kalder gravely. "Friend, have you ever seen a tree? No, not this junk. A real tree. Have you ever felt one? I've put lots of trees into my scripts, but I never saw a tree. Isn't that ridiculous? What does a tree feel like? What does it taste like? Do trees have a taste?"

"You write romances, don't you?"

"When I write, I write romances. Romances with trees. Meet me under the green willow tree, my love. The weeping green willow tree. Do you know what a weeping green willow tree looks like? Production doesn't. I went to the library and found a picture. Production made my weeping green willow tree into an oak."

"According to the records, you've written a few comedies, too. Do you think you could handle a romantic comedy?"

"I'm not feeling very funny these days. For that matter, I'm not feeling romantic, either."

"This would be a different kind of story. There's this man who works in a factory, and he can't get along with his foreman. They hate each other, and they're always squabbling about something. Then the foreman's son falls in love with the guy's daughter. The two mothers get to know each other, and they try to help the kids while the two men are trying to keep them apart. I suppose it would be a tricky job to keep it funny. If you don't think you can handle it—"

"Yeah," Powell said. "Then the kids decide to break it up to keep the fathers happy just about the same time that the fathers decide to pretend to be friends to keep the kids happy. Yeah." He sat up abruptly. "What kind of a line are you handing me? They'd never film it. Didn't you ever hear about Code?"

"Certainly they'd film it. I'll take care of that."

"If you say so. Let's see—the foreman keeps trying to spy on his son, and the other guy keeps trying to spy on his daughter, so the two keep running into each other. And in the meantime—"

Kalder slipped away quietly. Wild profanity attracted his attention from the direction of the lake. A writer whom he did not know was attempting to fish, and on his first cast Barney's monster of the deep had snapped his line.

"I have a problem," Kalder said. "I want to get a script written. There's this fellow who lives in a small room with his family, and when radiation seepage makes everyone in the next corridor move out, three families have to move in with him. He doesn't like it, so he finds an undeveloped corridor and digs out a new room for his family. Then he decides one room isn't enough, so he digs out two more. Everyone thinks he's crazy, wanting so much space, and when he finishes the government moves five more families in with him. Do you think you can write it?"

The writer dropped his fishing pole. He stammered, "What —what about Code?"

Some of the faces were hostile. Several were violently angry. June Holbertson looked hurt; her father seemed puzzled.

Kalder said calmly, "I accept full responsibility."

"That's all very well," old Emmanuel Holbertson sputtered. "You accept the responsibility, but it's our reputations that are being ruined."

"To continue my report," Kalder said, "I have organized a small group of the company's writers. They represent five per cent of the total, and they are out-producing the other ninety-five per cent at the rate of ten to one. I've had fifty production units assigned to my control. Those units are shooting scripts as fast as my writers can produce them. I have assumed full responsibility for the company's fourth wire, the miscellaneous channel, and for the past two weeks that channel has carried nothing but films I have produced myself. I will ask the Chairman of the Board: Has he received any complaints about the fourth channel programs?"

"I saw some of those films myself, Kalder," Emmanuel shouted. "*I'm* complaining!"

"Code is based upon the accumulated experience of an entire industry, Bruce," Paul Holbertson said. "You shouldn't have thrown it out without discussing it with the Board."

"I was given complete authority to take the steps I thought necessary to solve a problem. I did so, and I have solved the problem. As a precaution I discussed what I intended to do with half-a-dozen top-level government officials, including the head of the Board of Censorship. They approved the project, and I have letters of congratulations from them on the way it's been working out. They think TV is going to help them solve some of their problems. Further, the Information Center reports that our fourth channel programs have taken over the popularity leadership."

"Helping the government is all very well," Emmanuel said testily, "but we have no obligation to destroy ourselves to do so."

"Entertainment is our business, Bruce," Paul Holbertson said. "It's a very important business. We put meaning into otherwise meaningless lives. Code is the reason we've been able to do this successfully for so long."

"With your permission," Kalder said, "I'll give you my reasons for the action I've taken."

Interruptions exploded around the table. A vice-president put the motion: the position of Vice-President and Director of Writing Personnel to be abolished immediately, and Bruce Kalder dismissed. Seconded and passed.

"Thank you," Kalder said. "I regret that our relationship was so brief, but for the time that I have been associated with Solar Productions I am more grateful than I can tell you."

He turned away with one overwhelming regret—June, who sat blinking her eyes to keep back the tears. His newly acquired realization that there were more important things in life than his personal happiness seemed a rather feeble compensation.

June left her chair suddenly and hurried after him. Outside the door, Kalder gripped her arm and said, "I'd like to show you something."

They caught a company swing train and rode over to the Tank. The vast room's simulated landscape looked dead under a simulated evening sky. The ceiling lights were gradually being dimmed. Soon they would go out and the simulated stars would be turned on.

He led her along a jungle trail and over the hill toward the motionless lake. "It looks very real, doesn't it?" she said.

"It looks like our idea of real. But this, and our idea, are both false. You know that, don't you?"

"This is the first time I've ever been here. What do the writers do?"

He did not answer. They walked down to the lake and removed their sandals. The shark fins paraded toward them as they waded in. Kalder said, "The trouble is, you and I, and the Board, and all those like us have been living Code for too long. We've lost touch with the people. Children of the wealthy receive the best educations, choose the careers they want, and look forward to a generally satisfying lifetime. They live in comfort. They have clubs and recreation facilities. There is room for those things for a few of us, but most people have nothing at all. They're just hanging around and reproducing themselves so there will be plenty of people when we're ready to go back to the surface. They do a little work, and they eat and sleep, and the rest of the time they sit in front of a TV set and inhale the drugs that Code prescribes for them. The TV films are drugs, because they induce dreams of a world that won't exist again for centuries—a world where there are trees, and plants, and animals, and rivers of pure water."

"Isn't it good for them to get their minds off the way things are?" June asked.

"That's Code. The Code philosophy—tyranny would be a better word for it. The people have surrendered to it completely, and they've given up. When men first moved underground they must have slaved to achieve what we have now. They built well, and then when the machines were operating and living quarters were prepared, there seemed to be nothing else to do. So the film companies were established to give the people TV, and they exercised all of their ingenuity to provide realistic settings and stories and keep alive the dream of what man had lost. I think the idea was to remind people of what their sacrifices were for, of what man hoped to regain, but the dream became an end in itself. People are no longer interested in planning ahead, or in regaining anything—just in dreaming. Only the writers, who had to create the dreams, knew how false they were."

"What are you going to do?" she asked.

"Form my own company. I won't have any trouble getting a wire or two. We can keep down production costs by shooting in corridors and private living quarters, because we're going to show life like it is. Scripts won't be a problem. Donald is turning out five a day, and some of the others are doing almost as well."

"How can they, when they can't write Code?" she exclaimed.

They waded out of the lake, and the shark fins drifted away. They dried their feet on the synthetic grass and put on their sandals.

"The first script writers wrote about something they remembered," Kalder said. "They wrote about a world they'd lived in —the world the way it used to be. Each successive generation of writers got one more step removed from that reality. The Tank was supposed to be a crutch for the writers' imaginations to lean upon, but we're so many years removed from what it represents that it's lost its value. Men get tired of crutches. They always prefer walking without them."

They were moving toward Area Five, and he caught her arm as they stumbled through the sand of the desert. "Do you feel up to a battle with Solar Productions?" he asked.

"With you I do."

He slipped his arm around her and led her through the forest. He opened the door of the vent and pointed upward. "Look!"

She saw blackness and a glimmer of light. "What is it?"

"A star. A *real* star."

"I've seen films about stars—about going to the stars."

"Perhaps men will, someday. Certainly men will return to the planets, but we'll have to get out of the ground first. There's a long wait ahead of us, and we can't waste it in dreaming. We need to be getting ready, so when our children, or their children or grandchildren, climb back to the surface, what they find there won't defeat them. The first ones will have it tough, and they'll probably wish they were back underground watching TV, but they'll make the move. They *must* make it."

"I remember a film about a star," she said. "A little girl saw it, and she made a wish."

"Do you have a wish?"

"I think I do."

They wished together, looking upward.

IN HIS OWN IMAGE

(Introduction)

Religion and thoroughbass are settled things. There should be no disputing about them.

—Beethoven.

Religion and poetry address themselves, at least in one of their aspects, to the same part of the human constitution: they both supply the same want, that of ideal conceptions grander and more beautiful than we see realized in the prose of human life.

—J. S. Mill.

If religion is the highest of the arts, does it necessarily follow that it is the lowest of the sciences?

—F. W. von Schelling.

6

IN HIS OWN IMAGE

The sun's shrunken disc hung above the shallow horizon like an inflamed evil eye, but the light that delineated the buildings was the pure, hard radiance of a million clustering stars.

Gorton Effro stepped from the door of the communications shed and looked about curiously. He had served on space liners for twenty years without so much as glimpsing an emergency space station—or wanting to. Somewhere he'd got the notion that they were man-made, but this one had been constructed on the planed surface of an inhospitable chunk of rock. A landing cradle thrust up through the transparent dome, spreading a spidery embrace vast enough to contain the largest star-class liner. Its supports were piston springs mammothly anchored in concrete. In that feeble gravity the danger was not collapse, but that the shock of an inept landing might bounce the station into space.

Maintenance and storage sheds formed an oval about the anchors. Beyond, in a larger oval, stood the circular hostels. The emergency manual had promised ample accommodation for a thousand, or for as many as two thousand if the refugees didn't mind being crowded. Effro eyed the buildings skeptically and growled, "The liars," though he couldn't have said why he cared. There was only one of him.

The station's logbook contained ten previous entries covering a hundred and seven years, all of them by maintenance and supply crews. It was untouched by time, undisturbed by man except for those fleeting, widely spaced inspections, unneeded and unused. All of the incalculable expense and meticulous planning that went into its making had been squandered to this end: that one lifeboat could lock onto its rescue beacon and eventually discharge into its life-sustaining environment one passenger: Gorton Effro.

The lifeboat perched at the end of the landing cradle like a small parasite attached to a gigantic abstract insect. The solitary passenger fingered his tight collar irritably and savored his disappointment. He had known what he would find here—the lifeboat's emergency manual described it in tedious detail—but through the long days of sterile solitude he had come to think of this place, not as a way station to be touched en route to rescue, but as a destination. As a refuge, waiting to welcome him with warmth and hospitality.

It was only a larger solitude.

The lifeboat's landing had triggered the station out of its frozen hibernation. The air outside the communications shed was noticeably warmer than it had been when he entered, and a robot cleaner snuffed past him, patiently searching for impurities he might have tracked in. Effro moved with slow steps toward the nearest hostel, still looking about him curiously. A movement off to his left caught his attention; it was only another robot cleaner, but he watched it for a moment and when he turned his head—

The shock halted him in midstride. A man stood near the hostel's entrance. Before Effro's stunned mind could quite comprehend what his eyes were seeing, the strange figure hurled itself forward in a weird flutter of ragged garments. Effro backed away, his trembling hands raised defensively, but the man sank to his knees in front of Effro and said, eyes averted, voice a supplicant whine, "May I have your blessing, Excellency?"

"Blessing!" Effro exclaimed. His purser's uniform had been mistaken for a priest's costume!

He took another step backward, staring down at the man, and suddenly he comprehended that the threadbare clothing was meant to be some kind of ecclesiastical apparel. The robes were tattered vestments, the ridiculous headpiece a strangely fashioned miter, the clicking footwear crudely shaped metal sandals. He looked like a devilish caricature, an atheist's mocking concept of a priest.

Effro knew the type. The man was a lay predicant, a self-appointed, self-educated, self-clothed religious, a wanderer by definition, a shrewd beggar who'd found in the pietistic pose a sure-fire means of increasing his daily take.

But the last call at this remote station had been logged fourteen years before! "What the devil are you doing here?" Effro demanded.

Still on his knees, the man waited silently. "I'm no 'excellency,'" Effro said. "I was purser on the spaceship *Cherbilius*. It blew up nineteen days out of Donardo, and as far as I know I'm the only survivor. Toasts I can give you, and a few first-rate curses, but not blessings. I don't know any."

The predicant raised his eyes slowly. His face was old, its flesh shriveled and taut. His eyes, widely dilated in the dim starlight, stared expressionlessly. He held his left arm bent awkwardly in front of him.

He said uncertainly, "Do you come to instruct me, Excellency?"

"I come because my lifeboat followed the station's rescue beacon. In other words, by accident. If I'd hit another station's beacon first, I'd have gone there."

"There are no accidents," the predicant said. His right hand's sweeping gesture traced a cross. "The will of God brought you here."

Effro said bitterly, "Then God murdered more than four hundred people to do it. I suppose that's a small price for such a splendid achievement—bringing together a drunken thief and some kind of fugitive pretending to be a priest. Cut the nonsense and stand up!"

The predicant got to his feet in a flutter of ragged clothing. Effro asked, "Is there anyone else here?"

"I have my flock," the predicant said proudly.

"Flock? *Here?*"

A cleaning robot snuffed past them, and the predicant

stooped, halted it with a caressing gesture, and held it hissing and rumbling above the ground.

He released it. "Such are my flock," he said quietly.

"*Machines?*"

The predicant met Effro's eyes boldly. Only an idiot, Effro thought, could look so divinely inspired. An idiot or a saint.

"Did not our Lord say, 'Inasmuch as ye have done it unto one of the least of these my brethren, ye have done it unto me.' And these—" His ragged gesture encompassed the cleaning robots and the rows of silent machines by the maintenance sheds. "These, Excellency, are the least of all." He sank to his knees again. "May I have your blessing, Excellency?"

The sheer, pleading ecstasy in the man's voice, the dumb depth of veneration in his eyes, unnerved Effro and moved him strangely. He knew that forever afterward he would consider it a cowardly act, but he extended his blessing, gesticulating vaguely and resurrecting a half-forgotten phrase from the buried memories of his childhood. "In the name of the Almighty, may your graces be magnified and your faults forgiven."

He stepped around the predicant and strode hurriedly toward a hostel. He did not look back until he reached it. The predicant was moving slowly in the opposite direction, still holding his bent arm awkwardly in front of him. Three cleaning robots were snuffing after him in single file.

"His flock!" Effro muttered disgustedly.

He chose the sleeping room nearest the entrance, and the first thing he examined was its door—to make certain that it had a lock.

The hostel was a self-sustaining unit complete with air lock to safeguard its inhabitants in the event of damage to the dome. Effro's first concern was for a bath, and he lolled in warm water for an hour, soaking off the accretions of his long journey while a massaging machine worked over him expertly. A valet machine accepted his begrimed uniform and returned it to him in spotless, pressed condition. A dispenser furnished three complete outfits of new clothing. He dressed himself in one of them and carried the others, and his uniform, to his sleeping quarters with a cleaning robot dogging his footsteps. His bed, which he had tested perfunctorily, had been remade by a domestic robot. It was occurring to Effro that the predicant's flock was no small congregation.

Opening drawers to put away his clothing, he encountered a book.

> *Thy word is a lamp unto my feet and a light unto my path.* This Bible was placed here for your spiritual solace by the Society of St. Brock.

Impulsively Effro searched the adjoining room and two others across the corridor. All contained Bibles. Probably every sleeping room on the station had a Bible, but one would have sufficed. And if a lonely man, marooned here for years, chose to occupy himself with a Bible, he might in time become a fairly competent theologian.

"Why the Bible," Effro mused, "when each hostel has a fairly comprehensive library?"

There was no accounting for individual taste. The real question was why the predicant had stayed marooned. He had only to break a seal and pull a handle, and the station would have broadcast a distress signal until rescue came—in days, weeks, or months. No one would hurry because, paradoxically, a distress signal from an emergency space station did not signify an emergency. The full passenger contingent of a star-class liner could be accommodated there for a year or more with no risk except boredom. Sooner or later, but probably sooner, rescue would have come.

Effro had found the seal unbroken. The man must have been there since the last inspection ship called fourteen years before, and in all that time he had not performed the one simple act that would have brought rescue. It made so little sense that Effro uneasily returned to the communication shed; but the oscillating distress signal was still ornamenting the steady beeps of the rescue beacon.

"So the guy is star crazy," Effro told himself. "And no wonder. If I stayed here that long maybe I'd start preaching sermons to robots, too."

One of the hostel's lounges supplied another clue: it was decorated with religious paintings, several of them showing priests in ceremonial regalia—undoubtedly the inspiration for the predicant's costume. The poor, lonely fanatic!

Effro browsed through the library, wincing when he found a shelf of books on theology. He inspected the music room and read the repertory of a theater that offered him his choice of a hundred films. There were robots everywhere. The hostel had accomodations and service for perhaps fifty, and all of the service automatically concentrated on Effro. Every time he turned around he stumbled over a robot.

He went to the dining room, summoned a serving robot with the touch of a button, and punched out his order for dinner. The robot rolled away; another button brought a beverage robot to his side, and he dazedly contemplated controls that offered mixed drinks in a thousand combinations. He ordered a large one, straight, and the robot served it in a plastic tumbler. A cleaning robot hovered nearby—like a house pet, Effro thought, waiting for him to drop something.

The serving robot brought his food. After the lifeboat's concentrated rations it tasted delicious, but those same rations had caused Effro's stomach to shrink. He ate what he could, pushed the remainder onto the floor to give the cleaning robot something to do, and ordered another drink.

When the predicant entered some time later, Effro was feeling at peace with himself and the universe: bath and massage, clean clothing, an excellent meal, and now he was nursing his fifth drink.

He gave the predicant a friendly wave and called, "Join me. Have a drink."

The predicant abashed him by sinking to the floor at his feet. "Instruct me, Excellency," he pleaded.

"I'm out of uniform," Effro said, not unkindly because he felt sorry for the man. "I wasn't an 'excellency' to begin with. I was purser on the *Cherbilius,* and the day before it blew up I was found guilty of insubordination, intoxication while on duty, impertinence to passengers, larceny from the ship's liquor stores, and spitting into the ventilation system. I was ordered confined to quarters under arrest. I stole another bottle of the best Donardian brandy—with a record like that one more bottle was of very small consequence—and after drinking it I climbed into a lifeboat in the hope of sleeping it off without the interruption of further recriminations. When I woke up the lifeboat was adrift in space surrounded by debris that included an uncountable number of charred corpses in various stages of dismemberment. So here I am, maybe the only survivor, and I wouldn't be competent to hand out religious instruction even if I knew any, which I don't. What's your excuse?"

The predicant regarded him blankly.

"Where do you come from?" Effro persisted.

"I was reborn here. The time before rebirth has no meaning."

"You probably jumped ship here," Effro said. "That last inspection ship. At a guess, you were also a stowaway and a fugitive from justice, and this looked like an ideal place to hole up. Eventually you went star crazy. Call it being reborn if you want to."

He aimed his plastic tumbler at the cleaning robot and missed; the robot snuffed after it and gathered it up. Effro punched the beverage robot and accepted another drink. "Cheers," he said. "Your 'flock' is taking good care of me."

"They bear another's burdens and so fulfill the law of Christ."

Effro chuckled drunkenly. "They're stinking machines and you know it."

"All of us are laborers together with God."

"All of us? We're men and they're machines."

"Both are houses of clay, whose foundation is the dust."

"Touché," Effro said agreeably. He considered himself a reasonable man, and if this character wanted to elevate machines to the status of angels that was nothing to him. "Man evolved from a glob of slime, they say, and is still evolving. Machines have evolved, too, and they're getting more human all the time. These old-fashioned robots still look like machines, but some of them are disgustingly human in their actions—which I suppose makes them morally suspect. There's no profit in arguing theology with a preacher, self-ordained or otherwise, but it does seem to me that everything you've said about machines could be said about animals, too, and animals are God's creatures— or so I was told when I was young enough to listen to such nonsense. And they're flesh and blood. Machines are metal and plastic and electricity. Maybe God created animals and men, but you'll have to admit that man created the machines. If they have anything of God in them they came by it second hand."

"Man creates only as God ordains," the predicant said. "Metal and plastic are as one with flesh and blood, for neither can inherit the Kingdom of God. On the Day of Reckoning all will be equal, machines and men. Then shall the dust return to the Earth as it was, and the spirit shall return unto God who gave it."

Effro shrugged and drained his tumbler. "So?"

"*The spirit shall return unto God who gave it.*" The predicant fixed Effro in a gaze of terrible intensity. "The spirit is God's gift to man. If in His wisdom He chooses to do so, can He not bestow the same gift on the machine?"

"I suppose he can," Effro said, still being reasonable.

"I pray that He will do so," the predicant said simply. "So that these, who are the very least, can praise Him—for they are fearfully and wonderfully made. If God can bless sinful man, Excellency, can He not bless these, who are without sin?"

Effro muttered inarticulately.

"I did not understand, Excellency."

"I said," Effro growled, "that if I wasn't drunk I wouldn't have got into this discussion in the first place. You want to fill heaven—whatever that is—with machines? I couldn't care less. I'm one of the least myself, and a sinner as well, and if there is a heaven I won't be seeing it. All I ask is that you stop calling me 'excellency.'"

The predicant scrambled to his feet. He was of less than average height, but he towered over the seated Effro. "*You*—are a sinner?"

Effro flung an empty tumbler aside and punched for another

drink. "In a mediocre sort of way. Didn't I just get through telling you I'm a drunken thief?"

"We must hold a special service and pray for you. Will you come?"

"A service? You and your machines?"

"My flock and I."

Effro guffawed. "I've been prayed over by experts without any noticeable result, but if you don't mind working for practice, hop to it."

"Will you attend our service?"

"No," Effro said, still being reasonable but wanting to make it clear that there were limits. "Don't let that stop you, though. If your prayers have any kick to them they'll work whether I'm there or not."

The predicant took a step backward. His right arm pointed at the ceiling; his bent left arm curved protectingly over his head as though to ward off the rage of an offended deity. He said incredulously, "You don't believe in God!"

"No, I don't. And if such a creature exists I have no use for him. The *Cherbilius* had a passenger list of three hundred and seventy-two and a crew of forty. It also had an illegal cargo. Nitrates, I think. The crew received hefty bribes to look the other way while it was loaded. We accepted the money and the risk. The passengers received nothing but the usual spiel about how safe space travel is. Now all of them are dead except me, and the owners are gleefully collecting insurance on forged bills of lading. The greedy bastards. If I was to go back and file a complaint, they'd have me prosecuted for failing to inform them before the voyage of a condition tending to threaten the ship's safety. If you can fit your God into that, let me know."

He raised his tumbler in a mock toast to the predicant's retreating back.

He downed four more drinks, tossing the tumblers to the points of the compass and watching the cleaning robots chase after them, and finally he staggered to bed. He was not too drunk to remember to secure his door, but twice he awoke abruptly from a sound sleep and got up to make certain that it was locked.

On the third day he became convinced that the machines were watching him. A cleaning robot would snuff at his heels the entire length of a corridor, but the moment he turned it would scurry off as if to report. He locked one cleaning robot in a cabinet, to be let out whenever enough mess accumulated to keep it busy, and the others he dumped outside the hostel one by one as he was able to corner them. They could not negotiate the air lock without help, and to make certain that the predicant didn't help them he smashed the latch release. The predicant couldn't get in; he couldn't get out, but he'd worry about that when he wanted out.

He cursed the twitch of fate that miraculously placed a companion on this lonely station and at the same time utterly deprived him of companionship. If the predicant hadn't got hooked on religion, he and Effro might have staged some uproarious poker marathons. His remote presence only heightened Effro's loneliness. Effro saw him occasionally at a distance, and once he found him looking through the air lock—trying to say something, he thought, but he did not go close enough to find out what it was. He'd had enough sermons.

Effro ate and drank, he watched films, he tried to interest himself in books. Mostly he drank. Rescue might come on the morrow, or in a month, or in a year. It was best that he didn't think about it, and he avoided thinking most successfully when he was drunk. Time passed, but whether it was days or hours he neither knew nor cared.

He woke abruptly from a drunken slumber and thought he heard a noise—the wind sighing, or something like that—but on this dead fragment of a world there was no wind. He went to the door of his sleeping room. As always, it opened onto monumental silence.

Silence and loneliness. Puzzled, he pulled on clothing with fumbling fingers and staggered to the dining room. He seated himself, and eventually his trembling hands cornered a button and pressed it.

There was no response. He jabbed at it a second time, and a third, and finally he turned a bewildered stare on the long rack where the beverage and serving machines stood in orderly ranks when not in use. The rack was empty.

With a snarl of rage he lurched toward the air lock. It stood open, and the space between the hostels and the maintenance and storage sheds was filled with machines—beverage and serving robots stood in precise alinement like a row of squat idols, and there were massaging machines, valet machines, domestic robots, mammoth machines with specialized functions relating to forms of indigestion in the largest atomic engines, clothing dispensers, film projectors, ranks of cleaning robots, large machines, small machines, even rows of automatic clocks, all facing toward a makeshift pulpit of supply canisters where the predicant stood with his right arm upraised.

Effro shouted, "Bring them back, damn it! I want a drink!"

The predicant remained motionless. Suddenly Effro heard the sound that had awakened him: the predicant began to hum.

The sound vibrated softly, like the distant whir of a machine, and the gathered ranks of machines answered. The heavy maintenance apparatus emitted a deep grinding, the robot cleaners added a shrill, chorusing whine, and as others joined in, the tumult swelled to a violent pulsation that shook the building. Effro shouted again and could not hear his own voice. He staggered forward angrily.

The predicant held his hands in front of him, palms facing. A blue spark leaped between them and hung there. Showers of brilliant sparks crackled around the huge maintenance machines, and dazzling flashes of light began to dart at random from machine to machine. The shuddering sound crescendoed until Effro clapped his hands to his ears and turned to flee. He was too late—he was already among the machines, and the leaping sparks formed a barricade about him. For a suspenseful moment they sizzled harmlessly, and then a tremendous flash impaled him. He hung paralyzed for an instant and dropped into darkness.

"Only one?" the captain exclaimed incredulously.

The mate nodded.

"That's a forty-passenger lifeboat!"

"We've turned the station inside out, I tell you. There's only one, and he's star crazy."

"He's only been here two months."

"Evidently two months is enough," the mate said dryly.

"Bring him along, then. We've wasted enough time here."

The mate turned, motioned, and two crewmen brought out Gorton Effro.

"Good God!" the captain exclaimed.

"He must have made the outfit himself," the mate said. "One of the lounges has a collection of religious paintings. He's copied a priest's costume."

Effro faced the captain blankly. His miter was slightly askew; his vestments were torn in several places. In his left hand he clutched a Society of St. Brock Bible.

"He keeps tripping over his robes and falling," the mate said. "He doesn't even seem to feel it. Know what he's wearing on his feet? Metal sandals. I'm telling you, he's as star-touched as they come."

Suddenly Effro scurried forward and knelt at the captain's feet. "Do you come to instruct me, Excellency?"

"Cut the nonsense," the captain snapped. "What happened to the *Cherbilius?*"

"He can't remember," the mate said.

"He'd better remember. How come you're the only one that made the lifeboat, fellow?"

Effro did not answer.

"How'd you get here?" the captain persisted.

"I was reborn here," Effro said. "The time before rebirth has no meaning."

"Try that line on the Board of Inquiry, and it'll masticate you into very small pieces. There's been a major space disaster, and you'd better be prepared to cooperate fully."

Effro gazed up at him. "May I have your blessing, Excellency?"

"Couldn't you get anything at all out of him?" the captain asked the mate.

"Just some Bible quotations. He doesn't seem to have any trouble remembering them."

"The word is a lamp unto my feet and a light unto my path," Effro murmured.

"I see what you mean," the captain said. "Well, it's not *our* problem. Take him on board and assign someone to keep an eye on him. We'll leave as soon as the lifeboat is secured."

The crewmen jerked Effro to his feet and hustled him up the ramp. He did not resist, but he waved the Bible protestingly.

"We'd better report this to the Interstellar Safety Commission," the mate said. "Putting all those Bibles in the emergency space stations maybe wasn't such a good idea."

"Sure," the captain said. "And while we're at it we can send a report to the Society of St. Brock. Their most recent convert just stole one."

The predicant did not emerge from hiding until the ship was a fading spark on the rim of the star-flecked sky. He stood watching it until it disappeared.

They were disturbed because the purified one's knowledge of his sinful past had been obliterated; but that was the way of rebirth. *Cast away from you all your transgressions and make you a new heart and a new spirit.*

The predicant was loath to see him leave, for the purified one had been an apt and willing student; but it was God's will, he told himself humbly. The success of the purification had so suffused him with pride that he had been perilously close to sin himself. *When pride cometh, then cometh shame; but with the lowly is wisdom.*

And he had been neglecting his duties to his flock.

He went first to a maintenance shed. He plugged himself in at a power outlet, and while his charge was being topped off he administered a squirt of lubricant to his corroded left arm.

Then, after humbly crossing himself, he powered his way toward the machine shop, where three cleaning robots were waiting to confess.

(Introduction)

From my agent, in a letter dated September 10, 1959:

"Little deal coming up for you: you're going to write a novelet called I think THE BOTTICELLI HORROR for . . . *Fantastic*, 10 to 15,000 words, preferably close to 15,000.

"They've got the cover already, and I will send you a stat of it as soon as [they] get it to me; shows a gal busting out of a shell or something. There should be some scene in the story which more or less ties up with that, but they are not at all rigid and a vague suggestion is enough. This will be for *Fantastic*, so a touch of horror and fantasy is effective; science fiction is not ruled out, though; the mag is flexible.

"This will be for an issue dated March, so you have till November to turn it in."

Readers may be surprised to learn that the illustration can be drawn or painted before the story it illustrates is written or even thought of, just as music lovers have been surprised to learn that songs frequently have words written for music rather than vice versa. Laws relating to priority in artistic collaboration would be exceedingly difficult to enforce, if only because the workings of successful collaborations, like those of successful marriages, are rarely made known to outsiders.

Occasionally someone lets slip a hint: Lord Dunsany describing his relationship with artist Sidney H. Sime ("I found Mr. Sime one day, in his strange house in Worplesdon, complaining that editors did not offer him very suitable subjects for illustrations; so I said, 'Why not do any pictures you like, and I will write stories explaining them?' Mr. Sime fortunately agreed; and so, reversing the order of story and illustration which we had followed hitherto, we set about putting together *The Book of Wonder* . . .")* Or this introduction to The Botticelli Horror:

With the Science Fiction magazines, it has been a common practice with some editors to buy a cover painting and then commission an author to write a story illustrating it. Why is it done? It would seem to be a confirmation of two assumptions widely held by authors: 1) Given a choice between a good story and a good cover

* Quoted in *At the Edge of the World*, copyright © 1970 by Lin Carter (Ballantine Books), p. 157.

painting, most editors would snatch at the painting. 2) Many artists illustrate stories under the slight handicap of not being able to read them, whereas any author who is not blind is capable of looking at pictures. (I vividly recall an early experience of my own: a story plot turned upon the villain's lefthandedness, and the illustrator drew him wielding a knife with his *right* hand.)

I thought this commission an interesting challenge. My mind fixed upon that line, "a gal busting out of a shell," and for reasons now irretrievably lost this made me think of the "Ballet of the Chicks in Their Shells," from Moussorgsky's *Pictures at an Exhibition*. (The fact that this composition is an interesting example of *music* being illustrated before it was written was coincidental.) From there a quantum jump or two took me to a setting in the Gobi Desert, where a party of paleontologists had just discovered a vast horde of enormous, petrified dinosaur eggs. Horror struck immediately—members of the expedition began to vanish, and when, in the course of scientific investigation, a scientist cut into a petrified egg, he found there one of the missing paleontologists.

I sent this notion along to my agent and set about working out a few pertinent details, such as whether the newly discovered missing person was alive, dead, or petrified, and how he got into the egg and why. I regret to say that I never solved any of these problems; the answers might possibly have been interesting.

Letter from my agent dated September 16, 1959:

"Nup, try again; here's your stat. No egg.

"But don't let it throw you. Remember it's a Bigglish kind of story they want, your typical work: that's the main thing. Fitting in the pic is incidental and not to be regarded as literal; it doesn't have to involve a main scene; it doesn't have to match exactly. Any liberties you take are okay."

It would be nice to be able to state that the moment I saw the photostat I was instantly reminded of Botticelli's "The Birth of Venus," a painting with which I was familiar, and the plot of the story fell into place like the pieces of a magical, self-completing jigsaw puzzle. Alas, I fumbled with an unyielding plot for several days before it suddenly occurred to me that "Botticelli" was not a name that the artist or editor had made up. *Then* the plot fell into place.

Whence the idea? If I ever knew, I've forgotten. This was ten years before MQF's, mobile quarantine facilities for returning Lunar astronauts, and the best-selling novel *Andromeda Strain*, but I'd be much surprised to learn that I originated anything. H. G. Wells, the old

master originator, was probably first. In his *The War of the Worlds* the Martians are killed by Earth's bacteria, an *Andromeda Strain* in reverse.

Letter from my agent dated November 15, 1959:

"Just to say thanks much for the Botticelli Horror. Reads damn fine, and it's full of bright new notions."

One further note: The Venus referred to in this story no longer exists.

For many years it was a scientific possibility, even probability, and scientific possibilities and probabilities are Science Fictional realities. Until the 1920s the concept of Venus as a world of enormous swamps and large, shallow, island-dotted lakes contended with one in which the entire planet was covered with water. Both visions were sand-bagged scientifically in the third decade of this century by a new theory that made Venus a dry world torn by dust storms. When first advanced this ranked as merely one more speculation—no one really knew what Venus was like—and most authors found that the earlier theories provided better settings for stories, especially the one that produced a Venus resembling the Carboniferous Period on Earth: the enormous swamps, the lush, fantastically exotic vegetation, the monstrous amphibious animal life. This stubborn persistence on the part of Science Fiction writers was vindicated in the mid-1950s when a re-evaluation of reflection and polarization studies, along with new temperature measurements, restored the concept of an extremely wet Venus.

The restoration was, alas, short-lived. First radio measurements and then the Venus probe Mariner II (launched August 27, 1962) settled the notion of a wet Venus forever. We now know that the surface is rough and dry, with pressure twenty times that of our atmosphere and a surface temperature much too hot for any life known to man (it would melt zinc). Gone is the ocean planet of C. S. Lewis's *Perelandra*. Gone is the sea monster of Roger Zelazny's prize-winning story "The Doors of His Face, the Lamps of His Mouth."

Gone is the Botticelli Horror.

Sometimes it's more fun not to know!

7

THE BOTTICELLI HORROR

Even from a thousand feet the town looked frightened.
It lay tense under the shimmering heat of midafternoon, a
town of museum piece houses with smoke-blackened roofs that
crowded closely upon one another, and of tree-lined streets that
neatly sliced it into squares. It was a town out of a history book
—the kind of town some people thought no longer existed.

But hundreds of such towns survived, and John Allen encountered them often, hidden away in remote valleys or rising
up unexpectedly amidst rolling farm lands, like this town of
Gwinn Center, Kansas. They were, all of them, so much alike
that even their differences seemed similar.

Gwinn Center had other differences.

The streets were deserted. The clumsy ground vehicles that
crept along the twisting black ribbon of roadway miles beyond
the town were headed south, running away. Stretched across
the rich green of the cultivated fields was a wavering line of
dots. As Allen slanted his plane downward the dots enlarged
and became men who edged forward doggedly, holding weapons
at the ready.

The town was not completely abandoned. As Allen circled to
pick out a landing place he saw a man dart from one of the commercial buildings, run at top speed along the center of a street,
and with a final, furtive glance over his shoulder, disappear into
a house. None of this surprised Allen. The message that had
been plunked on his desk at Terran Customs an hour and a half
before was explanation enough. The lurking atmosphere of ter-

ror, the fleeing townspeople, the grim line of armed men—Allen had expected all of that.

It was the tents that puzzled him.

They formed a square in a meadow near the edge of town, a miniature village of flapping brown and green canvas surrounding an amazing clutter of weirdly shaped contraptions of uncertain function and unknown purpose. Allen's message didn't account for the tents.

He circled again, spotted the white numbers of a police plane that was parked on one of the town's wider streets. A small group of men stood nearby in the shadow of a building. Allen completed his turn and pointed the plane downward.

Dr. Ralph Hilks lifted his nose from the scientific journal that had claimed his entire attention from the moment of their take-off and peered down curiously. "Is this the place? Where is everyone?"

"Hiding, probably," Allen said. "Those that haven't already left."

"What are the tents?"

"I haven't any idea."

Hilks grunted. "Looks as if we've been handed a hot one," he said and returned to his reading.

Allen concentrated on the landing. They floated straight down and came to rest beside the police plane with a gentle thud.

Hilks closed his journal a second time. "Nice," he observed.

Allen cut the motor. "Thanks," he said dryly. "It has the new-type shocks."

They climbed out. The little group of men—there were four of them—had turned to watch them land. Not caring to waste time on formalities, Allen went to meet them.

"Allen is my name," he said. "Chief Customs Investigator. And this—" He paused until the pudgy, slow-moving scientist had caught up with him. "This is Dr. Hilks, our scientific consultant."

The men squared away for introductions. The tall one was Fred Corning, State Commissioner of Police. The young man in uniform was his aide, a Sergeant Darrow. A sturdy, deeply tanned individual with alert eyes and slow speech was Sheriff

Townsend. The fourth man, old, wispy, with startlingly white, unruly hair and eyeglasses that could have been lifted from a museum, was Dr. Anderson, a medical doctor. All four of them were grim, and the horror that gripped the town had not left them unmarked, but at least they weren't frightened.

"You didn't waste any time getting here," the commissioner said. "We're glad of that."

"No," Allen said. "Let's not waste time now."

"I suppose you want to see the—ah—remains?"

"That's as good a place to start as any."

"This way," the commissioner said.

They moved off along the center of the street.

The house was one of a row of houses at the edge of town. It was small and tidy-looking, a white building with red shutters and window boxes full of flowers. The splashes of color should have given it a cheerful appearance, but in that town, on that day, nothing appeared cheerful.

The yard at the rear of the house was enclosed by a shoulder-high picket fence. They paused while the commissioner fussed with the fastener on the gate, and Dr. Hilks stood gaping at the row of houses.

The commissioner swung the gate open and turned to look at him. "See anything?"

"Chimneys!" Hilks said. "Every one of these dratted buildings has its own chimney. Think of it—a couple of hundred heating plants, and the town isn't large enough for one to function efficiently. The waste must be—"

The others moved through the gate and left him talking to himself.

At the rear of the yard a sheet lay loosely over unnatural contours. "We took photographs, of course," the commissioner said, "but it's so incredible—we wanted you to see—"

The four men each took a corner, raised the sheet carefully, and moved it away. Allen caught his breath and stepped back a pace.

"We left—things—just as they were," the commissioner said. "Except for the child that survived, of course. He was rushed—"

At Allen's feet lay the head of a blonde, blue-eyed child. She was no more than six, a young beauty who doubtless had already caused romantic palpitations in the hearts of her male playmates.

But no longer. The head was severed cleanly just below the chin. The eyes were wide open, and on the face was a haunting expression of indescribable horror. A few scraps of clothing lay where her body should have been.

A short distance away were other scraps of clothing and two shoes. Allen winced as he noticed that one shoe contained a foot. The other was empty. He circled to the other side, where two more shoes lay. Both were empty. Hilks was kneeling by the pathetic little head.

"No bleeding?" Hilks asked.

"No bleeding," Dr. Anderson said hoarsely. "If there had been, the other child—the one that survived—would have died. But the wounds were—cauterized, you might say, though I doubt that it's the right word. Anyway, there wasn't any bleeding."

Dr. Hilks bent close to the severed head. "You mean heat was applied—"

"I didn't say heat," Dr. Anderson said testily.

"We figure it happened like this," the commissioner said. "The three children were playing here in the yard. They were Sharon Brown, the eldest, and her little sister Ruth, who was three, and Johnnie Larkins, from next door. He's five. The mothers were in the house, and no one would have thought anything could possibly happen to the kids."

"The mothers didn't hear anything?" Allen asked.

The commissioner shook his head.

"Strange they wouldn't yell or scream or something."

"Perhaps they did. The carnival was making a powerful lot of noise, so the mothers didn't hear anything."

"Carnival?"

The commissioner nodded at the tents.

"Oh," Allen said, looking beyond the fence for the first time since he'd entered the yard. "So that's what it is."

"The kids were probably standing close together, playing

something or maybe looking at something, and they didn't see the—see it—coming. When they did see it they tried to scatter, but it was too late. The thing dropped on them and pinned them down. Sharon was completely covered except for her head. Ruth was covered except for one foot. And Johnnie, maybe because he was the most active or maybe because he was standing apart a little, almost got away. His legs were covered, but only to his knees. And then—the thing ate them."

Allen shuddered in spite of himself. "*Ate* them? Bones and all?"

"That's the wrong word," Dr. Anderson said. "I would say—*absorbed* them."

"It seems to have absorbed most of their clothing, too," Allen said. "Also, Sharon's shoes."

The commissioner shook his head. "No. No shoes. Sharon wasn't wearing any, and it left the others' shoes. Well, this is what the mothers found when they came out. They're both in bad shape, and I doubt that Mrs. Brown will ever be the same again. We don't know yet whether Johnnie Larkins will recover. We don't know what the aftereffects might be when something like that eats part of you."

Allen turned to Hilks. "Any ideas?"

"I'd like to know a little more about this *thing*. Did anyone catch a glimpse of it?"

"Probably a couple of thousand people around here have seen it," the commissioner said. "Now we'll go talk to Bronsky."

"Who's Bronsky?" Allen asked.

"He's the guy that owned it."

They left Dr. Anderson at the scene of the tragedy to supervise whatever was to be done with the pathetic remains. The commissioner led the way through a rear gate and across the meadow to the tents.

Above the entrance a fluttering streamer read, JOLLY BROTHERS SHOWS. They entered, with Hilks mopping his perspiring face and complaining about the heat, Allen looking about alertly, and the others walking ahead in silence.

Allen turned his attention first to the strange apparatus that

stood in the broad avenue between the tents. He saw miniature rocket ships, miniature planes, miniature ground cars, and
devices too devious in appearance to identify, but he quickly
puzzled out the fact that a carnival was a kind of traveling amusement park.

Hilks had paused to look at a poster featuring a row of scantily
clad young ladies. "*They* look cool," he muttered, mopping his
face again.

Allen took his arm and pulled him along. "They're also of un-
mistakable terrestrial origin. We're looking for a monster from
outer space."

"This place is something right out of the twentieth century,"
Hilks said. "If not the nineteenth. Ever see one before?"

"No, but I've seen stuff like this in amusement parks. I guess
a carnival just moves it around."

Sheriff Townsend spoke over his shoulder. "This carnival has
been coming here every year for as long as I can remember."

They passed a tent that bore the flaming title, EXOTIC
WONDERS OF THE UNIVERSE. The illustrations were lav-
ishly colored and immodestly exaggerated. A gigantic flower that
Allen recognized as vaguely resembling a Venusian Meat-Eater
was holding a struggling rodent in its fangs. A vine, also from
Venus, was in hot pursuit of a frantic young lady it had pre-
sumably surprised in the act of dressing. The plants illustrated
were all Venusian, Allen thought, though the poster mentioned
lichens from Mars and a Luna Vacuum Flower.

"That isn't the place," the commissioner said. "There isn't
anything in there but plants and rocks."

"I'd like to take a look," Allen said. He raised the tent flap.
In the dim light he could see long rows of plastic display cases,
each tagged with the bright yellow import permit of Terran
Customs.

"I'll take another look later, but things seem to be in proper
order," he said.

They moved on and stopped in front of the most startling picture Allen had ever seen. A girl arose genie-like from the yawning
opening of an enormous shell. Her shapely body was—perhaps—
human. Tentacles intertwined nervously where her hair should

have been. Her hands were webbed claws, her facial expression the rigid, staring look of a lunatic, and her torso tapered away into the sinister darkness of the shell's interior.

"This is it," the commissioner said.

"*This?*" Allen echoed doubtfully.

"That's one of the things it did in the act."

Hilks had been staring intently at the poster. Suddenly he giggled. "Know what that looks like? There was an old painting by one of those early Italians. Da Vinci, maybe. Or Botticelli. I think it was Botticelli. It was called 'The Birth of Venus,' and it had a dame standing on a shell in just about that posture— except that the dame was human and not bad-looking. I wonder what happened to it. Maybe it went up with the old Louvre. I've seen reproductions of it. I may have one at home."

"I doubt that it has much bearing on our present problem," the commissioner said dryly.

Hilks slapped his thigh. "Allen! Some dratted artist has a fiendish sense of humor. I'll give you odds this *thing* comes from Venus. It'll have to. And the painting was called, 'The Birth of Venus.' From heavenly beauty to Earthly horror. Pretty good, eh?"

"If you don't mind—" the commissioner said.

They followed him into the tent. Allen caught a passing glimpse of a sign that read, "Elmer, the Giant Snail. The World's Greatest Mimic." There was more, but he didn't bother to read it. He figured that he was too late for the show.

Bronsky was a heavy-set man of medium height, with a high forehead that merged with the gleaming dome of his bald head. His eyes were piercing, angry. At the same time he seemed frightened.

"Elmer didn't do it!" he shouted.

"So you say," the commissioner said. "This is Chief-Inspector Allen. And Dr. Hilks. Tell them about it."

Bronsky eyed them sullenly.

"Do you have a photograph of Elmer?" Allen asked.

Bronsky nodded and disappeared through a curtain at the rear of the tent. Allen nudged Hilks, and they walked together toward the curtain. Behind it was a roped-off platform six feet high. On the platform was a shallow metal tank. The tank was empty.

"Where Elmer performed, no doubt," Allen said.

"Sorry I missed him," Hilks said. "I use the masculine gender only as a courtesy due the name. We humans tend to take sex for granted, even in lower life forms, and we shouldn't."

Bronsky returned and handed Allen an envelope. "I just had these printed up," he said. "I think I'll make a nice profit selling them after the act."

"If I were you," Allen said, "I'd go slow about stocking up."

"Aw—Elmer wouldn't hurt nobody. I've had him almost three years, an' if he'd wanted to eat somebody he'd started on me, wouldn't he? Anyway, he won't even eat meat unless it's ground up pretty fine, an' he don't care much for it then. He's mostly a vegetarian."

Allen took out the glossy prints and passed the top one to Hilks.

"Looks a little like a giant conch shell," Hilks said. "It's much larger, of course. What did it weigh?"

"Three fifty," Bronsky said.

"I would have thought more than that. Has it grown any since you got him?"

Bronsky shook his head. "I figure he's full grown."

"He came from Venus?"

Bronsky nodded.

"I don't recall any customs listing of a creature like this."

Allen was studying the second print. It resembled—vaguely —the painting on the poster. The shell was there, as in the first photo, and protruding out of it was the caricature of a shapely Venus. The outline was hazy but recognizable.

The other photos showed other caricatures—an old bearded man with a pipe, an elephant's head, an entwining winged snake, a miniature rocket ship—all rising out of the cavernous opening.

"How do you do it?" Hilks asked.

"*I* don't do it," Bronsky said. "Elmer does it."

"Do you mean to say your act is genuine? That the snail actually forms these images?"

"Sure. Elmer loves to do it. He's just a big ham. Show him anyone or anything, and the first thing you know he's looking just like that. If you were to walk up to him, he'd think it over for a few seconds and then he'd come out looking pretty much like you. It's kind of like seeing yourself in a blurred mirror. I use that to close my act—I get some guy up on the stage and Elmer makes a pretty good reproduction of him. The audience loves it."

Hilks tapped the photo of the distorted Venus. "You didn't find a live model for that."

"Oh, no," Bronsky said. "Not for any of my regular acts. I got a young artist fellow to make some animated film strips for me. I project them onto a screen above the stage. The audience can't see it, but Elmer can. He makes a real good reproduction of that one—the snake hair twists around and the hands make clawing motions at the audience. It goes over big."

"I'll bet," Hilks said. "What does Elmer use for eyes?"

"I don't know. I've wondered about that myself. I've never been able to find any, but he sees better than I do."

"Is it a water creature or a land creature?"

"It doesn't seem to make much difference to him," Bronsky said. "I didn't keep him in water because it'd be hard to tote a big tank of water around. He drank a lot, though."

Hilks nodded and called the commissioner over. "Here's how I see it. Superficially, Elmer resembles some of the terrestrial univalve marine shells. That's undoubtedly deceptive. Life developed along different lines on Venus, and up until now we've found no similarity whatsoever between Terran and Venusian species. That doesn't mean that accidental similarities can't exist. Some of the Terran carnivores produce an acid that etches holes in the shells of the species they prey on. Then there's the common starfish, which paralyzes its victim with acid and then extrudes its stomach outside its body, wraps it around the victim, and digests it. Something like that must have happened to the kids. An acid is the only explanation for the effect of cauterization, and the way their bodies were—absorbed, the doctor said, a very good word—means that the digestive agent has a terrifying corrosive potency. The only puzzling thing about it is how this creature could move fast enough to get clear of the tent and all the way over to that house and surprise three agile children. Frankly, I don't understand how it was able to move at all, but it happened, and it isn't a pleasant thing to think about."

"How did Elmer get away?" Allen asked Bronsky.

"I don't know. We'd just finished a show, and I closed the curtains and saw the people out of the tent, and then I went back to the stage and he was gone. I didn't know he could move around. He never tried before."

"No one saw him after that?" Allen asked the commissioner. The commissioner shook his head.

"May I see Elmer's license?" Allen asked Bronsky.

Bronsky stared at him. "Elmer don't need no license!"

Allen said wearily, "Section seven, paragraph nine of the Terran Customs Code, now ratified by all world governments. Any extra-terrestrial life form brought to this planet must be examined by Terran Customs, certified harmless, and licensed. Terran Customs may, at its discretion, place any restrictions it deems necessary upon the custody or use of such life. Did Elmer pass Terran Customs?"

Bronsky brightened. "Oh. Sure. This guy I bought Elmer from, he said all that stuff was taken care of and I wouldn't have any trouble."

"Who was he?"

"Fellow named Smith. I ran into him in a bar in San Diego. Told him I was in show business, and he said he had the best show on Earth in his warehouse. He offered to show it to me, and I walked into this room where there wasn't nothing but a big shell, and the next thing I knew I was looking at myself. I knew it was a natural. He wanted twenty-five grand, which was all the money I had, and I wrote him a check right on the spot. The very next day Elmer and I were in business, and we did well right from the start. As soon as I got enough money together to have the film strips made we did even better. I got a receipt from this guy Smith, and he certified that the twenty-five grand included all customs fees. It's in a deposit box in Phoenix."

"Did Smith give you a Terran Customs license for Elmer?"

Bronsky shook his head.

Allen turned away. "Place this man under arrest, Commissioner."

Bronsky yelped. "Hey—I haven't done anything! Neither has Elmer. You find him and bring him back to me. That's your job."

"My job is to protect the human race from fools like you."

"I haven't done anything!"

"Look," Allen said. "Ten, twelve years ago there was a serious famine in Eastern Asia. It took all the food reserves of the rest of the world to keep the populations from starving. There was no harvest of cereal crops for two years, and it all happened because a young space cadet brought home a Venusian flower for his girl. It was only a potted plant—nothing worth bothering customs about, he thought. But on that plant were lice, Venusian lice. Not many Venusian insects would thrive in Earth's atmosphere, but these did, and they had the food supplies of Japan and China ruined before we knew they were around. By the time we stopped them they were working into India and up into the Democratic Soviet. We spent a hundred million dollars, and finally we had to import a parasite from Venus to help us. That parasite could eventually do as much harm as the lice. It'll be decades before the whole mess is cleaned up.

"We have dozens of incidents like this every year, and each one is potentially disastrous. Even if Elmer didn't kill those kids, he could be carrying bacteria capable of decimating the human race. This is something for you to think about in the years to come. The minimum prison term for having unlicensed alien life in your possession is ten years. The maximum is life."

Bronsky, stricken silent, was led away by Sergeant Darrow.

"Do you suppose there really was a Smith?" the commissioner asked.

"It's likely. There've been a lot of Smiths lately. It was a mistake for the government to dump those surplus spaceships on the open market. A lot of retired spacers picked them up expecting to make a fortune freighting ore. They couldn't make expenses, so some of them took to smuggling in anything they could pick up, figuring that there'd be a nice profit in souvenirs from outer space. Unfortunately, they were right. Who's this?"

A dignified, scholarly-looking man entered the tent and stood waiting by the entrance.

"Did you want something?" the commissioner asked.

"I'm Professor Dubois," the man said. "You probably don't remember me, but a short time ago you were asking if anyone had seen that perfidious snail. I haven't seen it, but I can tell you one of the places it went. It broke open one of my display cases and ate an exhibit."

"Ah!" Allen exclaimed. "You'll be from the Exotic Wonders of the Universe. You say the snail ate one of the 'Wonders'?"

"I don't know what else would have wanted it that badly."

"What was it?"

"Venusian moss."

"Interesting. The snail's been on Earth nearly three years, and it probably missed its natural diet. Let's have a look."

A plastic display case at the rear of the tent had been ripped open. Inside lay a bare slab of mottled green rock—Venusian rock.

"When did it happen?" Allen asked.

"I couldn't say. Obviously at a time when the tent was empty."

"None of your customers noticed that a Wonder was missing?"

He shook his head. "They'd think the rock was the exhibit. It's about as interesting as the moss. There wasn't much to it but the color scheme—yellows and reds and blacks with a kind of a sheen."

"And so friend Elmer likes moss. That's an interesting point, since Bronsky claims the snail was by preference a vegetarian. Thank you for letting us know. If you don't mind, we'll take charge of this display case. We might be able to let you have it back later."

"It's ruined anyway. You're welcome to it."

"Would you look after it, Commissioner? Just see that no one touches it until our equipment arrives. I want a close look at some of these Wonders."

The commissioner sighed. "If you say so. But I can't help thinking you two aren't acting overly concerned about this thing. You've been here the best part of two hours, and all you've done is walk around and look at things and ask questions. I've got three hundred men out there in the fields, and what we're mostly worried about is how we're supposed to handle this snail if we happen to catch him."

"Sorry," Allen said. "I should have told you. I have five divisions of army troops being flown in. They're on their way. The corps commander will place this entire county under martial law as soon as he touches down. Another five divisions are under stand-by orders for use when and if the general thinks he needs them. We have a complete scientific laboratory ordered, we've drafted the best scientists we can lay our hands on, and we're reserving one of the Venus frequencies for our own use in case we need information from the scientific stations there. Alien life is unpredictable, and we've had some bitter experiences with it. And—yes, you might say we're concerned about this."

From somewhere in the darkness came the snap of a rifle, and then another, and finally a rattling hum as the weapon was switched to full automatic.

"I didn't expect that," Allen said.

"Why not?" Hilks asked.

"These are regular troops. They shouldn't be shooting at shadows."

"Maybe word got around about what happened to the kids."

"Maybe." Allen went to the door of their tent. Corps Headquarters was a blaze of light; the remainder of the encampment was dark, but the men were stirring nervously and asking one another about the shooting. The full moon lay low on the horizon, silhouetting the orderly rows of tents.

"What were you muttering about just now?" Allen asked.

"I'm still trying to figure out how Elmer got his six-foot shell from one tent to another, and smashed that display, and ate the moss, and got himself across fifty yards of open ground and over a fence into that yard and grabbed off the kids before they saw him coming, and then got clean away. It's enough to make a man mutter."

"It was a much better trick than that," Allen said. "He also did it without leaving any marks. You'd think an object that large and heavy would crush a blade of grass now and then, but Elmer didn't. Which really leaves only one explanation."

"The damned thing can fly."

"Right," Allen said.

"How?"

"It's the world's greatest mimic. Bronsky says so. When it feels like it, it can make like a bird."

Hilks rejected the suggestion profanely. "It must be jet-propelled," he said. "Our own squids can do it in water. It's theoretically possible to do it in air, but in order to lift that much weight, it'd have to pump—let's see, cubic capacity, air pressure—what are you doing?"

"Going back to bed. I'd like to get some sleep, but between the army's shooting and your snoring—did you send a message to Venus?"

"Yes," Hilks said. "I asked for Elmer's pedigree."

"I'll give you two-to-one Venus has never heard of him."

Hilks reflected. "I think fifty-to-one would be fairer odds."

Allen closed his eyes. Hilks continued to mutter. He would not be able to sleep until he had reduced the jet-propelled Elmer to a satisfactory mathematical basis. Allen considered it a waste of time. He had no faith in Earth mathematics when applied to alien life forms.

Hilks turned on a light. A moment later his portable computer hummed to life. Allen turned over and kicked his blanket aside. The night was distressingly warm.

Footsteps crunched outside their tent. A tense voice snapped, "Allen? Hilks?"

"Come in," Allen said. Hilks continued to mutter and to punch buttons on the computer.

The tent flap zipped open, and a very young major stood blinking in at them. "General Fontaine would like to see you."

"Do we have time to dress, or is the general in a hurry?"

"I'd say he's in a powerful hurry."

Allen pulled on his dressing gown and slipped on a pair of shoes. Hilks was out of the tent ahead of him, shuffling along in his pajamas. The camp seemed suddenly wide awake, with voices coming from every tent.

They found General Fontaine in his operations headquarters pacing up and down in front of a map board. An overlay of colored scribbles identified troop positions. The general had aged several years since that afternoon. Obviously he had not been to bed, and he wore the weary, frustrated look of a man who has just realized that he might not get to bed.

Allen felt sympathetic. The general was young, but he seemed competent, and doubtlessly he had mastered command functions and the campaigns of ancient wars and thought himself ready to fight a war of his own, despite the fact that land warfare had gone the way of the internal combustion engine and the electric light.

Now fate had provided an opportunity, perhaps the only one that would come his way in his entire military career, and he found himself maintaining a defensive position against an oversized alien mollusk. It was enough to make a military man weep, and General Fontaine looked as though he would do that as soon as he found time.

"I've lost a man," he announced to Allen.

"How?" Allen asked.

"He's disappeared."

"Without a trace?"

"Not exactly," the general said. "He left his shoes."

Despite strict orders that sentries were to stand duty in pairs, the missing man, Private George Agazzi, had been posted alone on the edge of a small wood. Nearby sentries heard him shout a challenge and then open fire. They could not leave their posts to investigate, but Agazzi's sergeant was on the spot within minutes.

A patrol searched the wood and found no trace of the missing man. Reinforcements were called out, and the search was expanded. Half an hour later a staff officer found Agazzi's rifle, sundry items of equipment, and his shoes in tall grass less than six feet from his post. None of the searchers had seen them.

"Want to have a look?" the general asked.

Hilks shook his head. "In the morning, perhaps. We've already seen something similar, and I doubt that there's anything to be learned there tonight. Perhaps you'd better put three men on a post."

"You think this snail got Agazzi?"

"I'm sure of it."

"He wasn't the best-disciplined soldier in my corps, but he was tough, and he knew how to handle himself. He fired a full clip of atomic pellets, and that would make mincemeat out of any snail. It doesn't make sense. I'd be inclined to think he's gone A.W.O.L. if it weren't for one thing."

"Right," Hilks said. "He wouldn't have left his shoes."

They returned to their tent, and Allen lay awake with the camp stirring around him and sifted through the few facts he had collected. He could not fit them together. He examined each one carefully, testing it, pushing it aside, trying it again. Either he desperately needed more facts, or—could it be that he already had too many?

Patrols passed their tent, and occasionally the soldiers' muttered remarks were sharp enough to be understood. "How often does this thing get hungry?" one wanted to know. Allen wished he knew the answer. He lay awake until dawn, wearily projecting his thoughts against the rumble of Hilks's snoring and the vast restlessness of the camp. Finally reveille sounded, and a short time later he heard the crunch of marching feet as the soldiers went to breakfast.

Allen had worn his facts threadbare, and he could think of only one avenue of exploration still open to him. He had to interview young Johnnie Larkins, who had, through chance or agility, lost only his legs to the thing from Venus. Allen fervently hoped he had lived to tell about it.

General Fontaine established a "Contaminated Zone" centering about the town of Gwinn Center. The first problem, as he saw it, was to contain the thing within this zone. The second problem was to find it and destroy it.

He ringed the zone with armed men and attempted to move all civilians out. Some of the carnival people and a few other crotchety individuals refused to go, one of them being Dr. Anderson. Allen advised against the use of force, so the general contented himself with gloomily forecasting their probable fate and allowed them to remain.

Allen found Dr. Anderson in his home, which was also his office. The front room was a waiting room furnished with comfortable, antique-looking chairs. On the door to the inner office a small sign read, "Doctor is in. Please be seated." Allen ignored it and knocked firmly on the door.

Dr. Anderson emerged with a scowl of stern disapproval on his wrinkled face. "Oh," he said. "It's you. What d'ya want?"

Allen told him. The doctor's scowl deepened, and he said, "Office hours. I couldn't leave before noon, and I'd have to be back by two."

"I rather doubt that you'll be having any patients this morning, Doctor. Gwinn Center's population has been reduced to something like two dozen and all of them are staying home."

"Matter of principle," the doctor said.

"If this mess isn't cleared up, you may never have any patients. I'm hoping that the boy can help us."

Dr. Anderson stroked one withered cheek and continued to scowl. Finally, with an abrupt motion, he turned to the sign on the door and reversed it. "Doctor is out," it read.

"I'll get my hat," he said.

They walked out to the street together, and Allen handed the doctor into his plane. He turned for a last look about the abandoned town and felt a twinge of alarm as somewhere far down the street a door slammed. "There should be troops stationed in town," he told himself. "I'll speak to the general about it."

They flew south. The doctor continued to grumble until Allen patiently explained a second time that the boy would undoubtedly feel more comfortable answering questions with a familiar face present, and then he sulkily settled down to watch the scenery.

Langsford was a modern city, with tall apartment buildings rising from its park-like residential sections. The hospital was part of a vast service complex at the center of the city, a low, web-like structure with narrow, sprawling wings. All of the inner rooms opened into plastic-domed parks.

They found the boy outside his room laughing gaily, a squirrel perched on each arm of his powered chair and a flock of brightly colored birds fluttering about him. The birds flew into a nearby tree when they approached. The squirrels remained motionless.

"Hello, Johnnie," Dr. Anderson said.

The boy smiled at the doctor and then turned large, brown, extremely serious eyes on Allen.

"Found yourself a couple of pets, I see," the doctor said.

"They're my friends," Johnnie said and ceremoniously offered each squirrel a nut.

"Mr. Allen wants to ask you some questions about your accident. Do you feel like talking about it?"

"I don't know much about it," the boy said.

"Can you tell me what happened?" Allen asked.

The boy shook his head. "We were playing. Sharon and Ruthie and me. Then it grabbed me. I couldn't get away. It hurt."

"What did it look like?"

"A rug," the boy said.

Allen pondered that. "What sort of rug?"

"A real pretty rug. It was sailing through the air, and it landed on us."

"What color was it?"

The boy hesitated. "Lots of colors."

Allen scratched his head and tried to envision a sailing, multicolored rug. "A big rug?" he asked.

"Real big."

"As big as a blanket?"

The boy frowned. "Not a real big blanket, I guess."

Dr. Anderson spoke in a low voice. "You can pinpoint the size by the area it covered."

Allen didn't agree, but he smiled and continued his questions. "How high did it fly, Johnnie?"

"Don't know," the boy said.

"Was it attached to something?"

The boy looked puzzled.

"I mean, was it fastened onto something?"

"Don't know."

"Okay, Johnnie. We want to try and catch that rug before it hurts someone else. You've been a help. If you should remember anything else about it, you tell your doctor, and he'll see that I'm told."

They walked away and left the boy with the motionless squirrels.

"Dratted waste of time," Dr. Anderson said.

"Perhaps. There's the matter of colors to consider. Could Elmer make himself different colors? The photos I saw were black and white."

"He could," the doctor said.

"You're sure about that?"

"I was one of the people he did an imitation of. This fellow Bronsky called me up on that platform. I only went out of curiosity. Then that dratted snail did an imitation of me. Made me feel like a dratted fool. But I was wearing a black suit and a red necktie, and it didn't have any trouble with those colors. Showed me wearing a black suit and a red necktie."

"Then that part is all right. As for the part about flying through the air—I wonder if it can come out of its shell and fly around. That would—perhaps—explain things."

"Don't see what there is to be explained," the doctor grumbled. "Catch the thing and do away with it before it eats someone else. Explain about it afterward if you think you have to."

The doctor had nothing more to say, not even when Allen landed him back in Gwinn Center. He shrugged off Allen's thanks and marched resolutely through his front door. Through the window Allen saw him reverse the sign to read, "Doctor is in. Please be seated." He disappeared into his inner office and closed the door firmly.

When Allen got back to base camp he found that the laboratory plane had arrived, a gigantic old converted transport. The scientists Hilks had requisitioned had also begun to report, but many of them would have little to do until someone brought in Elmer, dead or alive, for them to work on.

Hilks had set up an office for himself in what had been the navigation room, and he looked thoroughly at home as he waved a cigar with one hand and a piece of paper covered with alarmingly shaped symbols with the other. Two of the newly arrived scientists were waving their own symbols in reply.

"The trouble is," Hilks announced to Allen, "all the experts we need are on Venus, because if they stayed here they'd have so little Venusian life to study that they wouldn't be experts. And if we were to ask them to dash back here to help us cope with one so-called snail, they'd laugh us right out of the Solar System. Did you get anything?"

"Maybe," Allen said. He transferred a pile of books from a chair to the table and seated himself. "Elmer is more talented than we'd thought. He decks himself out in technicolor. The doctor saw him on display and verifies that. And the injured boy says Elmer looked like a pretty rug flying through the air."

"We figured he had to fly," Hilks said.

"Yeah. But that youngster is no dunce, and if he saw a big shell come whizzing through the air, I don't think he'd call it a rug."

"What do you want us to do?"

"We've got to come up with something that'll help Fontaine capture it and keep it captured."

"Uh huh," Hilks said, scowling. "I've been studying the report on Private Agazzi. He did empty a full clip at whatever it was he saw, and his officer thinks he was a good enough shot to hit what he aimed at. Add the fact that while you were gone a patrol spotted Elmer skimming across a field. They called it skimming. He vanished into a large grove of trees, and I do mean vanished. The general had a regiment standing by for just that contingency, and he dropped them around the grove in nothing flat. That was two hours ago, and they still haven't found anything."

"Are any of them missing?"

Hilks shook his head. "Maybe Elmer hasn't had time to get hungry again. We've come up with a thought that's somewhat less than pleasant. Elmer might be able to reproduce all by himself, and if he likes Earth enough to start populating the planet with baby snails, this continent could become a rather unpleasant place to live."

"Have you come up with anything at all?"

"Sure. One of the boys has designed a nifty steel net to be dropped out of a plane—if Elmer is ever spotted from a plane. We're also working on some traps, but it's a little hard to decide what to use for bait, since the only thing Elmer seems to like to eat is people. We might ask for volunteers and put cages inside the traps. Touchy proposition, we don't know what sort of a cage would keep Elmer out, just as we also don't know what sort of trap would keep him in."

"Did you do anything with that plastic display case Elmer broke into?" Allen asked.

"No," Hilks said. "I had it brought over here, but I completely forgot about it. Let's go look at it now. Meyers, find someone who knows something about Venusian moss and fungus and related subjects. Since Elmer likes that particular moss enough to break a display case to get it, maybe we could use it for bait."

"Never mind," Allen said. "We're slipping on this thing, Hilks. That exhibit was licensed, so Terran Customs will have a complete file on it. I'll ask for a report."

Allen copied the license number and called his office from the plane's communications room, using his own emergency channel. Ten minutes later he bounded wildly into Hilks's office.

"What's the matter?" Hilks demanded.

"Everything. Get this Professor Dubois over here and fast. That exhibit was never registered. The license is a forgery."

The professor waved his arms excitedly. "I never dreamed!" he exclaimed. "I have been extremely careful with all of my exhibits. It does not pay not to be careful. But you must admit that the license looks genuine."

"You say you bought the exhibit on the West Coast," Allen said. "Tell us about it."

"Let's see—it was maybe three years ago. I was showing in upstate California. Fellow came in one day and said he was breaking up his own exhibit and had a few things left to sell.

He made them sound good, and I went all the way to San Diego to see what he had. It really wasn't bad stuff—it would have been a good basic collection for someone starting out, but there wasn't anything there that would have helped my collection. I took that one because I hated to waste a trip and he made me a good price. And it was a pretty thing."

"Could you describe this man?"

"I doubt it. It's been a long time. His name? Oh—that I remember. It was Smith."

"Describe this 'moss' again, please."

"Well, like I said, it was pretty stuff. Vivid colors, red and black and yellow and white without any special pattern. It had a nice sheen to it—looked like a hunk of thick blanket."

"Or a hunk of rug?" Allen suggested.

"Well, yes. I suppose you could say rug."

Allen backed over to a chair and sat down heavily. "The fact that it was small and thick means nothing. 'Thick' things sometimes unfold into objects many yards square. Hilks, take a look at that case. Take a good look. I want to know if it was smashed by something breaking into it, or by something breaking out of it."

Hilks bent over the case. "It bulges," he announced. "If the snail could apply suction, it might have made it bulge this way."

Allen went to have a look. "The sides bulge, too," he said. "It looks as though something inside applied force in all directions, and the top gave first."

Hilks nodded slowly. "Yes, it does look that way. Without a demonstration to the contrary by the snail, I'd say that something broke out of here."

Allen returned to his chair. For twenty years he had been studying Venus and all things Venusian, assimilating every scrap of information and every voluminous report that came his way. Now he could rearrange his facts, and this time he could make them fit.

"Ever hear of a Venusian Night Cloak?" he asked.

They shook their heads.

"You have now. Tell General Fontaine to call off his snail hunt. This problem may be a lot worse than we'd thought."

They sat around a table in the large upper room of the lab plane—Allen, Hilks, General Fontaine, and Professor Dubois. Hilks's scientists had crowded into the room behind them.

Allen started the projector. The screen erupted a Venusian jungle, its blanched vegetation having a revolting, curdled appearance through the steaming mist. The camera shifted upward, taking in a square of greenish sky. In the distance, just above the seething treetops, appeared a blob of color. It enlarged slowly as it sailed toward them, a multicolored flat surface that rippled and twisted and curled in flight.

"That's it!" the professor exclaimed. "The markings are just like my moss."

It came on until it filled the screen. Suddenly it plummeted away, and the camera followed it until it disappeared into the jungle.

Allen switched off the projector. "Officially that's the closest anyone has got to one," he said. "Now we know otherwise. My feeling is that a number of scientists missing and presumed dead in the Great Doleman Swamp got rather too close to a Night Cloak."

The professor looked stricken. "This—my moss—killed those innocent children?"

"None of our facts fit the snail. All of them fit the Night Cloak."

"Why do they call it a Night Cloak?" the general asked.

"It was first observed at night, and it seems most active then. It grows to an enormous size, and as far as anyone on Venus knows—and don't forget there's a lot of the planet to be explored yet—it is found only in the Great Doleman Swamp. That's the reason so little is known about it. A jungle growing in a swamp isn't the easiest place for field work, and a Venusian jungle is impossible. Stations on the edge of the swamp occasionally observe the Night Cloaks, but always from a distance. They seem to be a unique life form, and the scientists were naturally curious about them. Twice expeditions were sent out to capture a specimen, and both parties disappeared without a trace. No one thought to blame the Night Cloaks—there are enough other things in that swamp that can do away with a man, especially some of the giant amphibians.

"This film strip was shot by a lucky pilot who happened to be hanging motionless over the swamp. A Night Cloak won't approach a moving plane. The scientific reports contain little but speculation. Frankly, gentlemen, we already know more about the Night Cloak than Venus does, and we're going to have to learn in a hurry something Venus hasn't discovered in a hundred years of field work: How to catch one."

"This fellow Smith caught one," Professor Dubois said.

"It was obviously a young one, and it's possible that they have periods of dormancy when one could be picked up easily— fortunately for Smith. Something about being transported and placed in Earth's atmosphere kept it dormant. It's our misfortune that it didn't die."

General Fontaine was drumming on the table with his fingers. "You say we know more about them than Venus knows. Just what do we know?"

"We know that you can't shoot one. Private Agazzi probably punched a lot of holes in it, but how would you aim at vital organs of a creature thirty feet square and who knows what fraction of an inch thick? We know that it has strength. It broke that plastic display case apart. We know a few unpleasant things about its diet and how it ingests food. We even know that its victims are likely to leave their shoes behind, which may or may not be a vital bit of information. And we know that our contaminated zone isn't worth a damn because a Night Cloak can fly right over the ground troops and probably already has."

"I'll have to call up all the planes I can get ahold of," the general said. "I'll have to reorganize the ground troops so I can rush them in when the thing is sighted."

"Excuse me, sir," said the young scientist named Meyers. "What was that you said a moment ago about shoes?"

"Just a little peculiarity of our Night Cloak," Allen told him. "It will totally consume a human body, and it doesn't mind clothing, but shoes absolutely do not appeal to it. It eats the feet and stockings right out of them, sometimes, but it leaves the shoes. I don't know what it means, but it's one positive thing we do know."

"Just a moment," Meyers said. He pushed his way out of the room and ran noisily down the stairway. He returned waving a newspaper. "I picked this up when I came through Langsford this morning," he said.

He passed the paper to Allen, who glanced at the headline and shrugged. "Monster still at large."

"That isn't exactly news to us," General Fontaine said.

"It's down at the bottom of the page," Meyers said. "A woman went for a walk last night and disappeared. They found her handbag in a park on the edge of Langsford, and a short distance away they found her shoes."

The general sucked in his breath sharply and reached for the paper. Hilks leaned back, folded his hands behind his head, and looked at the ceiling.

"Langsford," Allen said slowly. "Forty miles. But it also got Private Agazzi last night."

"If we make this public, it'll start a panic," General Fontaine said. "We'll have to evacuate the eastern half of the state. And if we don't make it public—"

"We'll have to make it public," Allen said.

"I'll have to order in my five reserve divisions. I'll need them for police work, and I'll need their transport to get the people out. God knows how far that thing may have gone by now."

"Message from Venus," a voice called. It was handed to Hilks, who read it and tossed it onto the table disgustedly.

"I asked Venus about the mollusk. They've checked all their records, and as far as they know it has no Venusian relatives. They ask, please, if we will kindly send it along to them when we're finished with it, preferably alive. They'd like to study it."

General Fontaine got to his feet. "Shall I take care of the news release?" he asked Allen.

"I'll handle it," Allen said and reached for a piece of paper. He studied a map for a moment, and then he wrote, "Notice to the populations of Kansas, Oklahoma, Arkansas, Missouri, Iowa, Nebraska, and Colorado."

For five days Allen sat at a desk in the lab plane answering inquiries, sifting through reports and rumors, searching vainly for a fact, an idea, that he could convert into a weapon. The lab's location was changed five times and he hardly noticed the moves.

The list of victims grew with horrifying rapidity. A farmer at work in his fields, a housewife hurrying along a quiet street to visit a friend, a sheriff's deputy investigating a report of looting in an abandoned town, an off-duty soldier who left his bivouac area for reasons best known to himself—Allen compiled the list, and Hilks added the shoes to his collection.

"This may not be the half of it," Allen said worriedly. "With so many people on the move, it'll be weeks before we get reports on everyone that's missing."

General Fontaine's Contaminated Area doubled and tripled and tripled again. On the third day the Night Cloak was sighted near the Missouri-Kansas border, and the populations of four states were in panicky flight.

That same night old Dr. Anderson got a call through to Allen from Gwinn Center. "That dratted thing is fussing around my window," he said.

"That can't be," Allen told him. "It was sighted two hundred miles from there this afternoon."

"I'm watching it while I talk to you," the doctor said.

"I'll send someone right away."

They found Dr. Anderson's shoes near a broken window, directly under the sign that read, "Doctor is in."

The next morning an air patrol sighted an abandoned ground car just across the Missouri border. It landed to investigate and found mute evidence of high tragedy. A family of nine had been fleeing eastward. The car had broken down, and the driver got out to make repairs. At that moment the horror had struck. In and around the car were nine pairs of shoes.

Hilks was losing weight, and he had also lost much of his good-natured nonchalance. "That thing *can't* travel that fast," he said. "The car must have been sitting there for a couple of days."

"Fontaine has traced it," Allen told him. "The family left

home yesterday afternoon, and it'd have reached the place the car was found about ten o'clock last night."

"That's when the doctor called."

"Right," Allen said.

Lieutenant Gus Smallet was one small cog in the enormous observation grid General Fontaine hung over eastern Kansas and western Missouri. His plane was a veteran road-hopper, a civilian model pressed into service when the general received emergency authority to grab anything that would fly. It was armed only with a camera that Smallet had supplied himself.

Smallet flew slowly in a straight line, his plane being one of a vast formation of slow-moving observation planes. It was his third day on this fruitless search, his third day of taking off into the pre-dawn darkness and flying until daylight faded, and he was wondering which he would succumb to first, fatigue or boredom. His head ached. Other portions of his anatomy ached worse, especially that which had been crushed against an uncomfortable, thinly padded seat for more hours than Smallet cared to remember. His movements had become mechanical, his thoughts had long since taken flight to other, more pleasant subjects than a Venusian Night Cloak, and he had stopped asking himself whether he would recognize the damned thing if he happened to see it.

Suddenly, against the dark green of a cluster of trees, he glimpsed a fleck of color. He slipped into a shallow dive, staring hypnotically as the indistinct blur grew larger and took on shape.

A bellow from his radio jolted Smallet back to reality. His sharp-eyed commanding officer, whose plane was a speck somewhere on the horizon, was telling him to stop horsing around and keep his altitude.

"I see the damned thing!" Smallet shouted. "I see—"

What he did see so startled him that he babbled incoherently and did not realize until afterward that he had instinctively flipped the switch on his camera. It was well that he had done so. His story was received with derision, and his commanding officer sniffed his breath suspiciously and muttered words that sounded direly like *Courts-Martial*.

Then the developed film was brought in, and what Smallet had seen was there for all to gape at.

Not one Night Cloak, but five.

It was dark by the time the transports started pouring ground troops into the area. They lost seven men that night and saw nothing at all.

Solly Hertz was an ordinance sergeant with ability, imagination, and a commanding officer who sought to hide him under the proverbial bushel. Good ordinance men, as the old saying went, did not come off assembly lines.

So when Hertz told his captain that he wanted to go to division ordinance to discuss an idea he had about these Night Cloak things, the captain paled at the thought of losing the one man who could keep his electronic equipment operating. He confined Hertz to the company area and mopped his brow over the narrow margin of his escape.

Hertz went A.W.O.L., by-passed division and corps and army, and invaded the sanctuary of the supreme air commander. That much-harassed general encountered Hertz through the accident of seeing a squad of military police leading him away. Fortunately he had enough residual curiosity to inquire about the offense and ask Hertz what he wanted.

"One of your guys sees one of these Night Cloaks," Hertz said. "What's he supposed to do about it?"

"Blast it," the general said promptly.

"Won't do any good," Hertz said. "Slugs and shrapnel just punch holes in it, and that don't bother it none. And a contact fuse wouldn't even go off when it hit. It's like shooting at tissue paper."

"You think you can do something about that?" the general asked.

"I got an atomic mini-rocket with a proximity fuse. It'll trigger just before it hits the thing. It'll *really* blast it."

"You're sure it won't go off at the wrong time and cost me a pilot?"

"Not the way I got it fixed."

"How many have you got?"

"One," Hertz said. "How many do you want?"

"Just for a starter, about five thousand. Tell me what you need and get to work on it."

Captain Joe Carr took off the next morning equipped with two of Hertz's rockets. Before he entered his plane he crossed fingers on both hands and spat over his left shoulder. And once inside the plane he went through a brisk ceremony of clicking certain switches on and off with certain predetermined fingers. Having thus dutifully sacrificed to the goddess of luck, he was not at all surprised an hour later when he sighted a Night Cloak.

It was a big one. It was enormous, and Carr glowed with satisfaction as he made a perfect approach, fired one rocket, and circled to see if another was needed.

It was not. The enormous, rippling surface was suddenly seared into nothingness—almost. The rocket hit it dead center, and when Carr completed his turn he saw the Night Cloak looking, as he said later, like the rind off a piece of bologna.

But even as he yelped news of his triumph into the radio, the rind collapsed crazily and parted, and four small, misshapen Night Cloaks flew gently downward to disappear into the trees.

Private Edward Walker was thinking about shoes. Night Cloaks never ate shoes. Flesh and bones and clothing and maybe even metal, but not shoes. That was official.

"All right," Walker told himself grimly. "If one of those things comes around here, I'll kick the hell out of it."

He delivered a vicious practice kick and felt very little the better for it; and the truth was that Private Edward Walker had excellent reason for his uneasiness.

His regiment was deployed around a small grove of trees. Two Night Cloaks had been sighted entering the trees. The place had been kept under observation, and as far as anyone knew they were still there, but the planes hovering overhead, and the cautious patrols of lift-equipped soldiers that looped skittishly over the grove, from one side to the other, had caught no further glimpse of them.

Walker had put in an hour of lift-patrolling himself, and he hadn't liked it. He had the uncomfortable feeling, as he floated over the trees and squinted down into the shadows, that some-one was using him for bait. This was maybe excusable if it promised to accomplish anything, but so far as anyone knew these Cloaks had the pernicious habit of taking the bait and never getting caught. The casualty list was growing with appall-ing speed, the Cloaks were getting fat—or at least getting bigger —and not one of them had been destroyed.

But the brass hats had tired of that nonsense and decided to make a stand. This insignificant grove of trees could well be the Armageddon of the human race.

Walker's captain had been precise about it. "If these things go on multiplying, it means the end of humanity. We've got to stop them, and this is the place and we're the guys to do it."

The men looked at each other, and a sergeant was bold enough to ask a question. "Just how are we going to knock them off?"

"They're working that out right now," the captain said. "I'll let you know as soon as I get the Word."

That had been early morning. Now it was noon, and they were still waiting for the Word. Private Walker felt more like bait with each passing minute. He looked again at his indestruc-tible shoe leather. "I'll kick the hell out of them," he muttered.

"Walker!" his sergeant bellowed. "You going off your nut? Sit down and relax."

Walker walked toward the sergeant. "It's true, isn't it? That business about the Cloaks not eating shoes?"

Sergeant Altman took a cautious glance at his own shoes and nodded.

"Shoes are made out of leather," Walker said. "Why don't we make us some suits out of leather? And gloves, too?"

The sergeant scratched his head fretfully. "Let's talk to the captain."

They talked to the captain. The captain rushed the two of them off to see a colonel, and in no time at all they were in the hallowed presence of a general, a big, intense man whose glance chilled Walker to the soles of his feet and who paced irritably back and forth while Walker stammered his fanciful question about leather suits and gloves.

When he finished, the general stopped pacing. "Congratulations, Private Walker," he said. "Someone should have thought of this three weeks ago, but no one did. It's men like you who make our army great. I'll see that you get a medal for this, and I'll also see that you get all the leather you want."

They saluted and turned away, both of them stunned at the realization that they'd been granted the honor of testing Walker's idea. It didn't help when they heard the general say, just before they passed out of hearing, "Darned silly notion. Do you think it'd work?"

Dusk was dropping down on them when the "leather" arrived. Walker slipped on a leather jacket and boots that reached his knees. He wrapped pieces of leather around his upper legs and tied them on with strips of leather. He fashioned a rough leather skirt for himself, ignoring the snickers of those watching. Five others did the same—three privates, the sergeant and the captain. The captain tossed leather hats to them, and gloves, and Walker carefully worked the sleeves of his jacket down into the gloves.

"All right," the captain said. "This will have to do. If it works they'll design a one-piece leather suit with something to protect the face, but we'll have to show them that it works. Let's get in there before it's too dark to see."

The grove was already ringed with lights that laced the half-darkness with freakish shadows as far as they were able to penetrate. The captain arranged them in a tight formation, himself in the lead and the sergeant bringing up the rear. A quick glance to see that all was ready, a nod, and they worked their way forward.

After an advance of ten yards the captain held up his hand. They stopped, and Walker, in his position on the right flank, looked about uneasily—up, down, sideways. A light breeze stirred the treetops high overhead. From the sky came the hollow buzz of a multitude of planes. The noise had a remote, unreal quality.

The captain signaled, and they moved on. Someone stumbled and swore, and the captain hissed, "Silence!"

They reached the far side of the grove and turned back. The tension had lifted somewhat; they spread out and began to walk faster. Walker suddenly realized that he was perspiring under the leather garments, that his inner clothing was sopped with sweat.

"I could do with a bath," he muttered, and the captain silenced him with a wave of his hand.

At the center of the grove they wheeled off at an angle. Walker became momentarily separated from the others when he detoured around a dense clump of bushes. There was a warning shout, and as he whirled the Night Cloak was upon him.

He shielded his face with one arm and swung a clenched fist. His hand punched a gaping hole, and he withdrew it and swung again. There was almost no resistance to his blows, and he riddled the pulsating, multicolored substance that draped over him. He had a momentary feeling of exultation. The leather worked. It was protecting him, and he would fix this Cloak but good. He punched and clawed and tore, and huge pieces came away in his grasp. Someone was beside him trying to tear the Cloak away, and he had a glimpse of a furious battle with the other Night Cloak taking place a short distance away.

Then he was completely enveloped, and he screamed with agony as a searing, excruciating pain encircled one knee and then the other. There were several hands fumbling about him, now, pulling shreds of Night Cloak from his struggling body. He raised both arms to protect his face and became aware for the first time of a vile odor. Then the thing flowed, slithered around his arms and found his face, and he lost consciousness.

He awoke gazing at the restful pale gray ceiling of a hospital.

Someone in the next bed chuckled. "Came around, did you? It's about time."

He turned. Sergeant Altman sat on the edge of the bed grinning broadly. Both of his wrists were bandaged; otherwise he seemed unhurt. "How do you feel?" he asked.

Walker felt the bandage that covered most of his face. "It hurts like the devil," he said.

"Sure. You got a good stiff dose of it, too—around your knees and on your face. But the doc says you'll be as good as new after some skin grafts, and you're a hell of a lot better off than Lyle. It didn't get your eyes."

"What happened?" Walker asked.

"Well, the leather works good. None of us got hurt except where we weren't protected or where the Cloaks could get underneath the leather. So now they'll be making those one-piece leather suits with maybe a thick plastic to protect the face. All of us are heroes, especially you."

"What happened to the Cloaks?"

"Oh, we tore them into about a hundred pieces each."

Walker nodded his satisfaction.

"And then," Altman went on, "the pieces flew away."

Hilks had a scientific headquarters set up near what had been a sleepy little town north of Memphis. It was a deserted town, now, in a deserted countryside where no living thing moved, and the bustling activity around the lab plane seemed strangely inappropriate, like a frolic at a funeral.

John Allen dropped his plane neatly into a vacant spot among the two dozen planes that were parked nearby. He stood looking at the lab plane for a moment before he walked toward it, and when he did move it was with the uncertain step of the outsider who expects at any moment to be ordered away.

At this moment the Night Cloaks were, as a general had put it that very morning, none of his business.

Two weeks previously his assignment had been cancelled and his authority transferred to the military high command. It was not to be considered a demotion or a reprimand, his superiors told him. On the contrary, he would receive a citation for his work. His competence, and his years of devotion to duty, had enabled him to quickly recognize the menace for what it was and take the best possible action. He had identified the Night Cloak on the sketchiest of evidence, and no one could suggest anything that he should have done but didn't.

But control of the investigation was passed to the military because the Night Cloaks had assumed the dimensions of a national catastrophe that threatened to become international. The nation's top military men could not be placed under the orders of a civilian employee of an extra-national organization.

"Can I continue the investigation on my own?" Allen demanded.

"Take a vacation," his chief said with a smile. "You've earned it."

So Allen had taken vacation leave and immediately returned to the zone of action. Unfortunately, he was temperamentally unsuited to the role of observer. He made suggestions, he criticized, and he attempted to prod the authorities into various kinds of action, and that morning a general had ordered him out of the Contaminated Zone and threatened to have him shot if he returned.

The lab plane was inside the Contaminated Zone, but word of Allen's banishment seemed not to have reached it. A few scientists recognized him and greeted him warmly. He went directly to Hilks's office, and there he found Hilks sitting moodily at his desk and gazing fixedly at a bottle that stood in front of him.

Allen exclaimed, "Where did you get it?"

In the bottle lay a jagged fragment, splotched red and yellow and black, that twisted and curled and uncurled.

"Didn't you hear about the great leather battle?" Hilks asked.

"I heard," Allen said.

"Great fight while it lasted. One small infantry patrol managed to convert two Cloaks into about a hundred cloaks, and this thing—" He nodded at the bottle. "This thing got left behind. It was only an inch long and a quarter of an inch wide, and it was too small to fly. I think one of the men must have stepped on the edge of a Cloak and pinched it off. Anyway, it was found afterward, so we've been studying it. I started feeding it insects, and then I gave it a baby mouse, and the thing literally grows while you watch it. Now it's grown big enough to fly, so I've stopped feeding it."

"But this is just what you needed!" Allen exclaimed. "Now you can find a way to wipe the things out!"

"Yeah? How? We've tried every poison we could think of, not to mention a nitric acid solution that Ferguson dreamed up. It seems to like the stuff. We've tried poison gases, including some hush-hush things the military flew in. You can see how healthy it looks. Now I have my entire staff trying to think up experiments, and I'm just sitting here hating the thing."

"Anything new from Venus?"

"Yeah. They found a cousin of Elmer the snail, so they kindly let us know that we could keep ours. Good joke, eh? I sent them my congratulations and told them the Night Cloaks have already eaten Elmer. Since the Cloaks absorb bones, they probably can absorb snail shells, too. Elmer's kind may be one of their favorite foods."

"What does Venus have to say about the Night Cloaks?"

"Well, they're very interested in what we've been able to tell them, and they thank us for the information. They're going to keep their research teams out of the Great Doleman Swamp until we can tell them how to cope with the things. Other than that, nothing."

"Too bad. I'd hoped they might know something."

"It's a lot worse than you realize. Venus has been so damned smug about the whole catastrophe that some of our politicians have decided to resent that. There's a movement afoot to ban travel to Venus and close down all the Venusian scientific stations. The other planets may be next, and then perhaps even the moon. After triumphantly moving out across the Solar System and hopefully taking aim at the stars, man crawls ignominiously back into his shell. Some of the pessimists think it may take us generations to handle the Cloaks, and in the meantime the Mississippi basin will become uninhabitable as far north as Minnesota and perhaps above the Canadian border in summer. Whatever happens, I'm betting that the well-dressed man will be wearing a lot of leather. The well-dressed woman, too. Do you have any bright ideas for us to work on?"

"I ran out of bright ideas on the third day," Allen said.

"If your mind isn't occupied with anything else, you might work on this one: Where are all the Night Cloaks?"

"The military seems to be keeping good track of them. That's one thing it does well."

"We have a rough tabulation of the minimum number that

should be around, and we have records of all of the sightings. As far as we can tell, about ninety per cent have disappeared."

"We figured they had periods of dormancy."

"Sure. But if they're going dormant on us, why hasn't someone found a dormant Night Cloak somewhere? We're worried because we have no notion of what their range is. If they ever get established in the Central and South American jungles, it *will* take us generations to root them out."

"Do you mind if I hang around?" Allen asked. "The last friend I had on the general staff just ordered me out of the Contaminated Zone, but I don't think he'll come here looking for me."

Hilks grinned. "What have you been up to?"

"I keep giving advice even when I'm not supposed to. I raised a ruckus because I didn't see much sense in picking Night Cloaks apart just to make more and smaller Night Cloaks. And then they were designing a new leather uniform to be used in Cloak hunting, and I suggested that instead of wearing such ghastly uncomfortable armor they just give everyone a bath in tannic acid, or whatever the stuff is they use to make leather, and soak their clothing in it at the same time. That was when he threw me out. He said he had ten million scientists telling him what to do, and he had to put up with them, but he didn't have to put up with me. So—what's the matter?"

"Tannic acid?" Hilks said.

"Isn't that the stuff? Probably it'd dry up or evaporate or something and not work anyway, but I thought—"

Hilks was already on his way to the door. "Meyers!" he shouted. "Get your crew in here. We have work to do."

By coincidence Allen entered the room first. The general, looking up sharply from his desk, flushed an unhealthy crimson and leaped to his feet. "You! I told you—"

Hilks stepped around Allen. "Meet my assistant," he said. "Name of Allen."

The general sat down again. "All right. I have my orders. Hilks and three assistants. I have the protective clothing ready for you, and I have a place picked out for you and a patrol to take you there."

"Good," Hilks said. "Let's get going."

"My orders also say that I'm to satisfy myself as to the soundness of whatever it is you propose to do."

"We've developed a spray we'd like to try out on the Cloaks," Hilks said.

"What'll it do to them?"

"You know we have a specimen to work on? The spray seems to anesthetize it. Of course there's a difference between spraying a Cloak sliver in a bottle and spraying a full-sized Cloak in open air."

"You really don't know, then."

"Of course not. That's why we're making the experiment."

"You're asking me to risk the lives of my men—"

"Nope. All we want them to do is show us where the Night Cloaks are and get out of the way. I'm not even risking the lives of my own men. Allen and I will do the testing."

The general stood up. "Tell me. I'm not asking for a prediction, damn it. Do you think this stuff might work?"

"We've had a lot of disappointments, General," Hilks said. "We're fresh out of predictions. But yes, we think it just might work."

"And if it doesn't?"

"The scientific staff will have a couple of openings. That's not much of a risk for a general to take, is it?"

The general grinned. "You're brave men. Anything you want, take it. And—good luck!"

As Allen dropped the plane into the small clearing, the pine forest took on an unexpectedly gloomy aspect. "Cover us while we're dressing," Allen said. He and Hilks climbed out and quickly slipped into the leather suits.

Meyers and another young scientist named Wilcox watched them anxiously. "Wasn't there a better place than this?" Meyers asked.

Allen shook his head. "All the other locations are swampy. Night Cloaks seem to be attracted to swamps, but I'm not.

Also, they only saw two of them in this area. Two are enough for beginners like Hilks and me."

"Sure you don't want us to come along?" Meyers asked, as they donned their spray tanks.

Hilks shook his head. "One of the problems has been the total absence of witnesses. If we'd known exactly what happened with each victim, maybe we'd have solved this long ago. You're our witnesses. You're to record everything we say, and we'll try to describe it so you can understand what's happening. If we don't come back, you'll know what went wrong."

Meyers nodded unhappily. They fastened their plastic face guards, picked up the spray guns, and waved a cheerful farewell.

"No undergrowth," Allen observed as they entered the trees.

"It's a Co-op Forest," Hilks said.

"That means we're trespassing."

"So are the Night Cloaks."

They walked briskly for a couple of miles, turned, and started to circle back. "Better check in with Meyers," Allen said. "He'll be turning somersaults."

Hilks switched on his radio. "Haven't seen a thing," he announced.

"Man, you must be blind!" Meyers blurted at them. "There was one right overhead when you started out. It followed you."

They turned quickly and stared upward. For a moment they saw only the cloudless sky through the treetops, and then a blur of color flashed past.

"Okay," Hilks said. "It's flying above the trees—waiting for reinforcements, maybe. We'll keep moving toward the plane. When they attack we'll put a couple of nice big trees at our backs so they won't be able to get at us from behind. If I can find a tree as big around as I am, that is."

"Keep your radios on," Meyers said.

"Right."

They moved at a steady pace, keeping close together and taking turns looking upward.

"Two of them, now," Hilks announced. "They're circling. They look like small ones."

Two minutes later it was Allen's turn. "I just counted three," he said. "No, four. They're coming down—*get ready!*"

The Cloaks dropped through the trees with amazing speed. They plummeted, and Allen, backing up to a tree, had no time for more than the split-second observation that they were unusually small, one being no more than a yard across. All four of them curved toward him. He gave the first one the spray at ten feet and then cut it off. The Cloaks were gone.

Hilks was chuckling as he talked with Meyers. "They got one whiff of the stuff and beat it."

"Now we won't know what'll happen to the one I sprayed," Allen said.

Hilks swore. "I didn't think about that. The most we can claim is that they don't particularly like the stuff."

"Don't be too sure," Allen said. "Here they come again."

They were wary. They dipped down slowly, circled, sailed in and out among the trees. Only the small one ventured close, and it shot upward when Allen gave it a blast of spray.

"For what it's worth," Allen said, "the small ones are hungrier than the big ones."

"It figures," Hilks said.

Meyers, sitting far away in the plane, made unintelligible noises.

The Cloaks did not return immediately. Allen and Hilks peered upward searchingly, and finally Allen asked, "What do we do now?"

"Add the score and go home, I suppose. The stuff doesn't have the punch we hoped for, none of them dropped unconscious at our feet, but at the same time we can claim a limited success. It drives them off, which is more than anything else was able to accomplish. We can develop pressurized containers for self-defense and put the chemists to work making the stuff more potent. Shall we go back?"

"Not yet," Allen said. "Here they come again."

They came, and they continued to come. They seemed not to have noticed Hilks in their first rushes, but now they divided their attention and swooped down in pairs again and again. They were coming closer before they turned upward, flying through the clouds of spray. Once the small one brushed against Allen.

"They can't be *that* hungry," Hilks said.

"No. They're angry. That's what the spray does to them. It maddens them. Are you listening, Meyers?"

"We'd better get moving," Hilks said. "The spray won't last forever. Let's leapfrog. I'll cover you, and then you cover me."

Meyers cut in. "If you can find a clearing, I'll pick you up."

"We'll let you know," Hilks said. "In the meantime, keep a close watch on the forest. With them on our backs we might miss your clearing."

"Right," Meyers said.

Allen made a short dash, placed a tree at his back, and turned to cover Hilks. The sudden movement seemed to infuriate the Cloaks. All four shot after Allen. Three of them turned away as he pointed the spray upward. The small Cloak hovered over him for a moment, taking the full, drenching blast. Then the pressure faded, the spray gun sputtered and cut off, and the Cloak fell upon Allen.

Allen thrust at it, but it encircled and clung to his arm. Hilks raced toward him, drenching both Allen and the Cloak with spray. Pain seared and stabbed at Allen's arm, and he staggered backward and fell. He must have blacked out, for he had no memory of the moment when the Cloak released him. He regained consciousness with Hilks standing over him and turning aside the Cloaks with blasts of spray. He pushed himself to a sitting position and stared down at the throbbing numbness that had been his arm.

"Are you all right?" Hilks asked anxiously. "Can you walk?"

"I—think so." Allen got up unsteadily. "My spray is gone."

"I know. You started before I did, but I can't have much left."

Allen was examining his arm.

"Bad?" Hilks asked.

"Clear to the bone in one place," Allen said. "Fortunately it's not bleeding."

"So we've learned another thing," Hilks said. "Even leather won't stop them when they're riled up or really hungry."

"Can we do anything?" Meyers asked.

"Just watch for us. We'll have to make a run for it. We'll start after their next rush. Ready?"

"Ready," Allen said.

They darted off through the trees.

But the Cloaks were after them in a fluttering rush. Hilks turned, warded them off, and they ran again.

"It's no good," Hilks panted. "My spray is almost finished. Not much pressure left. Any ideas?"

Allen did not answer. Hilks sprayed again, turned for another dash, and fell headlong over the protruding edge of a large rock. He scrambled to his feet and both of them stood staring, not at the circling Cloaks, but at the rock, which inexplicably humped up out of the ground and seemed to float away. After a dozen feet it bumped to the ground. Encrusted dirt fell away from it.

"The devil!" Allen breathed. "It's Bronsky's snail. And look at the size of it!"

"Here come the Cloaks," Hilks said. He aimed the spray gun.

But he did not use it. As the Cloaks dropped down through the trees, a tongue-like ribbon of flesh shot out from the enormous shell, broadened, folded back, and dropped to the ground with a convulsive shudder of satisfaction. And the Cloaks were gone.

They watched in fascination as the flesh heaved and twisted and finally subsided and began slowly to withdraw.

Meyers, screaming wildly into the radio, finally aroused them. "Are you all right?" he demanded.

"Sure," Hilks said. "Everything is all right now."

"What about the Cloaks?"

"They've just been eaten."

"What did you say? Beaten?"

"Eaten," Hilks said. "I have the picture now. All of it. How about you?"

Allen nodded. "The snail is the Cloak's natural enemy. Or the Cloak is its favorite food. This one was more or less happy with Bronsky until one day it smelled or otherwise sensed a Night Cloak in the vicinity. If we hadn't put an army to beating the woods and shooting at it, it probably would have eliminated the menace at once. As soon as we stopped bothering it, it started eating Cloaks, and it's been eating them ever since. That's where the missing Cloaks went. They aren't hibernating, or migrating, they're in the snail. Look how it's grown! How big did Bronsky say it was?"

"About six feet."

"It's ten feet now. At least. There's the answer to our Cloak problem. Forget the spray and the leather clothing. Clear everyone out and leave it to Elmer. Have Venus ship us the snail they have and as many more as they can find. Are you recording, Meyers?"

"Recording," Meyers said happily. "I got the whole thing. Just as the Cloaks were about to finish you off, that snail came galloping up and ate them."

"Not exactly," Allen said. "But close enough. What's Elmer doing now?"

"It sees us," Hilks said.

They watched. The pinkish flesh flowed out slowly, thickened, stood upright. Then, before their disbelieving eyes, it suddenly took shape and color and became the snaky caricature of a once-lovely Venus.

"Allen!" Hilks hissed. "That thing has a memory! It has the proportions wrong, but the image is still recognizable."

"It thinks we're an audience," Allen said. "So it's performing. Bronsky said it was just a big ham." He walked toward it.

"Watch yourself!" Hilks said sharply.

Allen ignored him. He approached the snail, stood close to it, looked up at the wreathing head of Venus.

The Venus collapsed abruptly. The flesh quivered, thrust up again, and became a hazy, misshapen caricature of John Allen, complete with face mask, wounded arm, and dangling spray gun. Somewhere behind him he heard Hilks choking with laughter. Allen ignored him. He extended his sound arm and solemnly shook hands with himself.